DEVIL'S PEAK II

GREIG BECK

**There's only one way out of Hell.
Fight your way out.**

SEVEREDPRESS

DEVIL'S PEAK II

WWW.SEVEREDPRESS.COM

ISBN: 978-1-923165-90-8

When I was young they told me there was no such thing as monsters.
They lied.

EPISODE 07

When the Earth's heartbeat stops, then the devil shall rise.

CHAPTER 01

The United States Geological Survey Headquarters (USGS), Reston, Virginia

Andrew Martinson and Phillip Zeng sat at each end of the claustrophobic monitoring facility, and were lost in their own duties. Around them were all manner of equipment monitoring earthquake data nationally, as well as the hundreds of shimmies, shakes, and full blown earthquakes from all around the world.

The data was correlated, analyzed, and then the AI programs would make a best guess on what and where the next geological shift would take place.

Martinson and Zeng were so used to the myriad beeps, pings and buzzes that to them they became part of the usual background noise. And it wasn't the music from the electronic symphony that caught their attention, but the lack of it.

Martinson lifted his head and frowned.

Something was different.

He turned to Zeng who was already staring back.

"It's stopped," Zeng said.

Martinson turned back and checked the seismological audio, and traced it back.

He scoffed softly and sat back. "Earth's heartbeat just stopped." He folded his arms. "I wonder what it means."

***

At the Vatican another private monitor registered the same thing. However this one generated a very different reaction.

The young priest trained in seismology raced up to his superior, Cardinal Belloni.

He bowed and was bade to speak and he looked up with wide eyes. "Earth's heartbeat has stopped."

Belloni shut his eyes for several seconds and after a moment more nodded once. "I'll tell the Holy Father." He sighed. "It seems the ancient enemy is finally coming for us."

CHAPTER 02

Australia, NSW, outskirts of Thrumster – the Simmons' farm

Jack Simmons was up late doing some paperwork, and hating every second of it. He surveyed the pile – bills, more bills, past due and final notices – he growled deep in his chest. Why would anyone be a damn farmer? he wondered.

The Simmons' farm just outside of the town of Thrumster wasn't a big one – two hundred acres holding a few hundred head of milking cows, a bull in another paddock, and in the barn several horses. It was hard work, and it never stopped. He couldn't remember the last time he took a day off.

His boys were both at university, Jesse studying economics, and Will doing computer science. Neither doing anything that was close to farming. And neither ever expressed any interest in it.

Good on them, he thought, as he wouldn't wish a life of backbreaking, thankless work on his worst enemy these days.

Margarete was already in bed, Neddy the kelpie was asleep under his desk, and the house was quiet.

But outside…

He paused to concentrate; he thought he heard a buzzing sound, thick and heavy, like an insect but deeper, more like that of a toy airplane.

It grew louder as if it passed overhead, and then went quiet – not fading away, just stopping.

Simmons sat listening for a moment more, but now silence reigned again. He looked down at Neddy who farted softly in his sleep. He smiled, knowing that if it had have been anything then the dog usually was the first to hear. But tonight, nothing.

After another moment he went back to his paperwork.

He'd give it another half hour, he thought with gritty eyes and drooping eyelids.

***

Out in the barn the horses snorted and stamped. The strange scent scared them. They didn't have great night vision, and the barn was near pitch dark, but they had a great sense of smell and excellent hearing, and they heard the sound of something big coming across their roof.

A large dark shape appeared momentarily in the high barn window and forced itself inside.

They heard it clawing its way across the ceiling and knew it was hanging above them in the darkness. The horses started to snort and move about. They wanted out. Something alien was in their home that smelt like danger and death. Some sort of predator.

The oldest horse, Nellie, the mare, stamped and snorted and turned to kick at her gate.

The thing above them dropped down and landed on top of her. She screamed at the revolting thing that clung to her. It was big, heavy and was covered in thick hair-like bristles.

Then she was either bitten or stung, and immediately fell silent. The other two younger horses soon suffered the same fate.

In the darkness the massive fly took its time laying eggs on the still living horse bodies. The eggs would hatch on them and feed, and each of the brood would carry in its gut a parasitic disease that no one on the surface of the world had ever encountered. It would be something that would infect the flesh, twist it, debase and deform it. It had no cure and it would be spread by the merest contact.

The fly suddenly stopped moving and seemed to freeze in place. The massive bristling thing shuddered and shook, and slowly a huge split appeared along its back.

In seconds more a bulbous lump of muscle appeared at the split, and gradually over the next fifteen minutes an even larger form of the Octavius Conti fly emerged.

It clung onto the empty shell casing for a while as its wings spread, filled with blood, and hardened. And then in seconds more the huge fly with the grotesquely human facial features was gone. On to grow more minions to spread its hellish plague across the country and then across the entire globe.

***

The bottle-shaped eggs swelled and hatched quickly, and the foot-long maggots soon ate the horses down to their bones. Then they crusted over, split down their backs, and from their husk bodies the fist-sized flies emerged.

They took to the air, spreading out in all directions. Except for one, who headed to the Simmons' house. Several also went for the local dam water that fed the town.

Like a small squadron of Kamikaze airplanes they dived at the water and on contact, they exploded, and the filthy contents of their bodies quickly mixed into the town's drinking water.

***

Jack Simmons woke to a feeling like someone was gripping the side of his face with a spiked glove – it stung.

He sat up in the darkness swiping a hand up and just caught something that let go and then darted away.

"*Ouch.*" He grimaced at the pain. "Fucking spider."

He gritted his teeth. His face already felt swollen and hot. It must have been a big huntsman given the size he felt. Those bastards were painful, but nothing like this.

"Fuck, fuck, fuck," he whispered, holding his face.

The pain was agonizing and getting worse, and was spreading down his neck; already his arms were feeling funny.

Simmons coughed, and tasted blood.

"Margie," he groaned from a rapidly numbing mouth.

There was no response.

Simmons coughed again, and this time felt something solid come up from his throat. And worse, it was moving.

He vomited onto the bedcover, and reached across to turn on the bedside lamp. With the light he saw his hand looked weird – the fingers were longer and darker.

"*Margie.*" He turned back and saw her still lying there.

He reached across and grabbed her hand, his fingers barely working now. "Margie, I'm sick."

Where his hand touched hers it felt hot. And wet.

"*Marhkeee…*" His mouth wasn't working properly and he leaned over her.

He saw then there was a massive boil thing on her neck, and he guessed she had been bitten as well.

He tried to release her hand, and found he couldn't. It seemed his hand was glued to hers, and when he looked down, he saw that now he couldn't even work out where his hand ended and hers began.

Margie seemed to lean closer to him then, and as their arms touched, the skin immediately zippered together.

"*Mrgghheetth.*"

He felt his skin burning all over and even his bones ached – he heard as well as felt them shifting beneath the skin, sliding, rearranging into different positions and shapes.

"*Mrggghhtthhh, wotthshappenggg oo eee*?" Simmons fell back onto the bed as his vision swam.

Margie seemed to move closer again, and now from his foot to his shoulder he felt the warm wetness as he bonded with her.

He heard a voice then – deep, commanding, and suddenly he heard Margie's thoughts as well as if they were in his own head. She was confused and frightened.

But most of all he was hungry. So hungry. But what he hungered for, revolted him at first.

But then the craving became intolerable.

And he knew what he had to do.

CHAPTER 03

USA, Texas, the Stoker Ranch

Addison lay in the darkness with her eyes open. She could feel the body heat emanating off Ethan in waves like he was on fire.

She hurt all over and especially down below. They had sex again. Just sex. Because she couldn't call it making love as it had been vigorous and brutal, and he had wanted to take her in ways they had never even talked about before.

She sighed. He was like a different person.

She rolled over and away from him because he smelled bad. He had stopped taking showers and there was a strange, sickly smell about him. And his breath was even worse.

Addison had tried to raise the subject about Drake, his older brother, and the guy who had literally marched through Hell to rescue him, but all Ethan could manage was a grunt, and telling her that he needed a bit more time to recover his strength.

She sat up and threw her legs over the side of the bed. She needed to talk to someone, and right now, there were only two people on the planet that could possibly understand what she was worried about.

She pulled on some jeans and a t-shirt, and paused to turn and look at him. She had come back from the seven circles of Hell. But had Ethan?

No, that was a stupid idea, she thought.

She went downstairs to the library to make a call.

CHAPTER 04

Rome, The Vatican, Operations Room-2

The Templar Knights sat in the darkened room and watched the screen before them. On it was the movement of the tracking device Leonidas had placed on the flying abomination.

It had first made its way from the Devil's Peak to the coastline of Australia, settled for a short time in a small town called Thrumster, and then made its way up the coast and crossed the Timor Sea toward Indonesia.

Isabella Romano had already given the Vatican superiors an update and then again to the room of assembled Knights – the apocalypse was upon them and for now, all they could hope to do was slow it until something arose that could stop it for good.

"The plague is here. And spreading," Isabella finished with.

"Two vectors," Leonidas said. "The flies, and those already infected, spreading by a bite or other fluids. It is aggressively contagious."

Isabella nodded. "For now, the only cure is a quick death to those infected. Because there is no coming back."

Cardinal Ferdinand Montebello folded his arms and paced at the front of the room. He stopped and turned. "And the sea beasts? The Hell spawn, what of them?"

Isabella shook her head. "No sightings yet. But I suspect they will harass the coastlines and shipping. They will try and distract the human race from what is going on with the infection, until it is too late to fight back."

He nodded. "I thought this too." He looked at the room. "Priority is to get a sample of the plague. We cannot begin to fight something we know so little about."

"Leonidas and I can go to Australia to this town of Thrumster." Isabella smiled sadly. "It seems communication has been cut to the two thousand residents. They know something is happening. But they will have no idea just how bad it is or is going to get."

Montebello nodded. "The others will be dispatched in two person teams throughout the world – to Indonesia, to other Asian countries. Our job is to educate the populations, find the vectors…" He looked at each of them. "And eradicate them all."

"And Drake Stoker?" Isabella asked hopefully.

Montebello shook his head slowly. "Right now, he is not a priority. And you know there is no way to get to him. If that changes, then we recognize the help he gave you and will do what we can." He dropped his arms. "Go, time is already against us. And take Marco. God bless you all in this that could be our final mission."

The group dispersed and outside Isabella turned on her phone. There was a message waiting from Addison.

She called back immediately.

***

"I don't believe it," Addison said. "You're leaving him down there?"

"I'm sorry, Addison. We have no choice," Isabella said softly. "There is no way to get to him. But the cardinal did acknowledge we owe Drake a debt. And if…"

"When?" Addison interjected.

"…*when*, we see an opportunity to retrieve Drake and Benson, I promise I will personally lead them in," Isabella finished.

Addison knew Isabella was right, but the guilt was still eating at her. Drake had thrown down everything for his brother, and saved her and Isabella's life many times. And Drake had lost a lot of friends along the way. But now he had paid the price.

She grimaced and squeezed her eyes shut for a moment. The thought of Ethan's brother being trapped in that horrifying nightmarish place made her feel like she was about to throw up.

"How's Ethan?" Isabella asked softly.

Addison's eyes flicked open. "He's…" she tried to think of a way to describe him.

She certainly didn't want to say he was changed, as for all she knew Isabella and the Templar Knights might drop in and cut his head off on suspicion alone.

"He's okay. Still recovering," she finished.

There was silence for a moment.

"Okay," Isabella said with the single word layered in skepticism.

"What are your plans now; next steps?" Addison asked.

"We need to go to Australia. A small town called Thrumster," Isabella replied. "The plague is out, and we need to obtain a sample. And also do what we can to stop its spread."

Addison looked up at the ceiling, as if looking through the wooden beams to see the sleeping Ethan.

"Can I help?" she asked. "I'm a biologist. And you know I know what's going on."

Isabella thought about it. They could use all the help they could get, but Addison wasn't trained as they were.

"Thank you but no. We can take it from here. You just stay put and look after Ethan," she replied softly.

"I'll try," Addison said. "But... can you keep me informed? Of anything?"

"I promise," Isabella said.

And then, "Addison?"

"Yes," she replied.

"I like that you called me. Please know that if you need anything, or are concerned about anything, anything at all, you call me anytime, okay?"

"I will. I will." Addison's brows came together. "Isabella..."

"Yes," Isabella waited.

There was silence for a few seconds.

"Um, nothing." Addison sighed. "Just be safe."

Isabella disconnected and held the phone up for a moment more. She didn't believe that everything was fine with Addison, and she was vague on Ethan's condition.

She certainly would stay in contact, to keep Addison informed, but also to keep an eye on her. And Ethan Stoker.

"We need to go," Leonidas said.

"On my way." She stuck her phone in her pocket, and they headed out.

Her team was small, at just three Knights – her, Leonidas, and Marco. Marco was one of the oldest Knights at thirty-five, but also one of the best trained. It was an honor to have him. Being given a larger team when all others were just in duos, and also the assignation of Marco was a testament to the importance the southern region was given.

The portal was there, and though it had been physically closed, the emanation point was there and when the Earth was brought low by the abominations and by the plague, then that could well be where the Devil chose to rise from.

"Thrumster, it's called," Isabella said. "Let's see what's happening down there."

CHAPTER 05

Australia, NSW, town of Thrumster

Thrumster was a smallish town in New South Wales with a population of just over two thousand people.

It was close to the larger town of Port Macquarie and had an older community and was nestled in amongst thick Australian bush land. The area was known for having a huge koala population, and also the fishing in nearby Lake Innes.

They didn't get all that many tourists in the summer months because it got frypan hot, and the snakes and funnel web spiders tried to find shade – be that in your tent, sleeping bag, or even shoes.

Chief Inspector Frank Hardcourt and a deputy, Nathan Fitzsimmons, were dispatched to see why the local constable outpost had gone dark, and no one seemed to be answering phones.

The pair of men were impatient to go in but they were told that there was an international team that would be coming to meet them, and they were to hold off entering the town proper until they arrived.

"Bugger that," Hardcourt spat.

They drove their Land Rover into the main street and Constable Fitzsimmons slowed; it was quiet, strangely quiet.

"Where is everyone?" Hardcourt asked the windshield.

"Hey, notice something else? There's no magpies or kookaburras," Fitzsimmons said back over his shoulder as he leaned out the window.

"Well, they don't exactly fly south for winter, do they?" Hardcourt replied. "And no dogs either. But fuck that, where are all the townsfolk? We gotta find them."

"Where to first?" Fitzsimmons asked.

"The cop shop. I know Eric Lanscomb, the chief constable. We need to find him as he'll know what's what," Hardcourt said.

"You got it." Fitzsimmons accelerated and turned into a side street that had the post office, empty, and one of the half dozen pubs in town, also empty. And at the end was the police station.

They pulled up out front and sat there for a few moments checking the street and then the small police station. There was no damage, but no people.

Fitzsimmons went to open the car door.

"Wait," Hardcourt said.

He lifted the mic and opened the police channel. "This is Chief Inspector Frank Hardcourt, for Chief Constable Eric Lanscomb. Do you read? Over."

He waited, but there was nothing but dead air.

He tried again.

"This is Chief Inspector Frank Hardcourt, for any police officers in the Thrumster region, please respond, over." Hardcourt waited, feeling a prickle on his neck. To say this was unusual was a mile from how it felt.

He snorted softly and replaced the small hand unit.

"We go?" Fitzsimmons asked.

Hardcourt nodded. "Yep." He shouldered open his door and slid out.

Fitzimmons did the same.

"Check your weapon," he said.

The young deputy glanced at him for a second or two, but then did as asked.

"You thinking there'll be trouble?" Fitzsimmons looked around slowly.

"I hope not, but…" Hardcourt exhaled. "An entire town of people don't just vanish for no reason."

"Yep." Fitzsimmons looked back at his boss with brows raised. "Aliens?"

Hardcourt scoffed. "You're a fucking alien."

It was coming into peak summer so even though it was still early it was already hot at about eighty-five degrees and low humidity.

"Let's go." Hardcourt headed toward the station steps.

It was a small single story building with a vacant lot next to it.

"Hold up." Fitzsimmons had his hand on his gun. "Got a body."

"What?" Hardcourt followed his gaze and saw a pair of boots sticking out of the long grass beside the station.

"Easy now. Spread out a little." Hardcourt pulled his weapon. "Let's have a little look," he said. "Keep your eyes open."

Fitzsimmons spread out to the left side and the pair of policemen approached carefully.

When they were within half a dozen feet they could see the prone man was well and truly dead.

Hardcourt grimaced. "What the hell happened here?" He looked up at his young partner. "Cover me." He holstered his weapon.

Fitzsimmons turned side on, quickly looked left and right, and kept his gun held in both hands but pointed at the ground.

Hardcourt crouched on his haunches and examined the young man. He saw that the body had been ruined. Most of the young man's clothing had been ripped away and the stomach was opened, but the contents were gone. His ribcage had been levered open and his lungs and heart were also missing.

Could a dingo do that? Maybe a pack of 'em, he wondered.

The man's mouth hung open and the jaw was so broken it hung down loosely on his ravaged neck. There was blood all over the face, but Hardcourt could see there was no tongue remaining and the stub was all frayed like it had been ripped out.

"Jesus Christ," he whispered, and closed his eyes for a moment.

The police chief breathed calmy through his mouth to slow his heartbeat but also so he didn't have to smell the open corpse.

There was something else. The other parts of the body he could see had bitemarks. Some looked human, but others looked like they had been made by mouths and tooth patterns very different from anything he knew of. And much bigger.

He slowly got to his feet.

"Might be an animal attack. Dingo pack," he said, feeling his stomach roil.

Fitzsimmons' eyes slid to him.

"Yeah, I don't believe it either." Hardcourt put his hands on his hips and turned about.

Fifty feet away on the long grass he could see something that looked like a pile of clothing.

"Hang on, might be another one." Hardcourt drew his weapon and crossed the grass and sure enough, there was an old woman just as ripped up.

"Fuck!" he said and holstered his gun.

"This is bad business, boss," Fitzsimmons said.

Hardcourt clicked his tongue in his mouth. "What bothers me is that it happened right next to the police station."

He drew in a deep breath and hitched his britches. "Something tells me we're not going to like what we find in there. Let's go."

***

Hardcourt and Fitzsimmons came back around the front of the building. There were two large bulletproof glass doors, both shut, and Hardcourt nodded to Fitsimmons who went up and peered in.

"Lights are on." After moment, he turned, "Nothing, no one there."

"We go in slow and quiet," Hardcourt said.

Fitzsimmons nodded and eased the door open. He slipped in, followed by Hardcourt.

The two men stood in the front meet-and-greet area and surveyed the damage – there were papers strewn everywhere, a computer smashed to the floor, and splintered furniture.

"Hey, look," Fitzsimmons pointed.

There were piles of clothing, mostly police uniforms, all scattered about.

Hardcourt toed one aside. "Ripped to shreds," he whispered. "Did someone bust in here and rip them from their bodies?" he cursed under his breath. "Keep your eyes open. Proceed."

They went around the front desk, and headed toward the rear where the administration offices were.

Hardcourt stopped to look at the water cooler from a company he knew called Thrumster Springs, a natural reservoir that was bottled and sold throughout the region – the huge four gallon container was half empty.

He frowned at it – the water looked cloudy or slightly discolored.

"Wait," he said.

He grabbed one of the paper cups, and placed it on the stand and then pressed the spigot lever. He put a few inches into the cup, and brought it close to his nose and sniffed.

Again there was something odd about it. Not so bad, but just not...right.

"You feeling thirsty, now?" Fitzsimmons asked.

"No." Hardcourt shook his head. "No, just something doesn't look right. Let's go on."

They went through the busted up offices and found more torn clothing. They checked them and found no bite or claw marks, but instead the ripping seemed to be mostly at the seams as if they had been burst open. A few had some sort of dark stain on them, not blood, and the smell was revolting.

"Phew." He dropped the cloth. It reminded Hardcourt of bad fish.

They came to a door and steps leading down to the cells. In towns like Thrumster they were mostly used as drunk tanks as there was little violent crime around these parts.

"Holy shit," Fitzsimmons whispered. "The freaking lock mechanism has been busted, and the door frame splintered."

"Someone wanted out of there real bad," Hardcourt said.

He gripped his gun. "Slow and steady now."

This time Hardcourt led, and for the first time he felt sick with fear.

The lights were out in the lower level, and the pair stood at the top of the steps for a moment. Hardcourt checked the lights – nothing.

"Of course not," he seethed.

Hardcourt unclipped the leather pouch on his belt that contained the high powered flashlight and slid it out – the black foot-long heavy flashlight doubled as a club and he switched it on and held it up in his fist.

Fitzsimmons did the same and the two white spotlights cut the darkness.

"Why don't we take it nice and slow. And quiet," Hardcourt said over his shoulder.

"Oh yeah," Fitzsimmons breathed.

The pair eased down one slow step at a time. Hardcourt had been to the station once before and still remembered the layout – down below there were three cells. They were old school types and had barred doors and open slots at waist level.

It only took them a few seconds to reach the floor and they paused, shining lights up and back down the concrete corridor. Once again there was torn clothing littering the floor and a food tray that had food and a drink bottle on it but had been dropped.

Hardcourt eased his weapon out and held it in one hand and over the top held his flashlight.

"Anyone in here?" he asked.

There was no response, but the tomb-like silence was as unnerving as the complete darkness.

The pair of policemen walked along the cells shining their lights into them, and as they got to the end they suddenly illuminated a white face at the bars.

"*Fuck!*" Fitzsimmons lurched backwards.

Hardcourt kept his light on the figure. The young man screwed his eyes shut and held an arm up in front of his eyes. He wore baggy denim jeans, had no shoes, and a camo t-shirt that read: 'make war, not love' on the front.

"Who are you?" Hardcourt asked.

The young man slowly lowered his arm but still squinted.

"Mark Menzies," he said.

"Why didn't you respond when we called?" Hardcourt asked.

Menzies hesitated for a moment. "I was scared."

"Come on, man, of what?" Fitzsimmons urged.

"The monsters," he said in a dry croak.

"Monsters," Hardcourt scoffed. "What are you talking about?"

"What day is it?" Menzies asked.

"Wednesday, mid-morning," Fitzsimmons replied.

"I've been in here for two days. I'm real thirsty," Menzies said and coughed.

Fitzsimmons ran his light up and down the skinny youth's body, and then along the floor. He saw a knotted sheet snaking outside the bars, where the youth had obviously tried to hook the water bottle. "And why are you in there, Mr. Menzies?"

Menzies shook his head. "Aw, I had a fight with Sheila again. And, well, she fell down and hit her head." He looked up with a crooked smile. "She called the cops." He frowned. "But it totally wasn't my fault. She tripped over the dog."

"Okay, whatever. Tell us what happened here. And don't fucking say monsters," Hardcourt warned.

He nodded and swallowed dryly. "At first it was normal like when I was brought in. Then around dinner time when I was in lock-up, Constable Johnson came down with my food. But all of a sudden he hunched over and started to scream." Menzies grimaced so hard his face creased in a dozen places. "And then he busted out of his clothing as he turned into a ..."

"Let me guess, a monster?" Fitzsimmons finished.

Menzies nodded. "That was the beginning. Because then I heard the alarms and screams and a lot of running." He pointed at the food and water. "He dropped it and went up the stairs like a Mallee Bull, and just smashed the door open. I mean, he really *smashed* it open." He sighed and his shoulders slumped. "I could hear them all running around up there – not talking, screaming at first, but then grunting and snarling. I just shut up and hunkered down."

Hardcourt and Fitzsimmons glanced at each other.

"Well, this is fucked up," Fitzsimmons said.

"Something weird is happening here," Hardcourt said.

"Ya think?" Menzies scoffed. "Hey, what's going on out there?"

"Nothing we could see; it's all quiet," Fitzsimmons replied. "Except for..."

Hardcourt knew he was going to say: *except for the bodies*, so shook his head.

"Except for what?" Menzies asked.

"Except, there's no one around," Hardcourt answered.

"Fine, then let's get the fuck out of here," Menzies said.

"What about your girlfriend?" Fitzsimmons asked.

"Are you kidding?" Menzies scoffed. "I'm only in here because of that bitch. She can go to Hell."

"A real gentleman," Fitzsimmons scoffed.

"Okay, you're coming with us," Hardcourt said. "We're going to do a quick check of the town, and then call it in."

Hardcourt turned and pressed the button for cell three on the wall. Luckily the power to the cells was still working and with a buzz-click, the door opened.

"Thanks." Menzies came out and then reached down to scoop up the water bottle, flipped the lid off and downed half of it.

"*Ahhh*, that's good." He kept his head tilted back. "Thought I was going to die." He lowered the bottle. "But I figured dying of thirst was better than dying of what was happening to these poor suckers." He pointed at the torn clothing.

"Shut up, and stay close," Hardcourt said.

The officers emerged with Menzies behind them. They still held their guns but switched off their flashlights.

"Hey, I have an idea," Fitzsimmons said.

"I hope it's a good one," Hardcourt replied.

"Yeah, well, all the new police comms systems are GPS linked." Fitzsimmons headed to one of the desk computers still working. "We might be able to track them if they're still wearing them. See where all the officers are."

"Do it," Hardcourt said and went to the glass doors and peered out. It was still dead as a door nail out there.

"On it." Fitzsimmons began to furiously type away, and in seconds slapped the desk top. "Got 'em." He smiled and pointed. "Most of them anyways."

Hardcourt came and looked over his shoulder. There was a grid map of the town, and a bunch of glowing dots were all congregated in one area.

Hardcourt frowned. "That's the old church. What are they all doing in there?"

"Or at least all their comm systems are in there." Fitzsimmons straightened. "What do you want to do?"

"Leave town," Menzies suggested.

The pair of policemen turned to him.

Menzies shrugged. "Look, Officers, there's something weird going on here, and if you'd seen what I did you'd want to leave town as well."

"Yeah, well, we can't do that until we find out what happened to our fellow officers." Hardcourt straightened. "And to everyone else."

"I know what happened to them," Menzies said softly.

The trio exited the police station and the officers quickly looked up and down the street. As before, the bright sunshine of the day normally would have been a warming and welcoming sensation. But today, the lack of sound, people, and even bird calls, just left them with an unsettled feeling.

Hardcourt opened the rover's back door. "In you get, Menzies. Unfortunately it only opens from the outside. So you get to stay put."

Menzies laughed with little humor. "Are you kidding? I want to stay here. I do not want to know what's going on in the old church."

They headed down the main street, slowly, and Hardcourt turned to the young man in the back. "I know most people up in these parts, and most of Thrumster. I don't recognize you; where are you from?"

"Newcastle," Menzies replied. "I came up for the fruit picking season two years back, and met my girl, Sheila Renfree, and kinda just stayed."

Hardcourt turned. "Bob Renfree's daughter? That's who you're messin' with?"

"Bob, yeah, that's her dad's name." He shrugged. "I don't have much to do with him." He guffawed. "He doesn't really approve."

Hardcourt shook his head. "It's a wonder Bob Renfree didn't tear your head off, fooling around with his daughter."

"She's twenty." Menzies looked away but then looked back with a grin. "And she ain't no little angel."

Fitzsimmons turned the corner and they slowed as they approached the old church. It had been due for demolition for a few years, and was deconsecrated. The old building was all sandstone and heavy wooden beams.

Hardcourt looked from the new church across the street, to the old church, and thought that the old one looked like a place of worship. But when he looked at the new one he thought it looked like a sterile office space or soulless box.

Fitzsimmons pulled in down the street. There was still no one and nothing moving, and oddly, no screech of a cockatoo, warble of a magpie, or even the squeak of parrots in the trees.

Hardcourt was first out, and Fitzsimmons slid out the other side.

The chief leaned back into the car and peered at Menzies. "You just sit tight. We won't be long." He shut the door.

"Fine with me." Menzies saluted and eased back into the seat, resting his head on the top and watching them through the front window.

***

Mark Menzies opened the water bottle again and drained it nearly all. He threw the bottle onto the seat beside him and let out a huge and revolting-tasting belch. He had a weird deep pain in his stomach. Not like he needed to take a big dump, or he'd eaten something bad, but more like things were starting to be pulled into knots inside him.

He worked his jaws – even his face tingled. It reminded him of the time he and a few of his buddies had bought some dried magic mushrooms and ate way too many – it made his entire body tingle and burn, and he ended up having a very bad trip.

He hadn't eaten anything in two days but strangely he wasn't hungry anymore – so he couldn't blame it on bad food. The only thing he'd had was the water.

He picked up the water bottle, and held it up to the light coming in the window. He thought he could see some tiny specks in there and it seemed a bit cloudy.

He tossed it back down on the seat, held his stomach and groaned. He felt like shit.

***

Chief Hardcourt and Constable Fitzsimmons headed toward the old church. The derelict sandstone and wood building had a weed-strewn yard and to one side there was a rusting wheelbarrow with empty flower pots inside.

From what Hardcourt understood the site hadn't been maintained as the old church was due to be torn down. However, the church had donated the site to the town so it could be made into a park with a playground.

As they got closer the first thing Hardcourt noticed was that the nailed boards that had been over the door had been pulled away. It matched what the locater had told them.

The pair climbed the few steps at the front and went to either side of the door. Hardcourt tilted his head, listening for a moment and then shook his head.

Normally, in a situation like this he'd call out, asking for the people inside to come out into the light. But after seeing the bodies in the lot beside the police station he decided that stealth might be the healthier option for both of them.

Hardcourt gave Fitzsimmons hand instructions and then counted down – three, two, *one* – they both went in, Hardcourt to the right and Fitzsimmons to the left. Both had guns held in both hands with the flashlights underneath.

There was nothing.

Hardcourt turned slowly, letting his heart rate ease back a little. The large room normally filled with pews was empty, dusty, and tomb silent.

He relaxed enough to take a few steps further in. "The vestry is at the back. And I know there's a basement for storage. Vestry first."

They went cautiously and slowly. The stone altar was still in place and also a dry baptismal font. At the front of the church behind the old altar was a pointed door. It was closed, and when Hardcourt tried the handle he found it locked.

He stepped back and looked down at the ground and didn't see any recent scuff marks. "If it's locked for us it was probably locked for them." He turned away. "The basement it is then."

The door was to the side and the pair approached quietly. This time the door was ajar, and Hardcourt gave it a gentle push. It swung open and steps led down into impenetrable darkness.

He reached in and flicked the light. Nothing.

"What a surprise," he muttered.

There was about a dozen steps to a small landing then it dog legged to the left, and then about half a dozen more.

"Stay alert." He bent to pick up a stick about a foot long that might have either blown in or fallen from the rotting ceiling. He then turned to look up at his young constable. "And if I start to back out quickly, you do too so I don't run into you."

"You got it," Fitzsimmons whispered.

Hardcourt led them down and winced at every step that squealed and groaned under their weight.

After a few minutes he made it to the landing. They shone their lights around but they weren't strong enough to reach the far corners. But from what they could see there were stacked things under tarpaulins, crates and boards leaning against the wall, and a jumble of old pews under a layer of cobwebs.

Toward the rear there was a mound of something that was just a dark lump in the gloom. Hardcourt stared at it, and the more he did the more his brows drew together – and that was why he brought the stick – he tossed it at the mound.

It moved.

Fitzsimmons leaned forward. "What the fuck is that?"

Both men focused their lights on the mound.

"Is that people in there?" Fitzsimmons asked in a voice that was a little higher pitched than normal.

"I don't know. But we gotta check it out. Could be our guys," Hardcourt replied. "Maybe they're hurt."

Fitzsimmons exhaled through his teeth. "Boss, are you sure we…"

"That's why they pay us the big bucks, Constable. Come on." Hardcourt advanced down the last few steps with arms outstretched and gun and light pointed at the mound. "Hurry up, I need your light."

Hardcourt had a primal sensation of fear and didn't want to go any closer. But he made himself. But only because he wanted to see what the thing was while also maintaining a safe distance.

As they walked slowly forward, Hardcourt smelled the coppery sweet smell of clotting blood. And now he thought he could hear something, like sliding, wheezing, and maybe a soft moaning.

"*Easy,*" Hardcourt whispered, and he wasn't sure if it was to Fitzsimmons or to bolster his own stretched nerves.

When they were a dozen feet away the thing began to come into focus.

"What the fu…" Fitzsimmons stopped dead.

Hardcourt took another few steps in front of his partner and stopped to stare in open-mouthed disbelief. And horror. It was people, maybe the entire police force, all jumbled together.

But they weren't lying on top of each other, they all seemed to be melted together. They were mostly naked, but there was the occasional blue of a police unform that was smeared in thick glutinous blood or some other extruded liquid.

Hardcourt's hand holding the light wobbled from fear – from the living pile, he saw arms extended, or trapped in the bloody mix. Feet stuck out, and there were the heads and faces, some only half a face, eyes rolling, and tongues lapping as if they were gibbering madly.

Others were backs of head, one with the short hair of a police haircut the only thing showing.

Fitzsimmons turned his head and threw up.

Hardcourt's teeth clamped together, and he backed up, knocking into Fitzsimmons. He barely heard the young man still gagging.

As Hardcourt watched with a shaking light, he saw the mass rise up. It balanced on multiple arms, legs, and even knees, and then along the front of the mass it split open with a wet tearing sound.

The slit widened and teeth came forward; tusks that were each six inches long and backward curving like he would have expected to see on some sort of prehistoric carnivore.

He was so terrified his mouth wouldn't work.

"*Fu-fu-fuuu…*" he could only manage.

Something shot out, like a cord, but rigid as a spear. Fitzsimmons, still with an elbow across his mouth to wipe away the vomit, looked up in time to catch the bloody red thing in the gut. With a grunt he was propelled backwards.

Hardcourt's mouth snapped shut as he felt it was hanging open. He went to go to his partner, but the man was suddenly yanked off his feet.

The spear-thing must have had an end like a fish hook or harpoon as it was being reeled in, and taking Fitzsimmons with it.

Hardcourt felt a moment of indecisive panic. He wanted to run, run away and never look back, but knew he couldn't leave his young officer. So he went after him.

Fitzsimmons was being reeled in towards the toothed maw. But when Hardcourt approached, another of the spears shot out and he had to dive out of the way or be speared himself.

When he rolled over and came back to his feet, Fitzsimmons screamed and was pulled into the giant mouth.

"No-*ooo*." Hardcourt heard the sickening crunch and bone as blood spurted to the ground.

"Bastard." Hardcourt lifted his gun and started firing into the mass of flesh.

But it was like hitting dead meat as the bullets smacked into the flesh, but no blood ran, just raw bullet holes punched into dead flesh.

And then the legs and arms underneath started to get moving, and like some sort of giant crab or insect it shuffled wetly toward him.

Hardcourt fired until his gun clicked on empty.

The mouth opened again like a giant raw wound and the lance shot out as before. Hardcourt fell back and the spear grazed him, cutting his shoulder.

He was on his back and heard, then saw, that the abomination was making its way toward him. He backed up, scuttling backwards, and dropped his gun in the process.

His shoulders hit the bottom step, and he turned and went up fast on all fours. He was out the basement door and through the church in seconds, putting his head down and sprinting hard.

He felt his heart hammering so hard it was beginning to hurt, and he regretted letting himself put on those extra pounds over the last few years.

Hardcourt leapt through the front door and suddenly felt the blessed sunshine on his face and sucked in a lung full of clean air, hoping it would take the stink away from his nostrils, and the slime that coated his mouth and throat.

He saw the police truck and the shape of Menzies watching him from the back seat. He knew he needed to call this in and get help. Lots of help.

He pulled the van door open and jumped in. Automatically he lunged for the radio, and didn't even think about Menzies not saying a word to him, or even asking what happened to Fitzsimmons.

In the split seconds he was wondering, he looked in the rear view mirror – what he saw didn't make sense.

He turned.

The kid, Mark Menzies, was gone or didn't look like Mark Menzies anymore. The thing in the back seat was hairless and looked like it had been skinned as it was all shining like it was wet or slimy. There was no nose and a pair of totally black eyes.

Its mouth dropped open revealing rows of needle-like teeth, and it coiled itself and sprang forward, coming through the mesh shield partition as if it were paper.

The last thing Chief Inspector Frank Hardcourt felt was something like a hundred daggers gripping his throat.

CHAPTER 06

Australia, Sydney, Eastern Coast

Isabella, Leonidas, and Marco disembarked from the flight and headed for the terminal. This time they had travelled under a Vatican diplomat passport, and all their luggage was branded with the diplomatic security clearance tags.

The luggage contents would have been hard to explain as there was a range of firearms, knives, three swords, black military fatigues, nano-masks, computer equipment, as well as a microscope and medical equipment. They were basically a moving armory and science division.

After clearing immigration, they found their smaller plane that would take them to Port Macquire, a medium-sized town a few hundred miles north and on the coast. This was the major hub town for Thrumster and where the tracker had told them the massive fly had headed to. And stayed. And now as the town had gone radio silent, this was the outpost they needed to get to.

Already, they were announced to the authorities as advisors, and were expected by the local police. Isabella wasn't anticipating any pushback from the authorities, and they would certainly assist where they could. But for now, they would need to be kept in the dark, as what they knew, and what they expected was unfolding, was too unbelievable for the locals to wrap their heads around.

The flight was only a few short hours and they arrived late morning to brilliant sunshine. They headed to their hotel and for now just wore civilian clothing.

Their cover story was they were researchers travelling from Italy that had experience with an infection that was spreading throughout the Asia Pacific region. In a way it was true.

One way or the other, they would need to split off and head to Thrumster – their prime objective was to kill the monstrous plague-spreading fly. But they also needed to obtain a specimen for a blood sample.

The Knights then needed to try and isolate the disease and hopefully their scientists could then work on a vaccination. Maybe even a cure. If that could be done they could stop the Hell plague before it even began.

For the meeting with the local police, the three Templar Knights dressed in dark suits, and the only weapons they took with them were a small gun in a holster in the small of their back.

For now, they were playing the professional, and needed to make a good impression on the local forces. Though they had support from higher ups, and plenty of international passes, the locals could make things difficult for them if they chose to.

Their first meeting was with Mike Lawler, chief of police for the district. He had over two hundred officers under his command and oversaw a Port Macquarie community of around forty-five thousand souls.

They entered the medium-sized office block, gave their names and were told Lawler was coming down. In seconds the elevator pinged and out stepped a middle-aged man, possibly late forties, with iron grey hair but looking like he kept in shape. It had to be Mike Lawler.

With him was a woman of about mid-thirties, short hair, brawny, and an I-take-no-shit look on her face.

The man's eyes went to the three in suits and sized them up quickly – the woman with the dark piercing eyes and athletic frame, and the two men that both radiated a fearless danger. One of them had on a backpack, that cut deep into his shoulders – meaning there was something really damn heavy in there.

"Mike Lawler," he said. "I've been expecting you." He turned over his shoulder. "This is Senior Officer Angela Bennet assisting."

Lawler turned. "Follow me."

A few of the more junior officers watched them pass by as they avoided the elevator and headed up the steps to Lawler's office. He hadn't shaken hands, offered them coffee, and seemed pissed off.

It made Isabella think things might be worse than she thought.

They entered the large office. Lawler sat in his huge chair behind a huge wooden desk, and Angela Bennet stood at his shoulder.

Isabella didn't wait to be asked if she could sit, and did so in the center. Marco was to her right and Leonidas to her left.

"Thrumster," she simply said and watched his face.

"Small town abut twenty miles out." His gaze was unwavering. "What do you know about it?"

Isabella probably knew more than Lawler as they had already tapped into the police band network and had heard the communications.

She remained impassive. "I know you've lost contact with the inhabitants, and that the entire population seems to be missing. I know two of your men went in there yesterday, and are also now missing, as well as all the police stationed in there."

"How'm I doing so far?" She raised her eyebrows.

Bennet's gaze was half lidded. "Now tell us something we don't know."

"I know you've got an infection in there, and I know if we don't get a sample and analyze it, then the larger community of Port Macquarie will be next, followed by the entire East Coast." She sat forward. "And I know we're wasting time. How's that so far?"

Lawler exhaled through his nose. "If that's the case it should be quarantined." He frowned. "Is it airborne?"

"We don't believe so. We think it is passed on physically – a bite, or ingestion or injection of infected liquid."

Lawler opened a desk drawer and took out a paper folder. He flipped it open and lifted some large photographs. He tossed them across his desk, and Isabella caught them.

They were poor quality, possibly taken by a surveillance drone. They showed a creature she knew well – one of the abominations, the things that looked like a cross between a dog and a skinned ape. And she knew, something that was once a human being.

She shrugged. "Sorry, I don't know your Australian species all that well." She looked up. "Is it a dingo?"

Bennet snarled, "That's not a fucking dingo, and you know it's…"

"At ease, Bennet," Lawler warned.

The female cop shut her mouth and Lawler looked unwaveringly at Isabella. "You want our help, and we want yours. It works best if we level with each other."

"I agree." She slid the pictures back. "This could be the result of the infection. We need to get in there and get a sample so we can begin work."

"We'll send a support team…" Lawler began.

"No, we work alone. You can help by closing off all roads and tracks in and out. Time is of the essence here, Chief Inspector."

"You're taking one of my people with you, otherwise you can go home now." His gaze was dead level. "That's not negotiable."

"That could be their funeral," Isabella replied.

Lawler mashed large fingers together on his desk. "You're taking Bennet." He lifted his chin. "So is it go, or no-go and you go home?"

Bennet's eyes were round at the unexpected offer of her services.

"Go. Obviously." Isabella half smiled. "We leave immediately."

"Ah, do I need some sort of Hazmat suit?" Bennet asked.

"No. Like I said, we think it's blood and mucous borne. Maybe in waterways as well," Isabella replied and then held up a finger. "Question, tell me where Thrumster gets its water from?"

"The Lake Innes," Lawler replied. "It's still full this time of year. It only feeds the town, but not the greater Port Macquarie area."

"Good, good." Isabella stood and faced the policewoman. "We should be done by nightfall. Take your own water, and be ready in twenty minutes."

Bennet nodded. "I'll take the off road utility vehicle. In case things need to be pushed through."

Isabella nodded and turned back to the chief. "Shut the roads in and out. I don't want any infected, ah, animals, getting away."

"You mean people." Lawler also stood.

Isabella smiled. "Both."

Isabella went to leave with her two Knights.

"Tell me," Lawler said. "What happens if you come across an infected person?'

Isabella searched for a diplomatic way to answer. "We try and avoid them." Her gaze was dead. "But if we are attacked, we need to respond with force to stay alive."

"Guess I need to be armed," Bennet said. "I'll kit up and meet you out front in the vehicle. Thrumster is only an hour up the highway."

"I wish it was further," Isabella said.

"Excuse me." Leonidas held his ground.

The group turned to him.

"Tell me. Has there been any reports in the area of large insects lately?" he asked.

Bennet snorted. "Insects? Buddy, this is Australia, there are bugs down here that would fight your Doberman for their last biscuit."

Leonidas looked to Isabella.

Lawler saw the look between them and grunted in mild amusement. "He means it, doesn't he?"

"He does," Isabella said.

Bennet frowned. "Like what?"

"Like giant flies, and I mean *giant* flies," Isabella replied.

"Giant flies?" Bennet began to shake her head, but then frowned. "Gillies?"

"Oh yeah, the Gillies farm," Lawler said and turned to Leonidas. "Hank Gillies has a farm about forty miles up the coast. He reported that a small plane was bothering his cattle. Could be related."

Leonidas worked a small screen and then turned it to Lawler. "Anywhere near here?"

Lawler grabbed the edge of the screen and looked at the map with the grid lines and the small pulsing red dot. "That's the Simmons' farm. It's a bit closer to town but near enough to the Gillies' place."

"We need to go there first," Leonidas replied.

"You tracking something?" Lawler asked.

"A vector." Isabella turned away. "We need to get going. Out front in ten minutes, Officer Bennet. Let's go."

In just on ten minutes Bennet appeared from around the corner of the building in a police SUV, and to her credit, she now wore tactical gear. Isabella was glad the woman was taking her seriously.

Isabella got in the front and nodded to her, and Marco and Leonidas climbed in the rear. Marco also hefted a long black bag in beside himself, and Leonidas placed another bag in the trunk that caused the vehicle to settle a little lower.

Bennet turned to him. "What are you bringing, the kitchen sink?"

He ignored her.

"Okay, well, Thrumster it is then." Bennet pulled away from the sidewalk. "Any idea where and what you want to see first?"

"We need to investigate something out at this Simmons' farm." Isabella half turned. "Call them."

"I already did at the station," Bennet said. "But I'll try again."

She dialed and put the phone to her ear.

Isabella could hear the endless ring, and not even an answer machine. Bennet shook her head and disconnected the call.

"Still nothing."

"Okay, we'll do our site visit. Depending on what we find we can then take a drive through the town to assess the situation," Isabella said. "We look for a live specimen to take a blood sample from. Hopefully we don't need to be going door to door."

"Damn right," Bennet said, and then: "What if we find survivors?"

"We do nothing. Odds are the people in the town are in various stages of succumbing to the contagion. We can't risk them getting close to us."

Bennet shook her head as she stared forward watching the road. "I'm not sure I can do that. I know some of the people that live in Thrumster."

Marco leaned forward between the seats. "Officer Bennet, you have to prepare yourself for things that are going to be beyond your experience and perhaps comprehension. Things that are highly dangerous and deadly."

She frowned and half turned as she drove. "I thought you said it was a disease." She shook her head. "I have a duty to the people of this district."

Isabella drew in a deep breath and let it out slowly. "Officer Bennet, no one, no matter who they are, no matter how healthy they seem, or what relationship you have with them, is getting in the truck with us. Do you understand?"

"We'll see." The policewoman's jaw jutted.

Isabella turned away, hoping the woman wasn't going to be a problem.

"Five minutes," Bennet said as they bounced along the old road that was crowded with bushland on each side.

In the back, Marco and Leonidas opened their huge bags and began to draw out their weapons and check them. Marco then drew out the swords, checked them, as each Knight had their own that was perfectly sized and balanced just for them.

He handed Leonidas his and reached forward into the front seat to give Isabella hers. She already had the back scabbard in place and held it between her thighs as Leonidas handed her a range of weapons. She checked their ammunition and readiness, and then slotted them into holsters and pouches.

Bennet cast a glance at the sword. "What the fuck is that thing?"

Isabella didn't bother turning. "It's a cultural thing."

"Cultural, my ass. You can't be carrying that around in Thrumster. You'll scare people."

Leonidas and Marco chuckled in the back.

Isabella grinned. "You have no idea what will be scaring the people of this town. And how is the sword any more dangerous than your gun?"

Bennet scowled. "For a start, I'm the cop, remember? And I'm not sure you're even supposed to have guns for that matter."

"Ask me how you feel about my weapons after we've completed our work here," Isabella said and nodded forward at the road. "Focus."

They were coming to a fork in the road, where one way forward had a huge arched sign that welcomed them to Thrumster, population two thousand three hundred, and the home of the koala bear.

"Simmons' farm?" Bennet asked.

"Yes," Isabella replied.

They took the other road, and sped along a less well kept road toward the farming property. In ten more minutes they came to the property and found the front gate was wide open. They headed in to the grounds.

"Five minutes," Bennet said and looked around. "Weird."

"What is?" Isabella asked.

"They usually have a few of their horses in the front paddock. Must have kept them in today," she replied.

The farm house homestead was a large two-story building sitting between the horse barn a few hundred feet back, and also a large garage and equipment shed. Bennet sounded the horn on their approach.

No one came out or even appeared at a window.

"There's only Jack and Margie, as the boys are away at school now," she said as she pulled up out front. "That ain't good," she said softly.

The front door of the house was smashed open. Not just the door busted outwards, but the frame on both sides was blown out like something way too big for the doorway wanted out. And in a hurry.

"We may have missed it." Isabella turned in her seat. "Leonidas?"

The Knight checked the grid map and locater. "It's still here. Inside," he said.

Isabella pulled her sword, and the other two Knights did the same. She turned to Bennet. "You better wait here."

"What?" Bennet bristled. "You're not in charge here."

"Fine, then draw your weapon." Isabella turned away. "Leonidas, Marco, take the downstairs. Bennet, you come with me up top."

The four of them moved cautiously inside and paused for a moment in the entrance area, just adjusting to the sounds and feel of the house, straining their ears and senses.

After a moment Isabella nodded and Marco and Leonidas went around the steps to the living areas. Isabella and Bennet went up the front stairs, and Isabella was relieved to see the policewoman held her gun now, two handed and pointed down, but ready.

At the top they paused again but only until they saw the main bedroom.

"Same as downstairs," Bennet whispered.

"Yes. This is where it came from," Isabella replied softly.

The bedroom door frame was burst open as though whatever had busted out downstairs had started out in there. On the frame was a glutinous red residue.

Isabella crossed to the room and peered in – the large bed was flattened to the floor, and the sheets were in a terrible state, torn, covered in the same blackish-red mucous as the doorframe and here it glistened like snail slime.

Isabella quickly went to the closets and small washroom and checked inside. There was nothing.

"Party has gone elsewhere," Bennet said.

"We check the other rooms," Isabella replied.

"Let's split up; get this over with," Bennet said.

The policewoman started down the corridor and Isabella grabbed her arm. "Listen, you find anyone in here, you don't let them get close to you. Got it?"

"I know what I'm doing." Bennet went to pull her arm away.

Isabella hung on. "I mean it." She let her go.

The pair went in opposite directions. Isabella went inside a room set up like a drawing room, with a huge picture window to look out over the pastures. It was an idyllic scene, and Isabella imagined the family sitting in here, drinking coffee or maybe beers after a hard day and just unwinding together.

What the fuck?

At the sound of Bennet's voice Isabella came out of the room fast and headed back down the corridor. She came to the room Bennet was in, the boy's bedroom, and saw the woman with her shoulders hunched and staring down at something huge on the bed.

"Damn." Isabella lowered her sword.

It was a fly carcass, or rather the empty shell of one. It was about seven feet long, perfectly formed, but hollow as a drum. At first it looked like the real Octavius Conti fly, but it was dark and nearly translucent.

Isabella walked closer and stared – it was the face she recognized. The features were human from the top lip upwards. Below that it had the long pad and bristled mouthpart of a blowfly.

"What the hell is this fuc…" Bennet's mouth snapped shut for a moment and she turned. "Hey, is this why you asked about giant flies? *This* is what you meant?"

"Yes." Isabella straightened.

"It's a fucking monster," Bennet wailed.

"That it is, and we're too late. It's shed its skin, grown, and taken off who knows where." She pointed to the red blinking dot stuck to it. "It's also shed our tracker."

"I don't believe this." Bennet rubbed her forehead.

"We check the rest of the property and out buildings. Then we go get our sample." Isabella exited.

***

In minutes more they were at the barn, and Leonidas and Marco pulled open the huge doors. They recoiled momentarily from the smell, and after a moment went into the large dark space.

In the center of the large hay strewn room were piles of red and gristle-covered bones.

"The horses," Bennet said. "They ate them?"

"The eggs." Leonidas pointed to the shell casings broken open upon the piles of ruined animals.

"What came out?" Bennet asked.

As if in answer, from out of the roofing a buzzing started and then a swarm of fist-sized insects came at them.

Bennet ducked, but Isabella, Leonidas and Marco were like a blur of motion, swinging their blades, chopping and slicing the air with almost impossible precision. In seconds more the flies were in pieces on the ground.

Bennet slowly got to her feet. "What the fuck? I mean literally, what the fuck is going on here?"

The three Knights kept their swords firmly gripped as they turned slowly, craning their heads upward to scan the rafters.

"This is what hatched from the eggs," Isabella said. "Another vector." She turned. "This is what the Conti fly is doing and will do; lay these everywhere and all around the world."

"We need backup," Bennet said.

"We are your backup," Isabella said and turned to step back and look down at the ground.

She frowned. A small amount of gas seemed to be rising from the fly bodies. "Oh no," she said. "We need a sample, quick."

Marco shrugged off a small pack he had over his shoulder and ripped it open. He took out a glass cannister and a pair of long forceps. But in just the seconds it took him, the fly bodies crumpled into a black mush as more gas rose from them.

In moments more they were just dark, greasy stains on the barn floor.

"Gone," Marco said. "It's non-viable now." He stood.

"We're too late." Isabella gritted her teeth and silently cursed through them. "Okay, we check the other buildings and then go into the town."

In minutes more they were headed back to the police vehicle. Bennet stopped and looked back at the smashed open doorway.

"What exactly came out of there?" she asked.

Isabella turned, having an idea of the glued together abomination that smashed its way out. Those poor souls didn't stand a chance.

"The flesh is weak, Officer Bennet," she said softly. "Remember that."

"That makes no damn sense," the policewoman retorted.

"It will soon." Isabella put her sword in the scabbard over her back. "Let's go, we still have work to do."

***

"Slow," Isabella said.

They moved past a few houses on large plots of land, and soon came to a main street. They then eased back to about twenty miles per hour, just coasting.

Isabella saw an abandoned pushbike, cars with doors open, and even what looked like a bag of groceries dropped on the sidewalk.

"This happened quickly," Leonidas said as they continued down the desolate street.

"No one," Bennet said. "Maybe I should give the siren a blast to draw out any survivors huddling in their homes."

"Not yet," Isabella said. "We might draw out something that we don't want to deal with just yet."

"Some *thing*?" Bennet half turned.

"Stop. Go back," Leonidas said after they went past a side street.

Bennet turned the car around and slowed. About a hundred yards further in there was a stopped police truck.

"There," he said.

"That must be Hardcourt and Fitzsimmons," Bennet said softly.

She headed in and stopped about fifty feet from the SUV. Even from where they stopped they could see the front windshield had been exploded outward, as if something had smashed its way out rather than in.

And the glass on the front hood was glittering like rubies in the sunshine meaning it was probably covered in blood.

Bennet went to exit, but Isabella put her hand on the female cop's arm.

"Wait." She looked around, and Leonidas and Marco did the same. "Okay, we take it slow and silent for now." She kept her eyes on the empty streetscape. "We just want a sample and then we exit."

"You know I can't do that," Bennet said. "Gotta find my fellow officers."

"Then you'll be staying," Isabella said as a warning.

"You think you're gonna fucking leave me here?" Bennet scoffed.

"No." Isabella's expression was deadpan. "You'll be dead. Or worse."

Bennet frowned. "Worse than dead?"

"Yes, Officer Bennet, there are some things worse than death." Isabella turned back to the street.

Bennet cursed under her breath. "And if it was one of yours, would you leave them behind?"

Isabella suddenly knew she was wrong and right – she'd left Drake behind. But she wanted to go back and get him.

Isabella refused to meet her eyes. "Just keep up."

The group stepped out of the vehicle and stood close to their vehicle in the street for several moments as they surveyed the landscape.

Bennet nodded to the other vehicle and headed to the driver's side, and Isabella to the passenger side while the two men kept watch.

As they approached they were aware of the silence and stillness in the air – there was nothing that seemed to be living in the town, not a person, dog, cat or bird. There wasn't even the usual zumm of the summer cicadas.

Bennet was first to the vehicle, followed by Isabella.

"Ah, shit." Bennet coughed, and stepped back with an arm over her mouth. Isabella stared in at the grisly tableau – there was blood everywhere. In the back there was shredded clothing, but in the front there was a male body, with the head missing, and most of the chest cavity exposed as if something had tried to burrow into the rib cage from above to get at the heart and lungs. And succeeded as both sets of organs were missing.

"I think that was Frank Hardcourt." She backed up, grimacing. "What the fuck is in this town?"

"A nightmare," Isabella said softly.

"I thought you said we were going to be dealing with a non-airborne contagion. That's no fucking effect of a contagion." She seethed, "*Look at him.*"

"It is," Marco said. "The contagion changes people. Makes them violent, different."

"Nope, we should leave. Get backup." Bennet started to walk backwards toward the van.

"No." Isabella rounded on her. "We came here for a sample and we're going to get one." She glared. "If you want to go back and hide in the car, that's fine, but you hand over the keys as you're not going anywhere."

Isabella held out her hand. "Or you suck it up, and come with us."

Bennet wiped her face with the back of her sleeve and then drew in a deep breath. "Sorry, I'm just…"

"Don't apologize," Isabella said. "This would tear at the mind of most people."

"You've dealt with this before?" Bennet asked.

"We have. And survived." Isabella smiled flatly.

Bennet nodded. "Fitzsimmons is still out there somewhere. I need to find him."

"Good. That's the spirit." Isabella stared for a moment more.

She wanted to tell the policewoman that Fitzsimmons would already be dead. But that would do nothing for her right now.

Isabella turned away. "Come on."

In front of the abandoned car was a blood trail. "Whatever took your officer's head went that way." She nodded down the street. "We're going after it."

The group of four headed down the street, and after another few minutes Leonidas held a hand up stopping them.

He pointed off to the side at the old church. "Front door's open."

Isabella shook her head. "Later, we follow the blood for now."

They came to where the sealed road ended and dirt took over. Leonidas went down on his haunches near the blood trail. "Look here."

He placed two fingers close to the dirt. The others crowded around and saw the weird print.

"That's too big for a dingo," Bennet said. "And even too big for a domestic dog like a shepherd or rottweiler."

"It's neither." Isabella scanned the area. "We're running out of time." She looked toward the west, where the sun was heading fast toward the horizon. "They're probably waiting for nightfall, and I do not want to be out here in the dark."

There was a tap running in a front yard, and Isabella went quickly to it, took out a sample jar and collected some of the water. She placed it in a pants pouch and returned to them.

"Door to door?" Leonidas asked.

Isabella looked around. "No, but we might have to change the game plan – call them to us. Set a trap."

"How many people live in this town?" Leonidas asked.

"Over two thousand," Bennet replied.

"We can't deal with an attack of that size," Leonidas said.

"We only want one. And only a bit of one," Isabella replied.

"What do you mean can't deal with an attack of that size?" Bennet's frown was like an axe wound in the middle of her forehead. "We haven't written off finding survivors yet."

Isabella looked to their vehicle which was now about five hundred yards from them. Close enough, she thought.

"We have," she said. "It's time for you to see what we're, *you're*, really dealing with." She drew her gun and fired it twice into the air. "Get ready."

Isabella holstered her gun and then pulled her sword. The other two Knights did the same.

Bennet shook her head. "This is not real."

From somewhere behind the buildings there was a hiss like that of a giant snake. Then came a whine and deep throated grunting.

"What is that?" Bennet asked softly.

"You're about to find out," Isabella said. "Draw your weapon. Don't let them get close."

Bennet did as asked.

From the top of the street something on all fours darted from one side to the other way too fast for them to make out.

From inside a house close to them there was the sound of something being knocked over. More grunts and whines.

Then a screen door slowly opened with a squeal. Something slunk out to peer at them.

"What. The. Fuck?" Bennet breathed. She lifted her gun.

"Don't shoot. Yet," Isabella said.

The creature was hunched over and had six legs. The face might have been of a man, but the eyes were totally black and there was no nose, just two slits like on a bat. The thing seemed to sniff at the air and its mouth hung open revealing rows of needles.

It emerged a little more, and they saw it wore the remnants of a tattered camo t-shirt.

"It's wearing clothes. That goddamn monster is wearing clothes," Bennet whispered shakily.

"Because it wasn't always a monster," Marco replied.

From up and down the street there came more noise and movement. In moments more they spotted a dozen more of the creatures, some with four legs and others with eight, moving like large spiders.

"Okay, we back towards the car. They should follow. When they attack, I'll take a sample, and then we are out of here." Isabella began to back up, keeping her sword pointed at the beasts.

Leonidas and Marco did the same, and Bennet kept her gun moving from one of the things to the other.

"I thought you said it was a plague. A sickness," she said.

"It is," Isabella replied. "This is what happens when you get infected." She exhaled in a whoosh of frustration. "This is why I know there are no survivors. These things are also carnivorous."

"Oh god," Bennet replied.

"Yes, good, call to him. You'll need him soon." Isabella turned to Bennet and saw the movement from the corner of her eye. "Behind us."

The attack came from all sides as if it was coordinated. Dozens came at them at first, and the Knights wielded their swords faster than the eye could follow. Creatures were beheaded, cut in half, or had limbs cleanly removed. There was no blood, just a thick tar-like substance that stained the road.

Bennet screamed as one latched its viper teeth onto her forearm. She clubbed at it with the butt of her gun, and it pulled back, taking a chunk of meat with it.

"*Fucker!*" she screamed, blasting after it.

Isabella just looked at her and then turned away.

The policewoman kept firing and thankfully, Bennet was a good shot and she managed to get head shots which was the only way to make them go down for good. Even the creatures that had limbs cut away kept coming at them.

Isabella saw Bennet's arm dripped with blood, and though it wasn't normally a fatal wound, she knew that what it meant was something far worse than death for the woman.

In minutes more one dived at Isabella and she cleanly took its head off. On its head was the remnants of long blond hair and she grabbed it up, and used the hair to tie it to her belt.

"Got it, we're out of here." She collided with Bennet. "Back to the car."

This time Isabella pulled her gun. "Let's make a hole."

There were creatures all over the vehicle and in front of them, and she, Leonidas, and Marco blasted away, as did Bennet.

There was a lull for the moment, and Isabella called for Leonidas to remove the bomb.

"Bomb?" Bennet scowled as she held her arm. "What freaking bomb?"

Isabella turned to her. "The town is lost. The infection has won here. We need to make sure we at least slow down the infection wave."

"You brought a freaking bomb into our town?" she yelled.

Leonidas ran to the car rear door, opened it, and yanked out the heavy bag. He opened it, displaying a mechanism that was all silver pipe and glass tubes of blue liquid. He set the timer for one hour.

"Sixty minutes. We need to be half a mile from here." He rose to his feet.

Bennet pointed her gun at him. "Turn that thing off. There will be no second warning."

"I'm sorry, Angela." Isabella swung her sword and beheaded the policewoman.

The head bounced away to land upright, with the eyes still wide with shock.

Isabella sighed. "But you were already lost."

Leonidas and Marco began to back toward the vehicle. Isabella ran to the policewoman's fallen body and grabbed the keys from her pocket. She turned. "Get in!" she shouted to the Knights and opened the door and jumped in the passenger side.

Marco got in and grabbed the wheel, Leonidas jumped in the back, and Isabella turned in her seat to toss the creature's severed head in behind her.

"Go, go!" Isabella watched as the remaining sunlight began to get shut out as more and more of the things piled onto the vehicle.

Their teeth snapped at them and using their multiple arms they beat at the glass. The horde battered and ripped at the car, but the steel and toughened glass held.

"We're safe in here. That's bullet proof..."

One of the things punched the windscreen hard enough to create a star crack. Then with a boom, the front left of the car sank down as a tire was punctured.

"Any time, Marco," she yelled.

Marco immediately put it in reverse and jammed his foot down hard on the accelerator. The car flew backwards, and after a few seconds he turned hard so the front of the vehicle swung around, and about half a dozen of the things slid off onto the road.

He put it in gear and punched it forward. With a crack and crunch, he ran over the bodies beneath the car, and exploded any that got in his way.

Marco accelerated again. "Hold on!" he yelled.

He then slammed on the brakes and the last of the things still clinging tight to the police truck flew forward. He put it in gear again and ran them over with a lot of bone splintering crunches.

This time he didn't stop or slow and kept lifting the speed out of the town.

Isabella looked back through the rear window and saw the gathering horde. There must have been several hundred and more coming in.

She bet it was the entire town. This had happened in just a few days. Without intervention and disruption, this would be the fate of the entire state, then country, and then the rest of the world.

"Not if I can help it," she whispered.

From the back seat Leonidas handed her a thick plastic bag with the severed head in it. She took it and held it up, looking at the monstrous features for a second. The dark eye swiveled toward her.

"Ugh." She dropped it and put her foot on it.

Underneath her boot she could feel movement – the damn thing was still alive, and if given the chance would have bitten her.

She checked her wristwatch – three minutes.

Isabella turned to look back through the rear window as the seconds ticked down. Exactly on schedule, there was a colossal *thump*, and then a massive glow from a few miles back. A small mushroom cloud rose into the air, and a breeze blew past them buffeting the bush surrounding the roar.

Isabella watched the smoke rise and the glow receded to a

conflagration and then she sat back, rested her head against the head rest, and let her thoughts turn back to Drake Stoker.

I'll get you, Drake. One way or the other I'll get you out, she silently prayed.

"Back into town?" Marco asked.

"No, we're done here," Isabella sighed. "Straight to the airport."

CHAPTER 07

Brisban International Airport – Passenger Terminals

The long gangway corridors each had large 747 planes all waiting in line like suckling baby animals being fed passengers.

Underneath, automated slides delivered bags up into their holds. Benny Anderson threw the bags on the carousel, and they were delivered up to Adrian Sherrod, who grabbed them and maneuvered them into a semblance of space-saving order inside.

The first and business class passenger bags were already done – stacked neatly and carefully, and strapped in. Now came the economy bags, and they were furiously thrown into place, some getting a kick if they didn't behave probably by slotting into a near perfect sized space for them.

As Adrian bent down to reach for another bag as it came up the ramp, the huge thing flew out of the hold over his head, ruffling his hair.

"Hey." He grabbed his head.

He watched the thing like a small airplane zoom away, heading to another plane further down the arrival tube.

"Did you see that?" he yelled.

Benny Anderson lifted his head. "*Huh*, what?"

"I said, did you see …?" he could tell by the vacant look on his colleague's face, he didn't. "Ah, forget it, just something that looked like a giant mutant blowfly came outta the hold."

Anderson grinned. "Yeah, sure, you better lay off the Jazz Cigarettes, mate."

He went back to tossing bags on the ramp again.

Sherrod sighed and rubbed the back of his head. For a few moments he thought he should tell someone. Then he guessed their response would be the same as Anderson's.

Not worth the trouble, and jokes, he thought.

He also went back to stacking the bags, giving his head a final rub.

***

The monstrous thing that used to be Octavius Conti, entered the next plane's baggage hold. Already its abdomen was swelling again.

He couldn't help himself, as he was being driven by a force far greater and stronger than his own will. He climbed along the inside of the roof, his strong clasping claws holding the ceiling where he went to the darkest corner. And just like in the previous plane, he squatted, and immediately began to deposit hundreds of vase-shaped eggs that stuck to the ceiling.

He would implant them in every plane he could get to, and when he was finished, would head to the coast to seed some of the container ships.

But he wouldn't rest. He couldn't rest. Not until he left the country and flew up the map towards Indonesia. There was a population of over two hundred and eighty million to feel the blessing of this Master's plague.

He had much to do, and he was being urged on to greater speed at every second.

CHAPTER 08

Hell – below, and far away

Drake Stoker and Clive Benson plodded along the stinking shoreline of slime, bones, and rotted nameless things, but never found the water. It seemed to be forever just out of reach.

Around them there was a decrepit twilight and the stink of rot and corruption filled their nostrils.

Benson stopped and bent over with his hands on his knees. "This is killing me."

Drake nodded, knowing what he meant. Walking through sticky, sucking mud that hung onto the boots was draining at every step. His thighs felt like jelly and his calves ached. Plus there was nowhere to stop and rest as there was no way he was sitting or lying down in the slime.

From time to time, he had seen worms as thick as his finger pull back below the tar-like substance, and once he pointed his light at several of them that poked above the surface, and he was sure they had tiny human faces.

More damned souls, he bet Isabella would have told him. Perhaps people who had sinned so badly they were cast out to the depths of Hell to spend eternity as worms pushing through the slime and putrescence.

The dismal lighting didn't give them much of a distance view, but out toward their right side, Drake was sure there was some sort of outcrop or upthrustings. If it was above the mud line, then it might be dry. It would be a good place to rest, and maybe if they could scale a little higher they could get their bearings.

"Over there," Drake said. "Might be high land."

"Works for me," Benson said and the pair continued their muddy slog.

They eventually came to the first of the things he had seen sticking from the mud, and it wasn't what he expected or wanted to see.

They stopped before it.

"Dinosaur?" Benson asked.

It was the bones of a giant animal of some sort. But the massive, toothed skull had one cyclopean eye, and the rib bones towered high above them.

Drake looked upwards. "About fifty feet, and that's with it lying down. Hundreds long. Bigger than a blue whale," Drake said." He pointed at the clawed feet. "And with legs."

"Old," Benson said. "I hope his relatives aren't hanging around."

From somewhere out in the darkness a low moan began to fill the air and continued for nearly an entire minute.

"You were saying?" Drake scoffed.

"Yeah, that ain't good." Benson turned about for a moment before facing his friend. "Captain, feet are killing me. Let's say we get off this mud flat, as my boots will begin to rot soon."

"Yep." Drake noticed Benson had been limping for a while.

They trudged on in silence and Drake's mind moved to another place and another time – one he remembered as being of sunshine, and bees on flowers, cold beer, and smiling faces. He wondered how Ethan was recovering. And how Addison was getting on. He also kept seeing Isabella's face.

I met an angel once. He smiled at the thought, and then, *I should have told her that.*

Yeah, if he ever got out of here, he was definitely going to ask her out. His heart beat a little faster, and he knew he was nervous thinking about doing that.

He scoffed.

For fuck sake, he thought. He was trudging through hell, and this is what made him nervous. He began to laugh.

"Something funny, boss?" Benson asked.

"Just thinking it's been a helluva day," Drake replied.

"Day? How many days?" Benson turned to look over his shoulder at his boss, his Reaper captain, and friend. "I've lost track of time." He stopped and frowned. "Weird. I'm not that hungry. Why not?" He looked to Drake. "Hey, dark thought; you don't suppose we're already dead, and just don't know it?"

"Do your feet hurt?" Drake asked.

"You know they do, especially my left one, and like a bitch," Benson said and grinned.

"Okay, then you're not dead." He chuckled softly and then nodded forward. "Land ho."

Ahead of them the slimy lake shore ended. It rose up towards something that could be some sort of weird growths like a giant petrified forest.

They walked up out of the slime, and Benson took his time as his limp was getting more pronounced. Drake stood on the small rise and looked about.

What he had at first thought was some sort of growths or ancient forest looked more like a city.

"Everything is melted," Benson said.

"Or decayed." Drake turned slowly.

They might have been buildings once but they were just the skeletal remains of structures now. And they were covered in some sort of slimy-looking growth that hung from them like black, greasy webbing.

"These are no ancient olden time's structures. They look more like they were a city from modern times." Benson looked around. "This doesn't make sense."

"Is it a city from the past, present, or future?" Drake said, and walked closer to a strange-looking mound of slimy growths. He peered at one and reached forward to pull some of the weed-like stickiness to the side to see better.

A skeletal hand rose up to grab his wrist.

"Shit." He jerked backwards and the arm came free, but still gripped his wrist. His momentum caused him to fall back as Benson lunged to him and gripped the skeletal limb. He tugged the thing free and flung it into the twilight darkness.

"That piece of fucking thing was alive," Benson said.

Drake got to his feet and they backed away from the thing he had thought was an odd- shaped lump of the slimy moss. But inside there might have been a person once. Now a skeletal figure.

Drake looked about. "There's more of them."

Planted around the decrepit buildings were more of the lumps.

Benson grimaced. "Like graves, but the people in them are rotted but not dead. Just damned forever."

"A damned city," Drake said. "The whole place is damned."

Drake and Benson carefully edged away from the slime skeleton to close in on one of the decrepit buildings and look up.

Drake then headed to the front steps, still looking up.

"No way," Benson said. "No way you are going in there?"

Drake turned with a grin. "And you can stay out front by yourself with all your living dead friends or come with me."

"Now that's a shit choice if ever there was one." Benson looked up and sighed. "I hate this place."

"When you get home, you can leave them a bad review," Drake chuckled.

"Home. Yeah, I'm just gonna think about that," Benson sighed.

Drake looked up again. "If we can climb, we can see how high we can get and try and get our bearings. We need a direction."

"In and out," Benson said.

Drake headed in, and Benson limped after him.

The two men eased in between two hanging shawls of slime. Where it touched the men it left long snot-like streaks, and Drake leaned away trying hard not to get any on his face.

Inside there was no furniture, nothing on the walls, and everything was out of shape and miss-sized. Doors were standard-sized on one wall, and double-sized on another. There was a fireplace that started three feet up from the ground, and a window at floor level.

"It's like a madman took a stab at building design." Drake looked around.

"Yeah, drugs are bad, man," Benson scoffed. "Creepy as fuck. Hey, stairs over there."

They eased through more of the seaweed-like drapes and found that the stairs were all differing sizes, and the amount of riser changed every turn they took.

After climbing about a hundred steps there were still no doorways and Drake wondered if they had entered some sort of fire escape. Just as he was going to call for an about face he came to their first exit. He had to wait for Benson who huffed and puffed his way up behind him.

The big man was fit, but his foot was really troubling him now. As soon as they took a break, he'd get the big guy to remove his boot so he could check it out.

Drake put his shoulder to the door, but didn't have to push too hard as the wood literally disintegrated like wet carboard and fell to the floor as mush. The pair of Reapers peered inside and then went through the opening fast.

They were on what might have once been a third floor, but in some areas the ceiling was eight feet high and in others they had to crouch as if the upper floor was in danger of collapsing down on them.

There were a few piles of things around the room that might have once been furniture and on the wall there were a few crooked frames holding faded pictures and a tarnished mirror.

Benson stopped in front of one and Drake frowned at another – it was a clouded mirror and he was drawn to it. He slowly walked closer as Benson called to him.

"Ugly mother fuckers." The big man nodded at one of the frames.

Drake turned away to where Benson indicated and lifted his flashlight to the picture.

It was of a family of four – two adults, two kids. They were dressed in olden style suits from perhaps the early 1900s, but their faces were grossly deformed – the little girl had a single eye in the center of her face, and the boy had a forehead crowded with a dozen dark and glassy eyes. And the mother was an abomination with a blank face, totally devoid of features save for a round mouth lined with needle teeth.

Drake grimaced, as there was worse to come – the man, the father, had a face distorted by blooms of tentacles where his mouth was supposed to be and his intense gaze burned with fervor or madness and stared back at him, penetrating him right to his core. In those eyes there was a deadness and darkness, and knowledge that he and his entire family were doomed and damned.

Drake blinked and looked away.

"Gives me the creeps." Benson shook his head. "It can't be real, right?"

"Just a nightmare, buddy," Drake scoffed. "And I'm still waiting to wake up in my bed back home." He swallowed dryly. "We finish our check then take five."

Drake went back to the mirror again on the other side of the room as if compelled to see into its depths. He looked into it – he felt a jolt right to his heart – there was Isabella looking radiant, fresh faced, happy, and staring right back at him.

She waved.

He smiled back.

I miss you, she mouthed.

For some reason, big tough Drake Stoker felt his eyes begin to water.

"I miss you too," he replied.

The image of Isabella raised her outstretched hand to him.

Come to me, she seemed to say.

"This is bullshit," he whispered.

But he still raised his hand to the mirror.

"You say something, boss?" Benson turned.

Drake stared. "I can see…"

The figure of Isabella suddenly lunged forward and grabbed his wrist. The shining woman with the warm dark eyes changed into some sort of hideous, reptilian abomination, and the clawed hands dug into his flesh.

Drake yelled in pain and fright.

Benson was beside him in seconds and gripped him around the chest as he was being pulled toward the mirror that had now turned to some sort of dark, swirling portal. Wherever it led, it certainly wasn't to the sunny, happy place where Isabella was.

Benson then began to punch the arm, and the hand released Drake, and grabbed him instead.

Benson was then the one being pulled toward the frame that was far too small to fit him in. Drake remembered what happened to Barak in the caves, and in a flash he pulled the sword that Isabella had given him and with one huge chop, brought it down across the arm.

It severed easily and the arm pulled back, the scaled hand dropping to the ground. But it wasn't still as it righted itself up onto its fingertips, and then like some sort of scaly crab it scuttled at speed around the room, up the wall, and then vanished into the dark portal that had been a mirror only seconds before.

"That wasn't Isabella," Drake laughed darkly. "I'm losing my freaking mind."

"We both are." Benson put his arm around him.

They both eased back from the portal that still swirled like dark muddy water.

"It's this place. Remember what they said, the Knights? This place will eat at your soul, your spirit. Make you despondent. We need to fight that as much as we fight those fucking monsters. We can't give up," Benson said.

Drake nodded and then turned to watch as his big friend limped away.

"Okay buddy, now that we got a few minutes, let me check that hoof of yours. And by the way you're limping it must be agony." Drake stood.

Benson didn't disagree and simply sat on the floor. He unclasped his boot and slowly dragged it off. He then rolled down a sodden dirty sock.

There was a massive lump there, on the ankle. It was red, and looked angry and painful.

"Looks like a bone break. Maybe compound by the way that lump is sticking out," Drake said.

He went to his friend and placed his fingers on the lump; it wasn't as hot as he expected.

He'd seen bone breaks before – some bad ones pushed a shard of bone up through the skin. But others didn't. The only option they had was for him to try and at least ease it back into place and then splint it. Benson would be a cripple at a time they might need to move over long distances, or at least move fast when called to do so.

He was about to lift his fingers away from what he thought was a bit of subcutaneous bone spur when he felt movement. He froze and looked up.

"Hey, did you, *ah*, feel that?" Drake asked.

Benson shrugged. "It's so damn painful all I feel is the pain, man."

Drake pressed the ankle swelling again, and this time he was sure if it – the mass felt softer now as if something had shifted under there. And watching closely he was sure there was something moving below the skin.

"Listen buddy, I've got news for you…" Drake began.

"Good or bad news?" Benson asked. "Nah, forget I asked that. There is no good news down here."

Drake continued to press the swelling. "Well, yeah, the good news is, I don't think there's a bone break there." He looked up. "But the bad news is, I think there is something alive in there."

"In there?" Benson pointed at his foot. "*In there-there*?"

"Yep." Drake exhaled through a pained grin. "In your foot."

Benson looked horrified. "Then get it the fuck out, man."

"On it." Drake pulled a pouch that was on his belt around in front of himself, and lifted out a small med kit.

There was an iodine swab which he rubbed over the lump, turning it a dark reddish-brown. Then he opened a small sachet that contained a sterile scalpel blade.

He looked up. "Need something to bite down on?"

Benson scoffed. "Yeah, a nice medium rib eye steak."

"You and me both, buddy," Drake laughed. "Here goes." He placed the scalpel blade on the lump and pressed, puncturing the flesh.

There was no blood.

He ran the scalpel along to the top of the lump for about an inch. And things got mad.

Like a jack in the box a large worm popped out that was as long as his finger. It glistened with Benson's blood and something slimy.

Drake pulled back and Benson cursed, holding his leg.

"*Get it, get it!*" Benson's lips had pulled back from his teeth.

The worm-thing turned its tiny head to Drake, and the small human-like face regarded him with a blank expression.

"Fa-*aaark*," Drake whispered.

It then swiveled its head to look up at Benson whose eyes looked about to pop out of his head. The thing then let out a tiny high pitched sound like a scream. It sprung from the lump, and slithered across the room to the open door and vanished outside.

Drake dropped his head for a moment and exhaled.

"Drake," Benson said softly.

"Yeah, buddy." Drake looked up.

"Can you please make sure that little ugly guy didn't have a wife and kids in there?" Benson asked.

Drake chuckled and checked the wound. The lump had collapsed, and was virtually flat now. Drake used the iodine patch to wipe all around the wound.

"All good," he said. "I'm gonna close it."

He then found other packets of needle and thread and closed the wound. He bound it in a clean bandage and Benson rolled his filthy sock back over it.

"If I get out of here without this sucker going septic I'll buy myself a lottery ticket." Benson got to his feet with Drake's help.

"If we get out of here I'll have felt like I won the lottery," Drake replied.

"I heard that." Benson nodded and put weight on it. "Yeah, yeah, that already feels better. That little sucker must have been nibbling on me from the inside."

"Must have picked it up walking on the seabed or seashore or whatever that was. I spotted a few of them poking their heads out," Drake said. "One must have latched onto your leg and climbed in your boot."

"*Yech*. Does my head in thinking about it." Benson shivered. "Give me a dozen fighters coming at me with guns and knives any day."

"Good man. I'll have you home dancing with the wife before you know it." Drake slapped the big guy's shoulder.

Benson's mouth turned down and he shook his head. "Nah, no more dancing there, my friend," he said as he continued to rub his calf.

Drake turned. "You and Patty still okay?"

Benson hiked huge shoulders. "Not really. No. She left me a year or so back." His eyes took on a faraway gaze. "I don't blame her. I was never home. And she said I scream at night when I have nightmares. Who'd put up with that?" He shared a broken smile with Drake. "And I'm not exactly a looker."

"I'm sorry to hear that, Clive." Drake sighed. "But when we get home, maybe we head out to a few bars, and find you a new wife." He grinned. "But I can't fix those looks, man. You were born with those."

Drake got to his feet and held out a hand. Benson grabbed it and the big man levered himself to his feet holding Drake's hand. "Deal," he said with a broad grin.

Benson walked around a bit and nodded. "Amazing. Feeling good."

"That's the way. Now let's see what we can see." Drake walked slowly toward some tattered curtains with the eerie twilight seeping through.

He eased up to the split and used one hand to gently open them a slit. He peered out, checking there was nothing just behind the decrepit curtains. It seemed clear so he pushed them wider and stepped out, followed by Benson.

They stood on a broken balcony where there was no railing and much of the platform had fallen away.

Drake exhaled. "Holy shit."

It was like an alien planet with a muted gloom for as far as the eye could see. Above them, there was an inky blackness but no stars, no moon, or rising or setting sun, just a dull glow that lit the landscape without chasing away a single shadow.

The city, if that's what it was, was broken, melted, or rotting down to nothing. Street after street was covered in something like weed, or soft vines that were more jelly than plant life.

"Look." Benson pointed. "Something moving over there."

Down one of the streets there seemed to be a sullen brooding silence and emptiness. But for only another few seconds because something like a skeletal elephant dragged itself down the center of the road. It was glistening black as if covered in oil and there were ribs showing on its back. It was low to the ground. Drake couldn't tell if it had multiple legs or no legs and moved like a huge slug.

As it came closer the men could see that there were dozens of smaller things climbing all over it like vermin. They scuttled over the hide, picked at it, pulling pieces from it, and stuffing them into tiny mouths.

The great beast passed by what might have once been an automobile and they could gauge its size – huge – and that meant that the revolting things climbing over it were human-sized.

"Is this what happens to the people that end up here?" Benson asked. "They eventually turn into things like roaches feeding off the hulk of giant decaying beasts."

Drake groaned softly. "I'll tell you right now, I ain't ever going to be that hungry."

Down another street came something that walked on all fours with two heads, and it stopped to sniff the air. Suddenly from the ground a flap was thrown back and something like a monster worm shot out toward it with its mouth open and thumping down over the creature. It stayed that way for several seconds and they saw its body undulating in some sort of peristaltic gulping.

Whatever the creature had been, and it was far bigger than a man, it was being chewed up and swallowed.

Drake shook his head and turned away to look out toward what might be a horizon. Miles away in the distance, there was the glint of something that might have been water.

"I still think taking to the ocean is the way to go," he said. "I just feel it."

"If we ever find it," Benson replied. "And we thought about finding a ship that might have washed in here somehow. But exactly how?" He laughed sadly. "Look around. Ask yourself this: exactly how did this city get here?"

Drake exhaled, feeling the physical and also mental fatigue. "There are cities from history that were destroyed and vanished. Like Sodom and Gomorrah. Maybe there were modern ones too. Destroyed and captured somehow."

"And how did they get here?" Benson looked upwards. "I mean, were they pulled in somehow?"

"I don't have all the answers." Drake grinned. "Or basically any answers. We're sailing in uncharted waters down here."

"So, we basically take a hike across Hell's landscape. Or we sail on Hell's waters?" Benson asked.

"That's about it," Drake replied. "So what do you want to do?"

"I don't want to do either," Benson replied. "But I know you want to do a little bit of sailing, and I have no real favorite option."

Drake could feel Benson continuing to stare at him.

He faced his friend. "Okay, what?"

"Just wondering. How do you keep going?" Benson asked. "I mean, look at where we are, and what's happened, and you're still pressing forward."

Drake half smiled. "Because we're in the shit. But we came to get Ethan out, and for that I give thanks. In my gut I feel Addison, Isabella and Leonidas all made it." He put a hand on his big friend's shoulder. "I'm sorry you're here, but we did our job."

"Yeah, that we did." Benson sighed, but then turned. "If we ever get out, just do me one favor…"

"Name it," Drake asked.

"Please don't call me for your next job," Benson laughed.

Drake laughed heartily and it felt good to do so – it made him feel human again. More than anything he wanted to get home, and also get his friend home. And then laugh with the sunshine on their faces and beers in their hands.

The pair looked out over the dismal and dark landscape. Things moved out there – deformed things, rotted things, things he knew were once human beings.

Drake began to turn away.

Help me.

He turned, frowning.

Help me.

Benson tilted his head. "You hear that?"

"Damn right I did." Drake stepped closer to the edge of the broken balcony.

Help me…Drake.

Benson frowned. "That sounds like…."

"Ethan," Drake replied.

"Nope. Can't be. It's just this place, it's Him, tricking us again," Benson said.

Drake continued to stare. He then brought his binoculars up and scanned the dark terrain. Something like a turtle moved through the mud creating a slime pathway. It seemed to turn for a moment, and he was sure it had a flat, white face.

Benson's hand came down on his shoulder. "Let's go, boss. I know what you're thinking, but there's nothing here but you and me."

"Yeah, yeah, you're right." He lowered his glasses.

"Ethan's home," Benson said. "It's you and me that are still in the shit."

Drake turned to half smile at his big friend. "Just like always."

Of all the Reapers he had brought with him, he was down to one. Drake knew he would move mountains to not lose him, no matter what.

"Do you think that's a sea out there?" Benson turned back to where they had seen the glint of something on the horizon.

"Might be," Drake said. "And I'm not sure travelling by water will be any safer than travelling over this terrible landscape." He squinted into the distance. "But something in my gut makes me feel that this is the right way to go."

"That's good enough for me," Benson said. "We stick to the shoreline, and find that water. Sail home, or row home."

"Buddy, even if I find two surfboards, we are paddling home," Drake laughed softly.

"Now you sound like Ethan," Benson grinned.

"Yeah, Ethan liked his surfing. And his damn rock climbing," Drake growled. "But I'll tell you that is something he is never going to do again. I guarantee it. Come on, big guy, let's go."

They headed back inside, skirting the weird mirror, and heading for the rear steps. The thought of seeing his brother again filled him with determination.

He would survive. And he would return to the sun no matter what.

CHAPTER 09

USA, Texas, the Stoker Ranch

Addison watched Ethan through the crack in the door. Her left eye stung and was a little blurry where he had hit her. She sniffed back tears confused about what was happening to them, to him.

There he was again, like every evening, talking softly on the phone to people all around the world, and she heard their names and knew none of them. And even more strangely, some people in other countries he'd adopt their language – where did Ethan learn to speak so many other languages?

She was sore all over, and many times throughout the day he would take her brutally – not love-making, but more a rough violation of her body as he rutted, exploded, and simply got up and walked away without a word, as if she was nothing more than a sex doll.

Addison had been in control of things her entire life, but now she felt lost and vulnerable. She had tried calling Isabella, but her phone just took messages and signed her off.

And then her mind had whispered: *that's not Ethan.*

Had something infected him infested him, down in those dark, dank labyrinths?

She needed to find out. And she had driven into the local church and filled a small vial with holy water.

A month ago, she would never have believed any of the things she had seen or was about to do. But right now, she was out of options, and if this little stunt meant nothing, at least she would feel better about it. It was stupid, sure, but if she went through with it then she could put a line through one horrifying scenario.

She made him a bourbon and water with the holy water, and knocked on his home office door.

He didn't turn, but continued talking on the phone.

She walked up beside him, and smiled, her black eye weeping, and placed the glass down on a coaster on his huge leather-topped desk.

He never bothered thanking her or even looking up. He reached for the glass.

She backed up a step, watching him.

He talked for a moment more, and then took a sip.

He froze.

Ethan slowly put the glass down. And then turned slowly in his chair toward her.

Around his lips there was red showing like a serious heat burn.

His eyes seemed to bug from his head, and he vomited.

Ethan rose to his feet and roared as gallons of liquid poured from him. And then it got worse as he grew, his body enlarging, twisting, and lumping right before her eyes.

She backed up, feeling her mind fragmenting at the sight. The reaction was a million times more than she expected.

Ethan's clothing began to split. Red fluid like watery blood soaked his tattered clothing and his face enlarged, bloated, and huge sores broke out over it.

He vomited again, and this time in amongst it pink and white sticks fell to the ground. In her horrified frozenness she saw they were bones, human bones, and her mind screamed at her – they were Ethan's bones.

She knew then that Ethan, her Ethan, had long ago been consumed and replaced by this thing.

The thing stomped toward her and her muscles finally unlocked and she turned to flee. But a large pocked arm shot out and grabbed her hair and yanked her off her feet. She was thrown violently to the ground.

Addison looked up. The monstrous being that glared down at her bore no resemblance to the handsome young man she was engaged to be married to.

A large foot came down on her chest, pinning her.

"Ethan," she croaked. "Please."

Ethan bent forward and grabbed her with one hand around the neck and lifted her. He brought her face close to his own twisted visage.

She grimaced and even though she found it hard to breathe, she could still smell the rotten charnel house stink coming off him, and she tried to turn away.

She knew then that Ethan was gone. He had been consumed down in those hellish caves, and what she had brought home was something far older and more evil.

"Your world is at an end," the beast said in a gravel deep voice.

It then began to squeeze, and she felt her neck begin to compress. In seconds more the air was cut off, and then the blood flow, and her head felt like it was going to explode.

But he didn't stop; Ethan continued to squeeze until the last thing Addison felt was the bones separating in her neck as his fingers came fully together with a wet crunch.

***

Ethan let her body slip to the floor like a sack, and went back to his desk to continue his calls.

He had much planning and preparation to do to ready the world for the Master's arrival.

CHAPTER 10

Getting a severed head on a plane was easy.

Isabella simply used her fake identification as a mortuary technician again, and had the object classed as an infected medical specimen.

It went through the x-ray machine just fine, and raised a few eyebrows, but as there was no metallic objects inside not a single boarding official wanted to take a look at it given the biohazard status.

She, Leonidas, and Marco travelled separately, and they met in Brisbane, the Australian capital city on the upper eastern coast. Their destination was the Church of St. Peter, a small sandstone building that was closed for renovations, and had been for years.

It was owned by the Vatican, and now it wasn't used as a church, but instead used as a form of safe house, prison for enemies of the Vatican, and even forensic laboratory with its own technicians.

Isabella, Leonidas, and Marco went around to the side, and down some steps. There was a heavily fortified door there with a passcode pad and fingerprint scanner.

She scanned her thumb, and the passcode pad lit up. She then inserted the code and the fortified door clicked open.

The trio walked along a dark corridor and Isabella knew they were being scanned and further identified. At the end another door clicked open, and a tall young man waited for them.

"Father Bertolli." She smiled.

The man returned the smile and stuck out his hand. "Call me Nico, please."

"Nico it is," she replied.

He shook each of their hands and waved them on. The corridors and rooms below the church were much larger and more expansive than the structure above.

Nico led them past rooms of technicians on computer screens and into the forensic laboratory. Inside there were several men and women and one older man looked up and clapped.

"At last," he said.

Nico nodded to him. "Father Enzo Adoni. He specially came back from leave when he heard what you were bringing us."

"Is this it?" he gestured toward the bag Isabella held.

"Yes, a severed head. I hope the material is still viable. I tried to keep it cold but…" She shrugged.

She remembered what else she had for them. "Oh yes, and a water sample. Looks a little weird and worth checking out." She took out the liquid and handed it over with the bag.

Father Adoni took the sample jar and held it up to the light, frowning as he did. "Slight discoloration. We'll have a look under the microscope to see what bugs are in there, and also do a chemical analysis for toxins."

He then turned and took the bag from her and went over to a silver laboratory table. The other technicians crowded around and he carefully unzipped the bag, peered in, and then lifted out the thing covered in picnic ice packs that was in a plastic bag.

He placed it on the table as gently as if it was a Ming Dynasty vase and then used surgical scissors to cut the bag open.

By then they had donned face masks and gloves, and he slowly peeled back the plastic revealing the gruesome head.

"Well, well, well." He turned it slowly so he could see it from differing angles. Adoni looked to Isabella as he straightened. "And this was once a human being?"

Isabella nodded. "Yes, and the change occurs quickly. The deformation can begin to occur within hours."

Father Adoni picked up a long steel probe and levered the fleshy lips open. "Very strong mandibles, and the dental patterns are not designed for chewing, more for ripping flesh free and gulping I assume."

He sighed. "I'd love to have a look at its digestive system."

"Not today, Doctor," Isabella replied.

Adoni bobbed his head and leaned forward again as he began his formal examination.

"No nasal root, nasal dorsum, or even nasal apex. Instead we now have vestigial slits for breathing, eyes with enlarged pupils totally covering the sclera for nocturnal vision."

He had rubber gloves on and he pressed the top of the head, feeling the skull. "Solid, heavy bone plating; I'll remove the brain later." He released it, and next called for a scalpel, forceps and sample jar.

"Let's take a sample and see what goes on at the cellular level." Adoni used the forceps to lift a flap of skin at the severed neck where it still looked moist and sliced away a tiny bit of grey flesh.

He dropped it in the jar, sealed it, and held it up. "This shouldn't take long." He nodded to Father Nico Bertolli. "Nico, please get them a coffee and something to eat. I'll call when we have something."

"Thank you. That sounds good," Isabella said and the trio were led out. They were taken to a room furnished like a parlor with cushioned couches, oak tables, glowing lamps, a coffee machine and even a chiller that had various cut sandwiches and cookies to choose from.

Marco sighed. "Yes, this will do."

He poured himself a coffee, grabbed a ham sandwich and a nut cookie, and went back to one of the couches and sunk into its luxurious comfort.

In moments more the Knights were sitting in silence, eating sandwiches or sipping coffee. Isabella stared at the dark liquid in her cup and let her mind wander.

She tried to think of different scenarios for rescuing Drake. Like one of those cube puzzles her mind twisted and turned looking at options.

The entrance through the Devil's Peak had been closed. But perhaps the hole she had opened below the ocean might be a way in. Could she get a submarine and travel in that way? Or maybe when the scroll was fully unfurled it might indicate another opening, somewhere far away and unexpected. That was possible.

She sat back and sighed. Isabella wondered then if he was even alive – or half alive and changed into one of the hellish abominations in the underworld. A lump grew in her throat at that thought and she swallowed it down hard.

"*No!*" she whispered.

If anyone could fight back against those things it was Drake Stoker. The man was made of iron and gristle, and his mind was just as strong.

But for how long? a voice in the corner of her head whispered.

Drake voyaged to the seven circles of Hell to rescue his brother, Ethan. And did it. And she bet that if he ever returned, the first thing he'd want to do is see how he was getting on.

That reminded her to call Addison. She stood up and walked a few paces away from her team and put a call through to the young woman.

The phone rang and rang until it went to voicemail. She didn't leave a message but promised herself she would call back later.

***

It was after two hours waiting that Father Nico Bertolli called for them. He led them into the laboratory and there stood a stony-faced Father Enzo Adoni.

"You have something? Some answers?" Isabella asked.

"I have something, but I'm not sure if it's answers. Or the answers we seek," he said grimly.

She saw that he had the projector attached to the microscope, meaning he was going to throw the images up onto the wall – good, she thought. Save them having to take turns crouching over the instrument.

"What do you know about human blood?" he asked.

She shrugged. "There are red blood cells and white cells, suspended in plasma. The red ones contain hemoglobin that makes them appear red. And they carry oxygen."

"Good, good. To expand, the human blood cells, which are primarily red blood cells or erythrocytes, with white blood cells, leukocytes, and one you missed called platelets or thrombocytes. And yes, all suspended in plasma. The plasma is the liquid component of blood, and it contains water, proteins, salts, fats, and sugars. Red blood cells contain hemoglobin, a protein that carries oxygen. White blood cells are part of the immune system and help fight infection. Platelets are involved in blood clotting."

He turned the projector on and an image was placed on the screen. It was all dark, and fragmented.

"You said this thing was alive only a few days ago, yes?" he asked.

"That's right." She looked back to the screen. "But I don't see anything there that looks like blood cells."

"You're right. Because everything has been degraded, and consumed. This is just excretory debris. *Shit*, if you like." Father Adoni paced for a moment. "If you hadn't told me this thing was alive a day ago, I would never have believed it. But it made me think that there was something missing here." He held up a finger as he paced. "Something missing that might have been there but was now gone, degraded, or dead. When the head was removed and the thing was killed, or at least stopped being animated, whatever was in the blood also died."

"So it is useless." Isabella sagged. "All that work."

"It made us think that whatever was in there was now gone. And then we wondered how it got there." He seemed to think on it for a moment. "Transmission vectors could be infection from an already infected human, or from insects bites…"

"Yes, that's how," she said, leaning forward.

"But the population of Thrumster was over two thousand souls. How was it possible for all of them to be infected so quickly? Were there million strong swarms of bugs there?" He raised his eyebrows.

She searched her memory, but there had been nothing like that. "No, not quite like that."

"And what is one way to get everyone infected so quickly?" He flat smiled. "Do a vaccination program. Or have them self-administer, by drinking the water."

He turned and changed the image on the projector. "This is from the water sample you brought us."

Isabella looked up at the new image and her brows came together as she stared at the horrifying things. "What is that? What are they?" she breathed.

"A parasite. We think," he said. "But not like anything we have ever seen before." He crossed to his bench top and picked up a small dropper that contained a tiny amount of red liquid.

"Blood," he said. "Now watch this."

He placed a drop on a slide and then magnified it. They appeared exactly as they expected to see from healthy blood cells. Magnified, it wasn't red as the plasma was clear, and the small red concave cells looked like little red pillows. There was also the spiked balls of white blood cells floating about.

Adoni brought forth another dropper. "And now I introduce a drop of the water."

He did so, and then on the screen they saw added into the mix were multi-armed microorganisms that began to grab the red blood cells and either consume them completely, or latch on and change them.

The white blood cells were quickly overwhelmed and consumed, and the others, the red cells that weren't consumed, elongated, warped, and became like jelly.

"What is happening?" Leonidas asked. "What's happening to the red cells?"

"They've been corrupted, changed for good. I believe that these parasites would move beyond the blood stream and attack every cell in the body – the flesh, the brain, eyes, bones, everything." He looked miserable. "Changing and warping the entire human physiology."

"The flesh is weak," Isabella whispered.

"And now the final test," Adoni sighed. "The proof of concept as it were."

Father Adoni drew some of the liquid up into a syringe and walked it over to a glass tank that held a white laboratory rat. He lifted the lid, picked up the rat, and expertly injected the liquid into its haunch. He then replaced it in the tank.

"I believe if the water was ingested, the changes might take a little longer. But if the infection is achieved via a bite, then it works the same as inoculation – rapid."

They all stared hard at the rat in the tank – at first it behaved normally, but then it stopped moving and began to shiver, then shudder.

It fell to its side and jerked spasmodically before opening its mouth and emitting an abnormally loud and deep growl. In seconds more the hair just fell from its body like powder.

Leonidas crossed himself.

They could then see the bones shifting beneath its skin. Bones lengthened or new ones formed and the muscles covering them shifted all over the hairless and now glistening body.

The rear end of the rat stretched and lengthened and they could hear bones popping and muscles and tendons stretching as if the flesh were made of putty.

Isabella grimaced.

One of Adoni's assistants backed away and turned her head.

The team was transfixed as they watched the rat turn into an abomination. In minutes more the change had completed or least it had slowed down.

In the tank, the medium-sized lab rat was now hairless at the front end, and the face was not recognizable as being from any mammal they knew – there was just a single eye, large and black and lidless. The long snout and mouth was gone and a round cavity full of small shark-like teeth remained. But travelling down the body was where the real nightmare began – there were four front arms, all spindly and ending in needle-like claws. The stomach went from hairless flesh to some sort of reptilian scales that lengthened and stretched until it had the tail of a snake that was red raw and left a trail of blackened blood or mucous discharge on the glass case's bottom.

Adoni exhaled despondently. "It is an aggressive universal mutagen."

"The Hell plague," Isabella said. "And it's out now."

"Can we stop it?" Leonidas asked.

"The fly. Octavius Conti is spreading it globally. We have seen the flies, large, fist-sized at a farm down the coast, and we have reports of them appearing everywhere. I believe he is laying eggs everywhere. Their bite is the inoculation, and then once infected, the others go on to infect more people, or more waterways."

"Waterways?" Adoni asked.

"Yes. I took that sample from a cooler fed by the local water supply," Isabella said. "I think the flies are diving into the water, and letting their disgusting bodies pollute the water that is drunk by the townspeople."

"We can't stop it everywhere. We can't blow everything up like we did in Thrumster," Marco said.

"I'd settle for being able to stop it *any*where," Leonidas replied.

"If the plague is out and in the wild, then the only real hope is some sort of cure or vaccine," Father Nico Bertolli said. He looked to Adoni. "Enzo, what are our chances?"

Adoni shook his head. "I've tried antibiotics, penicillin, even interferon to try and boost the body's own defenses. Nothing works against this abomination."

"There can never be no hope." Bertolli folded his arms. "We just need to look harder."

"I know, old friend, and we will." Adoni half smiled as he held up a single finger. "There is only one potential vulnerability I can see." He looked back at the multi-armed microorganism on the projected screen. "Do you know why viruses cannot be killed once they are in the body?" He didn't wait for an answer. "Because they are tiny and hide inside the cells. To kill the virus, you have to find it first, and then kill the cell. Not ideal. Our own white blood cells can identify infected cells and kill them, but they are wonderful in that they are selective. We have not found a way with our medicines to be that clever yet."

"We have vaccines against viruses." Leonidas frowned.

"We do. Sort of," Adoni replied. "We have immunizations against viruses, and how they work is they rely on the body's own defenses. We help prepare the body to defend itself from viruses. We give it a call to arms, so to speak."

He turned back to the screen. "So, can you see it?"

"We can. It's big, bad, and a nightmare." Marco stared at the revolting parasite.

Adoni turned back. "Yes, and that's just it – big – it's a big bug. So big it can't hide itself away inside the cell. And as long as it is free floating we have a chance against it."

"You mean we can prepare our own system against it like an immunization?" Isabella asked.

"Maybe, I'm not sure. So far this thing eats T-cells like they're popcorn before they can even fight back. They get overwhelmed. But I think that as it's free floating, we just have to keep trying things to find, attack, and kill the microorganism. Somewhere out there is our silver bullet." He smiled. "I'm hopeful." His smile was a little fragile.

Isabella caught it. "And?"

"And that was the good news. The bad news is that once it is in the system its effects are so fast, and so irreversible, it means it moves too quickly for us to ever stop it."

Isabella tilted her head back and shut her eyes for a moment. Her sigh turned into a groan.

"This is a nightmare," she said and tilted her head forward. "While we've been sitting on our hands for millennia, the Devil has been planning this since mankind walked upright."

"And the news gets worse," Adoni said. "The plague is out, and being spread far and wide. It means more countries will be working on a cure, but the speed of the spread also means we are in a race for the future of the entire human species."

"So, how do we fight something from Hell?" Marco asked.

Everyone turned to him.

He smiled. "With something from Heaven."

Isabella nodded and began to smile. "Okay, clever guy, go on."

"We know a lot about it, and Father Adoni can continue to investigate a cure or vaccine. But we need to get back to the Vatican, and search for different weapons." He raised his eyebrows. "Perhaps we haven't been sitting on our hands, and perhaps older and wiser heads than ours have been preparing for this time also."

"Maybe they know where to find our silver bullet." Isabella began to nod. "And we just need to look harder."

CHAPTER 11

Arakwal National Park, Byron Bay, East Coast of Australia

The Cummins family hiked along the bush track – Pete out front, the kids, Marty and Phillip next, and lastly, Frida trying to keep up.

"There's nothing to see," Marty, the youngest at ten, whined.

"Maybe they're hibernating because of the heat," Frida suggested.

"Well, some animals do stay out of the midday heat, but they don't hibernate this time of year." Pete looked around. "Strange though, as we were told there'd be kangaroos, wallabies, goannas, and all sort of parrots in the trees." He looked up at the branches, and saw nothing but leaves.

"I'm hot," Marty kicked in again.

"Stop being a crybaby, it's not that hot," Philip, twelve, shot back, never missing an opportunity to badger his younger brother.

"That's enough, Phillip." Frida sighed, and wiped her brow. "But must be time for a break soon."

Pete stopped and put his hands on his hips. "Soon." He turned to grin. "But this is going to make that dip in the hotel pool all the more satisfying, right?"

"*Aww*, I wanna be there now." Marty let his arms hang down heavily at his sides as if he was being tortured.

Pete took off his cap, wiped his brow with his wrist and stuck it back on. "Up ahead is a nice shady spot. We'll break for a snack there, okay gang?"

"Yay," Marty replied dismally.

In another fifteen minutes, they were underneath a large gum tree and Pete had broken out the coffee thermos, the cookies, and a few cut cheese sandwiches and soda for the boys.

The food vanished down the kids' throats like a magician's trick, and they immediately went off to scout.

"Don't go too far," Pete shouted.

He heard the boys using long sticks to whack their way through the bush. He was a little concerned, as he had read about the giant spiders, big bull-ants, and deadly snakes, and this time of year they were all out and about. But then again, they'd seen absolutely nothing and he was beginning to wonder if it had all been a tourist trap ploy.

He turned to Frida who sat staring off in the bush and holding her plastic cup with both hands. "I'm hot, and want to go swimming," he said and grinned.

She laughed, and turned to him. "Me too, but don't let the boys hear that."

"We'll head back when we finish here," he said.

She held up a hand and smiled. "I second that."

***

"*Poo*, what's that smell?" Marty said.

"Reminds me of that time the Fosters' cat got lost and they found it stuck in their wall after about three months, all boney and stinky," Phillip replied.

They continued on, and soon saw something odd up ahead in a small clearing. "Look, there."

Marty barged through the brush and held his stick out. "Is that a kangaroo? It's so big," he asked.

"A fucking dead one," Phillip replied.

"You used the bad word." Marty grinned and held a hand over his nose. "Stinks."

The boys looked down at it. The kangaroo carcass was as big as a man, reddish in color, and its stomach cavity was open and filled with things that looked like jelly golf balls.

"Is that what they look like inside?" Marty frowned.

"I don't think so." Phillip held out his stick.

"Don't, Phillip," Marty warned.

"I just want to see what they are," he said, and reached out further.

He couldn't quite reach properly so scooted forward another foot on his haunches. He then tried again, and this time the end of his stick just made it to one of the jelly balls. He prodded it, and as soon as he did, something emerged from inside the kangaroo's gutted body.

Phillip jerked upright, eyes like saucers and mouth open. Marty's eyes also bulged from his head.

It looked like a fly, huge, bigger than his dad's fist, but it had a weird tiny face, not like a fly's but more like a person's face, but with the stick-thing mouth parts.

The boys stared, frozen to the spot. The huge bug stared back.

And then it came at them.

***

"*Dad, Dad!*" The boys came crashing from the bush.

Pete was on his feet and running to them, and Frida dropped her cup.

Marty's eyes were wide. "Big fly, monster, dead kangaroo, stink, we followed the smell…"

Pete grabbed the boy's shoulders and looked into his face. "Slow down, slow down, and tell me," Pete said. "Phillip, you first."

Frida hugged Marty and Phillip swallowed dryly.

"We found a dead kangaroo, and pushed a stick into it. A big fly came out and followed us."

"A fly?" Pete relaxed and began to smile. "And it chased you?" He looked over Phillip's shoulder. "Must have turned back."

Pete felt something on the back of his shirt, and thought it was Frida scratching at him with her nails to get his attention.

He turned and smiled, and saw she was five feet away. The clawing sensation got to his shoulder, and down in front of him Phillip pushed back from him and screamed.

He pointed. "*There it is*."

Pete looked to his left and down into the face of the most grotesque thing he had ever seen in his life. He could have sworn it smiled up at him, before it darted forward and bit him on the side of his exposed neck.

The pain was excruciating. "*Shit!*" he screamed and slapped at it.

He just caught the end of it, feeling its weight and bristly oiliness as it zoomed away.

He placed his hand over the bite mark. It still stung.

"That's it," he said angrily. "Spiders, sharks, snakes, but no one said a damn thing about giant flies. Time to head back."

"Yay." The boys high-fived, the fly already forgotten.

CHAPTER 12

Australia, Eastern Coast – Port Macquarie

Police Chief Mike Lawler stood at the large window looking out at the dismal scene. Even the weather was conspiring to turn against them as thick, purple clouds boiled and swirled overhead, looking ripe and angry. Just looking at them gave him a sense of dread down deep in his gut. He could feel something bad was happening. And worse was coming.

He regretted not leaving when he had called for an evacuation. And now he couldn't as the entire large town had been quarantined by the Australian CDC – no one in, no one out.

He drew in a deep breath and let it out slowly. Ever since those Italian health specialists that had taken his officer, Angela Bennet, with them into Thrumster to check on some sort of infection things had gotten worse.

They went in, and mere hours later there came the huge explosion. And they never came back. Whatever happened in Thrumster was as bad as it got.

He sent another police team in there after them, and the radio calls had been insane, and horrifying. And then with a scream they were cut off, and that was the last he saw of them.

Lawler hoped the explosion signaled the end of it. But he was wrong because the first signs of the infection had come creeping out of the bush. First the animals had begun to flee in waves. Then it seemed to eat the forest as it came – everything turned black and rotten and seemed to melt before his eyes. Red veins that looked like they were pumping blood crept up over the building to strangle them.

Lawler sipped cold coffee from his vantage point and looked out over the township and towards the buildings closest to the edge of the forest. Many were covered in odd growths; things that looked like fungus, tendrils, but with their deep red color, he couldn't help thinking they looked like when skin had been pulled back to reveal the blood pumping veins beneath.

The quick thinking, decisive people were gone. They threw bags in cars and left when they could. The others that heeded the evacuation order for the outer suburbs refused to go home so they had to be put up

in sports halls, carparks, and vacant buildings in the other end of town.

There were entire families, grandparents, kids, pets, and the way they looked at him, haunted and silent, hoping for answers, broke his heart. Because he had none.

Maybe they were the lucky ones as the amount of people that either stayed or had vanished was alarming.

The sun was going down again, and night was worst. It seemed those revolting vein growths weren't the only thing creeping out of the forest. He'd seen the reports of the strange animals and deformed people, and the horrible abominations, and all of them had a taste for flesh.

None of his officers wanted to go anywhere near the town outskirts after dark. Especially after the first few went in and simply never came home. And every single officer demanded to take a shotgun with them.

Lawler sipped his cold and bitter brew again. He wondered what would happen to the people when those weird veins covered all of the town. As they were quarantined, they were supposed to be locked down. But if the nightmare that was coming at them began to push from one side, and the authorities pushed back from the other, there was going to be violence. And bloodshed.

Lawler smiled, remembering the tourism tagline for the city – *come visit Port Macquarie, where time does wonders.*

Because *time*, he thought, was one thing that they didn't have anymore.

CHAPTER 13

Los Angeles General Medical Center – Infectious Diseases Unit

Doctor Albert Finney stared in through the glass wall at the woman on the bed. Her name was Frida Cummins, mid-thirties, who arrived with her family yesterday evening and then fell sick. The other was her husband.

Frida, the father, Pete, and two boys, Marty and Phillip, all developed strange symptoms, with the husband Pete succumbing first. He was in the next room. The two young boys were being kept in separate quarantine rooms just a bit further along the corridor.

Right now they were all placed in induced comas, and Finney was absolutely lost as to what was happening and how to treat them.

Inside there was a nurse working in a hazmat suit. Underneath the suit she wore thick clothing as they had found that lowering the temperature seemed to slow the ravages of the infection down a little. And the ravages were monstrous.

Pete was farthest along, and his cell count of white and red blood cells continued to plummet while being replaced by the weirdest protein they had ever seen. It had to be an aggressive micro parasite, and was now being considered as a standalone organism.

But the thing was also acting as a mutagen, and not just corrupting his system's physiology, but also deforming the actual physical flesh.

Doctor Albert Finney knew the family had just returned from a holiday in Australia, and he knew of no blood infection even remotely similar from that part of the world. This was entirely uncharted territory.

They had just administered the strongest cocktail of anti-viral, anti-plasmodium, and antibiotics they had in their armory as they had at first considered it to be some sort of necrotizing agent.

Finney wasn't hopeful when he opened the microphone to the headset of Doctor Sonya Burrows. "Any improvement to the mother, Doctor Burrows?" he asked.

Burrows turned and shook her head.

He nodded, waved, and walked to the next isolation room. There were two beds inside with the two boys, both brothers corpse-like in their induced comas. And both suffering the same ravages of the parasite. He continued on to Pete's room. Pete was further along the path to whatever he was becoming.

They were now at the try anything stage. Finney had taken the extreme option of amputating the man's arm as it had begun to change into something not even remotely resembling human flesh.

In addition, it was displaying autonomous spasmodic movement – it seemed to have a life of its own.

To try and avoid the infection spreading back up his arm meant he decided to act quickly. So off it came mid bicep.

There were cameras fixed in his room and he focused in on Pete's face – the man had been quite handsome when he came in and had only been suffering from nausea, headaches and a strange pustulant rash. But now, his hair had all fallen out, and his nose had rotted away and collapsed into the nasal cavity.

Though his arm had been removed above the elbow, there was the nub of something showing at the end of the stump as if new bone was growing out through the bandages. And that was accompanied by further extrusions appearing at his sides over the rib cage.

Pete was now in a heavy plastic canopy that acted as a form of hyperbaric chamber that had increased oxygen content to his blood and cells to try and boost his immune system. They had also brought the temperature down and it was now at around thirty degrees in there. But so far, the microorganisms in his system were slowed but not stopped.

If, *when*, Pete Cummins finally succumbed there would be no autopsy. He was going to have the body immediately incinerated, such was his concern about the unstoppable nature of the disease or whatever it was afflicting him.

Doctor Finney had contacted the CDC and put them on alert at the borders. However, he knew that this thing was already inside the gates now.

He had just authorized one last experimental treatment which was a beefed up anti-parasitic which was a combination of *albendazole* and *mebendazole* at near lethal levels, in the hope they could at least paralyze the parasite and maybe slow it down to give them more time to work on Pete.

The nurse entered his room, and took the syringe to the drip bag and inserted it into the feed valve. She injected the yellowish fluid in slowly and it seeped into his vein.

As Finney watched the monitor he glanced at Pete's face and saw his eyes flicker, and then open. Finney felt a shock at the sight – they were totally black and in them he saw no remnant of a human being at all. They were more like the soul-dead eyes of a great white shark.

With all the trauma to his system, with the drugs keeping him in an induced coma, Pete Cummins still managed to move at lightning speed.

He lunged at the nurse, swinging his stump arm at her. But the stump wasn't a blunt end anymore; it now had a foot-long spike of something like dark bone extruding from it.

The spike went through the tough plastic curtain surrounding his bed and also through her hazmat suit, and by the way she doubled over, Finney knew it had penetrated her flesh.

She screamed and went down. Finney hit the alarm button, and called security. He saw the nurse go down onto the ground, and then to his horror he saw two things – the first was the spreading bloom of blood on her suit. The second was Pete rising from his bed and tearing open the plastic canopy.

He grimaced at their stupidity of not tying him down, but then again he had enough sedatives in him to stun a horse. In seconds more the security arrived, but they needed to suit up – this time just free working suits that didn't need to be connected to a tether that supplied oxygen and power.

They went in, subdued the man and locked Pete down. Then one of them dragged the nurse from the chamber.

Finney spoke again to security telling them to lock down the other members of the family as well. This thing was becoming dangerous and unpredictable. Finney looked back at the monitor and saw Pete back on the bed, his face fully animated now and jaws with needle-like teeth snapping at anything he could get close to.

Finney grimaced at the sight – there was no nose, the ears had become flattened to his skull, and the most bizarre aspect of the physiological change were the emergence of two new limbs branching from his sides.

For now they were tiny stick-like things that ended in claws, but he didn't doubt for a second that soon they would fill out, and then they too would need to be cuffed.

"What in God's name is happening?" he asked softly to no one other than himself.

This thing was debilitating, aggressive, and undoubtedly contagious as all Hell.

He suddenly froze at the thought.

Oh no, he spun away realizing that whatever this thing was, with the nurse spiked, she had been inoculated. The plague was now out of containment.

Doctor Albert Finney rushed from the room.

***

The security team exited the sealed chamber after all four of the Cummins family had been moved in together to a specially sealed quarantine room.

Beneath Pete's bed a small pool of dark liquid formed from where it had been dripping from the end of his stump. It wasn't blood, or plasma, or any other natural bodily fluid. Instead it was something dark and thick, a lot more like paste or jelly.

After another few minutes the dripping turned into a slow stream and soon there was a plate-sized puddle formed. The dripping stopped and then seemed to coagulate. The puddle gathered itself into a blob, and it stretched and slithered towards the next bed where Pete's wife Frida lay under her own plastic hypobaric chamber covering.

The blob then became a tendril and slowly climbed the gurney leg and reached in under the plastic sheet to find her. And then joined with her.

But it wasn't finished; the tendril came out the other side of her bed, and also slithered across to where the small form of Marty lay to his right. And from Frida's bed the tendril stretched out like a cable to find the teenage Phillip to her side.

In minutes more the beds were slowly dragged together.

***

It was twenty minutes later that Jose Moralles, one of the authorized quarantine nurses, entered the room to check on the family. The portable style decon suit he wore had a small oxygen pack and was not as thick and cumbersome as the standard heavy duty hazmat suits. In addition, it had a large plastic visor that kept slipping sideways, but through it he saw something unexpected.

"Who did this?" He lowered the electronic clipboard when he saw all the four beds had been pushed together to the center of the room. Further, the entire family now seemed to be all on the center one.

The thick plastic hyperbaric sheet was still partially over all of them, but now it was all misted up like there was a wet, humid air inside.

Jose's first thought was that the oxygen feed had stopped working and that allowed the respiration humidity to climb. And also the combined body heat was causing a rise in temperature.

He glanced at some room monitors and wasn't surprised to see that the room's internal temperature was now eighty degrees. It was supposed to be kept cool to slow down whatever infection was raging in their bodies.

"Dammit," he growled.

It was another complication. He'd have to get the technicians straight onto it. First he needed to do a quick site check on the family members to see if they had suffered any ill effects from their treatment environment being interrupted.

Jose frowned as he walked around the huge lump in the center of the four beds. He thought they were supposed to have been constrained. And from what he could see of the vacated beds, they were stained like they had shit themselves.

Maybe that was why the kids had climbed out of their beds, he surmised.

But even with that benign possible explanation his neck tingled and his primitive brain screamed at him to about face and get the hell out.

But his modern mind and perhaps own bravado told him to stay and do his job, check it out, and then call it in.

Jose went to the canopy. He unclipped and lifted the heavy plastic sheet and then reached forward to the hospital bedsheet covering the Cummins' bodies.

He paused. The sheet looked damp and putrid. He slowly looked around and saw the tray of instruments on a side bench and quickly crossed to it and grabbed a pair of long forceps.

He then used those to grasp the sodden sheet and pull it back.

Further. Further.

He stopped and stared, his brain not able to process what he was seeing.

There wasn't a single person there anymore. In fact it was hard to discern if it was any person anymore.

The thing he saw wasn't a person. Or even persons. Instead it was a huge lump of protoplasmic flesh with patches of hair here and there, glistening muscle on some areas and raw open wound-meat on another. And it wasn't still, it pulsated and moved with an unnatural and impossible life.

Jose dropped the forceps and backed up as the notepad fell from his hands.

"I need to call…"

He froze, transfixed.

"I need to…"

Part of the raw, wound-looking part of the mass seemed to unzip. It then opened with a sticky sound to become a long wet mouth. At first what he thought were teeth lining the edge were really fingers, big and small, all grasping as though excited at the thought of getting hold of him.

Jose's body was frozen, all except for his bladder that released a little squirt of pee into the front of his trousers. The shot of warmth in his pants seemed like a slap to his senses as he began to move then.

But so did the mass.

With a clattering of steel bed railings followed by the heavy thump of perhaps five hundred pounds of combined human flesh, the mass went to the floor.

But even as Jose tried to back up, the thing righted itself and came at him pushing beds and tables out of the way like some sort of giant soft shell crab.

Jose turned to run for the exit, but not quick enough as a spear of bone shot forward to impale his thigh, pass right through the meat, and then open like a hook to lock him in place and then reel him in.

He went to the ground and slid across the floor. He screamed so loudly he felt blood well up in his throat.

"*Help!*" he croaked.

He shot an arm out and grabbed onto a cabinet door handle that stopped his slide.

"Help!" he screamed again, louder this time, but he felt his strength ebbing away with every spurt of blood leaving his body.

He thought he might be gifted some time for rescue to come while he held on and stopped his slide. But instead, the thing rose up, with multiple hands and legs underneath it, and came scuttling towards him.

Fluid dripped from it to spatter the floor, and so close now, Jose saw fragments of hospital smocks peeking from folds in its disgusting merged flesh.

"Help me," Jose began to cry,

He looked toward the observation window and was shocked to see people there. They watched in absolute horror, but none made a move to enter.

Why would they? he thought.

Maybe they would call the armed security guards, but given they'd need to suit up in quarantine suits, it would be long over for him.

"*Madre de Dios,*" he screamed.

The abomination stopped.

Jose winced from pain and looked up at the thing now just a few feet from him. He could have sworn the ragged wound of a mouth curved up a fraction at the corners.

Then the words leaked out: *No hay Dios ni su madre aquí* – No God or his mother here.

Jose wailed as the thing rushed forward to cover him completely.

***

Through the observation room window, Doctor Albert Finney

watched through narrowed eyes as if to somehow blank out some of the horror playing out before him.

The others in the room that was crowded only a few minutes ago, now were mostly gone. Many had left in tears, feeling physically ill.

None had any suggestions as to what to do, and all options were thrown at him, from sealing the room up, forever, to going in there with axes and flamethrowers.

The flamethrower option appealed to him, but he needed to know more. He needed to know how a family that had been holidaying in Australia, where he would expect the worst things to happen would be snake or spider bite, or maybe even shark attack, had contracted something so horrible, so unheard of, he couldn't even begin to describe it.

Finney knew that whatever they were dealing with was one hundred percent contagious as the nurse who had been attacked only hours before was now beginning to show symptoms, as well as one of the guards who had escorted her to her room.

The CDC were on their way, but he doubted they would have experience with this either.

He sighed and closed his eyes for a moment. When he opened them the horror was still there. And now it had consumed, or assimilated, Jose into itself.

He could now see attached to the massive protoplasmic lump was some of Jose's hair and scraps of his uniform showing from the outside of the thing that now patrolled the room, looking for a way out.

For the first time in Finney's life he was confused and frightened. Very frightened.

CHAPTER 14

Eastern Chin, Yangzhou's Hanjiang district – Shaobo Lake

Hun Lee Soung slowly paddled his ancient fishing boat out over the glass smooth water. It was his favorite time, still before dawn, and so he was the first.

The air held a little chill, but was still balmy and the promise of a warm humid day was assured. He inhaled the smells of the lake, the fresh water, the reed beds on the banks, and the odor of his ancient boat smelling of old fish, gum resin for leaks, and flaking wood.

Hun Lee knew a special spot that was a little deeper than the rest, and he knew the big carp hung there in the green depths. He slowed his rowing and glided for a moment.

He smiled at his three beloved fishing cormorants lined up on the side of his small boat. Bo Bo, Mia, and Sun – all three had been hand raised by him, and had cords around the neck. They were used to shallow fish for small sprats, and would dive down, catch a fish and come back to the surface to hand it to him.

He had no children, so to him, his three 'girls' were his children.

The first twinge in the depths of his stomach was unexpected. He grimaced as the next was a little sharper and made him wonder about his eating choices the previous night.

It settled into a dull lump in his gut that made him feel miserable. He smelled something odd then and looked up. The still starlit sky had vanished and instead he caught the hint of deep purple clouds circling above like a tornado, unheard of in these parts.

The rain fell then. Huge, heavy drops and he pulled on his large cane hat. His mouth turned down as it pattered onto his boat and shoulders, large oily drops, and he held his lantern closer looking at it – it seemed more like mud than clear summer rain.

His birds sat still as stone and seemed immune to the shower and in seconds more it seemed over, and as the light of dawn was approaching he saw that the clouds had vanished, and something else; the surface of the lake had a brown frothy scum floating on it.

He hoped one of the large factories hadn't belched out its poisonous clouds toward their little Yanhu village. After all, every household in the village relied on the lake, and if it got polluted, it would be devastating for all of them.

Hun Lee resumed paddling, and he was disgusted to see that the scum on the surface discolored his oar. He stroked another few hundred feet and exhaled with relief as whatever it was, was now sinking below the surface.

He just hoped it wasn't poisonous and marred the fish's flesh. His stomach already seemed to be giving him trouble. And not just his stomach as he had a feeling of miserable depression as though something bad and unavoidable was coming and he wasn't looking forward to it.

He would not let his beloved fishing birds enter the water if he thought it dirty or dangerous. He reached forward and gently stroked each of their heads.

"You three can just watch this time," he said softly.

He rowed a little further and then slowed, lining up his boat on the marks – the tall reeds with a dead tree poking from them. The mountain peak in the distance, and on the other side of the lake, the small, abandoned hut that had been there since he was a boy and was now falling to ruin.

Hun Lee stopped rowing and after a few seconds his boat drifted to a stop. There was no breeze and no current so he would gently float where he was until he paddled elsewhere.

He baited his hooks with bloodworms, and then hoisted his three bamboo poles out over the sides and back, fastening their butt ends to the boat floor. He then took out an old tobacco pouch and some stiff homemade cigarette papers. He rolled one, lit it, and drew in the thick burning smoke and then let it out slowly through his nostrils.

The hair above his lip was stained an orange-brown from so many decades of smoking. But it was something he had enjoyed since he drew on his first cigarette as a boy.

His mind wandered as he stared at the small decrepit hut on the bank over the lake. He remembered as a boy when he and his brother, Hong Lee, had taken their father's boat and paddled across.

Inside they found old paintings on the wall and even a photograph of a man and woman in uniform, staring blankly at the camera. He wondered who they were; was it the man, the owner, and his wife from their younger days? He never found out.

He still missed his brother, even after over fifty years. When Hong was just twenty he went to the big city to make his fortune. Every year they waited for him to return, like the parable of the poor boy in rags who returns to his home village dressed in fine silks.

They received some mail from him for a few years, but then it stopped. And then nothing. He just hoped his brother found happiness wherever he was.

The tugging of one of his fishing lines snapped Hun Lee from his reverie, and he picked up the jiggling pole.

The water here was deep compared to the rest of the lake. He reeled the line in, and his brows came together – it didn't fight like a carp. Instead it felt more like a sullen weight, pulling just enough for him to be sure what he had was something alive as opposed to a clump of weed or sunken log. But not the jerking fight he would expect if he had caught a big head carp that was predominant in the Shaobo.

He slowly reeled in some more – twenty feet, fifteen, ten, five. Hun Lee looked over the side. The sun was still too morning-low for him to make out the fish, and he wondered whether he had caught the grandfather carp, big, old, and only a little fight left in him.

Then there was a swirl of movement on the surface as the fish must have been just under the boat now.

Then there came a thump as something knocked the bottom of the boat, and he glanced at the net he had tucked in against one of the gunwales. He hadn't needed it in years, but today might demand it.

The thump came again, heavier this time and it shook his boat. Hun's brows came together as he saw his three girls lift their wings for balance.

Suddenly the thump on the boat became a scrabble beneath the keel, and a shadow appeared just below the surface. And then that shadow lifted itself from the water.

Hun Lee pulled back in horror – the thing had a small pockmarked face with sores on the center of a bulbous flattened head, like someone had stuck a baby's face on the front of a big fish.

Then beside the grotesque face a tentacle rose up and slapped against the boat. Then another appeared, muddy brown, and this one too covered in ulcers. The creature blinked a few times, and then opened its mouth to wail. The sound grated on his nerves, and he saw inside the rubbery lips there was a ring of small conical teeth.

It began to lift itself higher and its weight began to drag the side of his boat down towards the water line. Just then the other fishing rods began to jerk and jiggle as they too had hooked something.

The glassy fish eyes of the thing fixed on him, and he saw its determination as it was desperate to get at him. The tentacles squirmed into his boat to pile in the bottom to coil and stretch like giant worms.

By then Hong had seen enough.

Hun Lee flicked the other rods over the side, and picked up the paddle, not to begin stroking away just yet, but to bring it down with a smack on top of the abomination's head.

More tentacles came over the front of his boat, and the others from the side behind him. They were all around him, and the boat was being pulled lower.

Hun Lee smacked at them, smacked at the grotesque things invading his boat, but it was like hitting a sack of flour and did not dissuade them at all. He called out then, his voice carrying over the still silent water.

In seconds more the first wave of water began to come over the side. The cormorants knew there was trouble and began to scream. But there was nothing he could do as the boat was anchored in place by the horrifying things invading his boat.

He knew they were demons, and he had no doubt that once they had his boat sunk they would grab him and take him down into the muddy depths. And perhaps one day, his small hut would be an empty enigma and the children would ask whatever happened to old Hun Lee, as they looked at the paintings and fading pictures still clinging to his walls.

His girls screamed again and flapped their wings. But they had the cords still tied around their necks and secured to the boat. If he and the boat went down, they were as doomed as he was.

Hun Lee could never let that happen. He dropped the paddle, picked up a fishing knife, and went to them, and one by one he cut the cords at their necks.

He widened his stance in the rocking boat and bent to kiss the top of each of their tiny heads and set them free. They squawked, complaining as they flapped their wings, but knew there was trouble and took flight, heading away to a far bank.

The water spilled over then as the boat went below the surface. In his last seconds above water, Hun Lee kept his eyes on the birds, wishing they would take his spirit with them.

The cold embrace of the tentacles revolted him, as they wrapped his legs, torso, and then neck.

As soon as his head went under, he felt the dagger spikes of the teeth on him. He didn't wait to die slowly, but instead opened his mouth and sucked in a huge draught of cold slimy water. His lungs spasmed, and his brain went into shock almost just as quickly.

Hun Lee's last sensation was of flying away to the far reed birds to be with his girls.

EPISODE 08

There are worse things than death.

CHAPTER 15

Drake Stoker and Clive Benson hunkered down behind a mound of rotted wood. Vermin like long slater bugs crawled in and out of it but the men ignored them and focused their binoculars on the dark water stretching before them.

Drake turned to look down along the shoreline and saw the towering creatures, each a hundred feet high, that he had at first thought were abandoned heavy machinery.

The skeletal creatures were on all fours at the water's edge and from time to time they reached forward to pick something from the dark water that wriggled like a caught worm in their colossal hands. They would then lift it back to stuff it into a hidden mouth under shawls of what might have been beard-like growths of either flesh or fungal extrusions.

Drake lowered his glasses, satisfied that each of them seemed rooted to the spot and made no effort to move as they fossicked in the stinking shallows.

He then turned back to the water and the object of their interest.

"What do you think?" he asked.

"Well, it's a boat. And still floating," Benson replied.

"Sitting low in the water. Could have a rotted hull," Drake said. "But beggars can't be choosers."

"Damn right." Benson lowered his binoculars. "So, how do we get to it? And don't say swim."

"How about we find something that floats, anything, and we use it to row or even paddle out on." Drake grinned at him. "Something like a surfboard."

Benson's eyebrows shot up. "Do I look like I'm built for surfing?"

"You can do it." Drake grinned and slapped Benson's upper arm. "Come on, let's look for something we can use."

The pair scouted the shoreline, moving fast but staying low. As they searched along what might have been a tide line, revolting things scuttled from their way, and from time to time, worms' heads popped from the black slime to peer at them with the horrifying human faces. This time Benson gave them a wide berth.

"Hey, forget the boat." Benson pointed. "Let's fly outta here."

Half stuck in the decrcpit mud was a small plane. It might have been silver once, but now it was covered in slime and there were things on it like barnacles, but they rose up on tiny sharp legs and moved off as the pair of men approached.

"That's one of ours," Drake said. "I think it's a Super Sabre. A jet from the mid-fifties. Years back I saw a model of one in my CO's office."

"How you spose' it get in here?" Benson asked.

Drake looked up at the miserable blackness above them. "How'd the city get in here? How'd we get in here?"

"Yeah, you're right, dumb question." Benson sighed. "The boat it is then."

They continued their search. There was little washed up, but in an hour they found the remains of another boat, this one smashed to pieces, and some of the planks with half-moon bite marks the size of which would have put a giant great white shark to shame.

However, the old boat being in pieces made it easier to select some of the largest boards to use as floats without having to resort to their knives to try and cut or lever some free.

They had no rope, nails, or anything to hold multiple sheets together, so each man took a piece and dragged them back to the waterline closest to the boat – even then it was still a good five hundred yards from them over dark water. And the water wasn't still; it swirled and bubbles popped at the surface.

Drake couldn't see movement, but he just had a gut feeling there were things living in there. *If anything down here could be called living*, he thought.

"Who's first?" Drake asked.

Benson rubbed his chin. "Do I go first and run into some monster? Or do I go last and get picked off from behind? Tough choice." He turned with eyebrows raised. "How about we go together?"

"Works for me. Besides, you're a much bigger target." Drake laughed, but felt nervous as hell. He drew in a deep breath. "Let's get this over with." He waded into the dark water, dragging his seven foot long and three foot wide plank of wood.

Benson did the same with an even longer chunk and together the men carefully paddled out. Drake had that weird flipping feeling in his gut from nerves as he tried to create as small a ripple as possible.

Beside him, Benson nearly slid off his plank and kicked, his legs thrashing for a moment, to climb back on.

"Will you cut that shit out?" Drake hissed.

Benson grimaced. "I'm tryin', man, but I ain't built for this," he grunted as he climbed back on. "Besides, this shit piece of wood is covered in slimy-ass moss."

Drake saw they had already covered about a third of the way, and was beginning to feel confident.

He kept his eyes on the boat, and was already mentally planning his climb aboard. He just hoped it wasn't in worse condition than it looked. He didn't want to climb up over the side and find it was full of stinking black water. And then they'd have to paddle back to shore.

Drake scoffed. He still had no idea where, or which way they were going to head. But he liked the idea of being on the boat.

First things first, he thought.

Drake dug his hand in the water about to pull forward again, when his hand touched something slippery. He snatched it back.

"Contact," he whispered.

Benson turned to him. He didn't say a word, but simply nodded. The big man then reached down to pull one of his blades from its scabbard at his hip.

Around the men the water swirled as something beneath them began to circle the pair. From the water's disturbance, Drake guessed it was big, and he suddenly remembered the sharks from the trip in.

"Dark water," Drake muttered. "I hate dark water."

The two men bobbed on their homemade surfboards for several minutes as something unseen glided beneath them in the impenetrable darkness.

"Benson," Drake whispered.

"Yeah," he replied dismally.

"Until whatever this thing is comes at us, we ignore it. We have to." Drake looked up. "We're nearly there."

"Ignore it?" Benson scoffed. "Well, if it ignores me, I'll ignore it."

The pair began to paddle again. They closed in on the boat, and at around twenty feet from it, a huge lump rose between them and the vessel.

"Oh fuck," Drake exhaled.

The thing was a mottled grey, and featureless.

The men stared, waiting for the thing to attack, but it didn't move. After a few moments, Drake began to paddle again.

"We go around it."

Drake and Benson began to go around the thing and as they did it floated closer. It turned around in the water.

"Oh, god no." Benson looked away.

But Drake stared, feeling the hairs on his neck rise – pressed into the grey mottled flesh was Gunner. Or at least the Aussie's face.

And then the face screamed.

"It's fucking Gunner. He's in there, man," Benson yelled over the man's agonized scream. "We need to get him out."

"How?" Drake gritted his teeth. "He's part of it."

He stared back at Gunner's face. The eyes rolled madly but never fixed on him. He saw then that there were other faces stuck there like boils on the side of a massive whale-like hide – he saw Thor, Brody, Vince, and all the others, all somehow pressed into the flesh and all screaming or wailing for help he could never give.

The thing glided closer. "Get away. Get the fuck away from me." Drake back-paddled. "That's not Gunner. It's not any of them," Drake yelled. "It's a trick to try and scare us."

"It's damn working, man," Benson yelled back.

"Keep paddling, we're almost there." Drake then pulled deep strokes on his plank and edged closer to the boat. He heard Benson behind him. The big man had given up any attempt at stealth and dragged huge swathes of water back with each stroke.

Drake felt something touch the back of his feet, and it was like he was given a jolt of electricity as he paddled harder than he ever had in his life until he came to the boat's stern, grabbed on, and began hauling himself to his feet on his makeshift surfboard.

He pulled himself over the stern wall and immediately turned back to throw his arm out for his friend.

"Come on, buddy, we're here." He stretched.

Benson got to the boat and then tried to stand on the wobbling planks of wood while trying to watch the plank, the boat, and also keep an eye on the surrounding dark water.

"Here you go." Drake stretched further.

Benson did the same and Drake grabbed his hand, and then the big guy scrambled over the railing and immediately lay on the deck, arms out, and breathing like he'd just run a marathon.

"Don't ever make me do that shit again," Benson gasped.

Drake grinned as he looked back out over the inky water – it was dead calm. There was no sign of their pursuer, and he wondered now if it had been real at all, or if it was something conjured by the Devil himself who was enjoying their torment.

He still couldn't get the images of his former Reapers' faces from his mind. The way they were somehow trapped in that sea beast, and had become part of it. He shuddered.

At that moment he realized that there were worse things than dying.

"Okay man, break's over," he said and turned back to the boat's deck. "We need to see exactly what we've got."

Benson groaned to his feet.

The men looked around at the deck, the rigging, and the superstructure – the boat looked to be an old seventy foot sail boat that had once undoubtedly been engine powered as well. The sails hung limp, and were streaked with mold and drips of stuff that looked like long bird shits, and Drake didn't want to know what sort of monstrous ass dropped them from above.

He leaned back over the stern and read the name. "The Hacienda," he said. "Name rings a bell for some reason."

Up top there was a wheel house, and Drake climbed to it. Frozen over the wheel was a body that was now just an age blackened skeleton, with jaws gaping in a perpetual scream. The flesh had long sagged to ribbons of rotten meat and the smell was of ripe corruption.

The man, he assumed by the size of the skeleton, gripped the wheel, but his hands seemed to have melted onto it, becoming part of it.

Drake sighed. "Sorry buddy, we might need that soon." He lifted his hands, not wanting to touch the disgusting corpse. In the end he just kicked out with his boot. The skeleton broke off at the wrists and fell to the side of the wheel house cabin with a clatter of bones. Unfortunately, the hands were still part of the wheel.

"We'll get those for you later," he said to the skull that stared hollowly back at him.

Drake went back down and joined Benson and the pair went to investigate the lower level. They stopped at the doors and Drake looked at his friend and grinned.

"Ready for this?"

"Hell no," Benson said, and shouldered open the door.

Inside, the men's lights illuminated a small area that was like a galley come dining area. There was a table that was stacked with plastic-wrapped, brick-shaped packages. One was open spilling a white powder to the table. There were also neat piles of money.

In a chair was another of the skeletons, this was exactly like the previous guy – age blackened, melted, and forever frozen as he lorded over the drugs and counted his money.

"Drug runners," Drake said. "Looks like they got their eternal reward."

"Lemme check out the guest suite," Benson said and lifted both his light and his handgun as he went towards a door that would have been to the sleeping cabins.

Drake followed him and Benson pushed the door open and looked inside. There were two small rooms, one larger than the other with a double bed and a small one with a bunk. Thankfully both didn't have a body and were cleancr than anything they'd seen down here.

"Small mercies," Drake said. "It's dry, and clean."

"I'm calling the double bed." Benson turned and raised his eyebrows.

"You're going to be able to sleep?" Drake scoffed.

"Nope, I just want a bed big enough to hide under." He grinned back.

They finished their search and headed back out to the living area and went to the table. There were some papers and Drake lifted one, shook it, and held it up to his light. "A newspaper. From the sixties." He turned. "You think this thing has been floating here for nearly seventy years?'

"I doubt it." He grabbed the skeleton in the chair and once again its feet and hands broke off. "I'm cleaning house. If we're going to be here for a while I'll sleep better knowing these assholes are at the bottom of the lake, sea, or whatever it is out there."

"I heard that. Over the side with all of it." Benson began to grab some of the drug packages as well.

Drake kept his mouth pressed closed as he lifted the skeleton, and together the men began tossing things over the side.

Twenty minutes later, Drake wiped his hands on his pants, satisfied with the cabin now. "Okay, I'll check the engines, but I'm guessing that is way too much to hope for."

"Well, not much of a breeze for the sails," Benson said and he slowly looked around. "While you do that, I'll go up to the wheelhouse and see if I can find us a direction that looks promising."

Drake grinned. "And the plan takes shape."

***

Benson went up to the wheelhouse and grimaced as he lifted away stuff that was draped over the wheel and around the small cabin-like room. It was like stinking seaweed that was turning to something like long strings of snot. And it stunk like shit.

He spotted the skeletal hands gripping the wheel, and used his blade to scrape them off. He turned and then saw the broken skeleton on the floor.

"You gotta go too, buddy."

He did a quick search until he found an old beach towel. He lay it out and pushed the bones and other crap onto it, went to the door and flung it all out into the dark water.

Benson winced and rubbed at his knee and thigh. It was the leg that had been infected before, and after a moment, he glanced around, and then took a moment to undo his belt and pull his pants down a ways so he could check himself out.

"Damn," he whispered.

Sure enough there were red and purple veiny streaks from his infected ankle to his thigh. As well as a lumped rash. And when he went to press one of them, it squirmed under his skin and slid away from his touch.

Benson closed his eyes for a moment and exhaled. "Seems you little suckers had babies before we got you out."

He slowly pulled his pants up and buckled his belt. He tilted his head back and looked heavenward.

"Lord, just give me enough time to get Drake home to his brother. That's all I ask."

He felt the painful squirm again, and he punched his thigh, hard. "And I ain't gonna make it easy for you little bastards, either."

He went back to work.

CHAPTER 16

Fifty miles southwest of New York – aboard the North Star cruise liner

Lieutenant Freshman frowned down at the radar. "I have a small object, two miles out, airborne, coming in at us from the west. Speed is approximately one-twenty miles per hour."

Captain Drinkwater turned. "That's slow for an aircraft. Is it a drone?" he asked.

Freshman slowly shook his head. "Could be, sir. Radar says non-metallic signature. Coming right at us."

"Albatross?" Drinkwater asked.

Freshman shook his head. "Signature is ovoid shaped and around seven feet in length. But no albatross wingspan."

"Not an albatross then. And too small for a light plane," Michael Ferrel, his second in command observed. He tuned to his captain. "Permission to put an armed man on deck."

Drinkwater rubbed his silver bearded chin as he thought about it. It was relatively slow moving, but he didn't like the way it was coming right at them. Good idea to have some sort of defensive option if it turned out to be something hostile.

"Permission granted," he said.

Ferrel turned away, and grabbed up one of the ship's internal mics and started issuing orders.

"Four thousand feet," Freshman said. "Bearing is unchanged and still approaching from the east."

Drinkwater watched as Ferrel and an armed man made their way onto the foredeck. He quickly and quietly escorted a few passengers who had been milling around to below deck, and then they took up a position close to the bow.

The captain lifted his glasses, watching for it now, his curiosity eating at him.

Freshman counted off the feet now to contact. And then finally Captain Drinkwater saw the dot appear on the horizon.

The thing came at them quickly, a black dot became a smudge, that became a buzzing bristling thing.

Ferrel and his armed man ducked as the massive insect landed on the deck. Its wings shivered and then folded.

"It's a fly," Drinkwater scoffed. "A gigantic goddamn fly."

Ferrel approached it, and his man had a pistol trained on it. The fly shivered its wings again, and Drinkwater craned his neck and stared through his binoculars – the fly didn't have those large muti faceted eyes or ugly hairy face he expected, but instead seemed to have a small round pink face. Almost human-like.

Drinkwater wished he had a bug expert to tell him what exactly he was dealing with here. Maybe they should try and catch it, he thought.

Out on deck, Ferrel flapped his arms at it, but the fly wasn't scared away. And why would it be? It seemed bigger and more formidable than the puny human trying to scare it away.

Ferrel took off his jacket and furiously flapped it at the monstrous thing, and then got within a dozen feet of it. And this time he got a reaction – the fly took off, not away from them, but straight at the pair of men, bowling over the guard before he could fire a shot, and picking up Ferrel in its multiple legs and flying off with him.

Ferrel screamed as the thing circled the deck and then dropped his second in command. Even from where they were they saw the blood smearing his shirt collar from the bite it had inflicted on him.

The fly zoomed overhead again, and then dropped to pass around the entire sides of the ship. Drinkwater rushed to the side trying to see where it went while also yelling orders for the injured men on deck to get assistance.

In the last seconds he had sight of it, he saw it come back around to the deck area of the ship. It headed straight for an open deck door where he knew the passengers were undoubtedly still milling around unaware of what was unfolding aboard the North Star liner.

Drinkwater lowered his glasses, his mouth hanging open.

Finally, he turned. "Get me a security team. We're going after it."

CHAPTER 17

New York, Manhattan – Manhattan Cruise Terminal, 12th Avenue

Benny Brown snatched up the ringing phone that was driving him nuts. "*What*?"

He was one of the Port Authority managers and right now at 6pm, things should have been quietening down, not going bananas.

His brows came together. "Say again?"

He turned to slowly look out the window of the two-story building overlooking the passenger terminals.

The cruise liner, the North Star, was ignoring its tug and coming in toward the dock, and still steaming in way too fast.

He glared, working the angles. In fact it looked like it was going to miss the dock all together and come in hard up at Pier 97 on the Hudson River Park.

"*Sonoffabitch*." He turned. "Steve, we got a damn runaway."

In seconds more things happened fast – this type of event wasn't usual, but was not unheard of, as many boats lost steering, or power, or the engines overcooked, or a hundred other things happened that would throw off their guidance and control as they came in to dock.

Benny couldn't remember how many repairs the dock had undergone over the years from misadventure. But right now, what concerned him was the North Star was coming in on the park, not too bad at this time of year as it was cooler and there would be less tourists. But the strange thing was no one onboard was answering – the entire ship seemed to have gone dark.

Benny scrambled his team and shouted into the phone as he watched the slow motion disaster unfolding.

Already there was a chopper overhead, a few drones capturing images, and the police onsite trying to evacuate the area.

He counted down the seconds as the massive thousand-foot, pristine white juggernaut of a vessel weighing in at about 120,000 gross tonnage came at them.

"Hold onto your fucking hats," Benny whispered.

Benny, and a few of the other office workers crowded at the windows and watched as the ship impacted with the Pier 97 water wall.

The North Star first cut a huge V into the wall ploughing in a good twenty feet before lifting slightly as the engines were still engaged and giving it power.

It kept going, ploughing up a few hundred feet of parkland before coming to a stop and he could see the churn of the propellor as it boiled the water behind as it continued to try and push the massive vessel forward.

Benny had binoculars to his eyes and still didn't see a single person on deck, or in the still well-lit wheelhouse.

"What the fuck is going on here?" he scowled.

First step was he had to get bodies onboard and turn the engines off before they overheated. Then he had to find someone in charge on that boat and kick their fucking butts.

Benny spent the next few hours coordinating the responses from the fire brigade, the local police, customs and immigration.

The first thing they did was fly drones over the top deck, and the magnificent little busy body machines peered in windows, and looked for open doorways. They found no sign of anyone, though it was important to note that all the ship's lights were on, and there didn't seem to be any sign of an attack at sea.

Next up, they needed to drop a couple of naval engineers on board plus a couple of armed support, and Benny would also attend and supervise himself.

He wanted to get onboard quickly before the ship's owners arrived and tried to take over the scene.

Not on his watch. He'd ensure culpability would be apportioned without fear or favor.

The chopper came down in the park, and the small group crouch ran under the blades and jumped in.

The chopper would be able to land on deck even though the huge ship was resting at a slight angle and being buffeted by the push of the still operating engines.

The pilot touched down lightly and they scurried out. Benny looked up, and saw that the sky was filled with drones – nearly all the local media organs had them, the police had them, as well as every Tom, Dick, and Harry with a few hundred bucks could get one and fly it right up to your bedroom window.

The first thing the group wanted to do was head to the bridge. Thankfully the deck doors weren't locked and the team of five went in. Immediately it was warmer and quieter, and the engineers went straight to the master console and checked the equipment.

Salvatore Mangione and Bella Azzopardi quickly saw there was plenty of fuel, all systems were online, and the communication system was still functioning normally.

Mangione went to the main computer and called up the ship's notes – not quite the captain's log, but it contained details of the operations that the senior officers regularly entered.

"Captain Robert Drinkwater," Mangione said. "Crew of forty-eight, and… four hundred luxury end passengers." He turned. "Everything online and working fine."

"Yeah, just a few things missing," Benny growled. "Like Captain Drinkwater, his team, and all those passengers."

"Gotta be somewhere on here," Mangione said.

Benny quickly checked the ship's online schematic and stepped back. "Well then," he said. "Let's go find them."

***

The ship was in four grand layers like a wedding cake – the top layer, the smallest, was for the wheelhouse, navigation, and instrumentation, and of course open deck entertainment.

The next level down was gaming, clubs, dining and catering. On down to floor three came to the cabin quarters for passengers and crew – in front was officers and first class, and rear for the crew and economy class. Next down was the engine room, workshops, storerooms, and maintenance. And then there was the lowest area, that was hardly a layer and was the bowels of the ship for ballast, waste, and some additional storage.

The group had walkie talkies and split into two teams. Benny went with one of the guards, Mike Jarvis, who was big, young and raw, and they would be team one. They would check the cabin quarters.

Team two was their two engineers, Mangione and Bella, and also the senior security, Allen Harper, who was oldest and most experienced. They'd check on the engine infrastructure in the bottom layer.

They all entered one of the elevators together – unlike buildings where the numbers rose the higher you went, it worked the opposite on a ship – the numbers elevated the lower you went.

"Creepy as fuck," Benny said.

"This ever happened before?" Mangione asked.

Benny snorted, and then thought for a moment. "Yes." He turned with a half-smile. "The Mary Celeste."

"Oh, good one," Bella laughed. "Hey, but seriously, you think they might have abandoned ship somehow?"

"Unlikely. All the lifeboats are still here. Not even the buoys are missing." He looked up as the numbers slowly rose on the elevator panel. "And no, I don't think aliens abducted them." He turned to wink at her.

Benny and Mike stepped out on level three, and Mangione and his small group continued on down to four.

***

Benny had on his makeshift toolbelt that he had made himself. It contained a flashlight, some basic tools, and a taser. He wanted to be ready for anything.

He knew that Mike had a sidearm if they needed one, and though he doubted they would need it, the weirdness was unsettling.

Besides, things like piracy happened. Bad people could make everyone jump over the side without lifeboats. He just doubted it could have happened so close to the mainland, and if it didn't, there was no way the boat could have threaded the needle and made it into the harbor so cleanly.

They came to the start of the first class cabins and Benny stopped and turned. "This is the first of the officer's cabins. Might as well start here."

He knocked – waited – then knocked again.

There was nothing so he tried the door and found it locked.

"Break it down?" Mike asked.

Benny shook his head. "Not just yet. Let's try a few more."

They went to the next and knocked again. And once again it was locked. On the third try they found the door ajar, and Benny eased it open.

"*Hello? Port security,*" he called.

There was no answer, and he raised his eyebrows at Mike who simply nodded. The pair went in.

"Shit!" Benny exclaimed

It was exactly what he didn't want to find – chaos, sprayed blood, and torn clothing strewn everywhere.

He picked up some papers from the desk. "Cabin belonged to Lieutenant Ferrel, second in command." He nodded to the washroom. "Check in there."

Mike did as asked and pushed the door open. He coughed.

"Shit, this is just as bad." Mike stood back.

Benny looked past him. The floor was covered in torn clothing that looked all greasy and stunk so bad it made his eyes water.

"What the hell happened here?" Mike asked with a forearm over his lower face.

Benny picked up a man's jacket that was split down the back as though it had burst open. It was covered in something like a grey, sticky mucous.

"What happened here?" Benny dropped the jacket. "Something weird and bad."

"We should call it in," Mike said.

"Not yet. There's over five hundred people on this ship and until we know something about their whereabouts, we hold off so we can calibrate our request. And their response."

The pair continued with their search and the cabins they could get into and found almost half of them contained the same evidence of something inexplicable and violent happening – bloody, torn clothing, stinking mucous, and no people or bodies.

Back out in the hallway, Mike paused. "Where are they all?"

"My gut tells me they didn't get off the boat." Benny exhaled.

Mike turned. "Maybe they're hiding."

Benny grunted, not ruling anything out. "You might be right, but why? Or from who?"

"We need to let them know it's safe to come out," Mike replied.

Benny pointed. "Hey, I've got a plan. You keep looking and I'll be back."

Mike raised his eyebrows. "By myself?"

"Yeah, I'm going to the command deck to issue a general announcement to the entire ship. I'll tell anyone and everyone to come out." Benny began to fast walk back to the elevator. He turned and grinned. "Great idea by the way."

"Yeah, you're welcome." Mike grinned nervously. "Just hurry back."

***

Mangione, Bella, and Allen Harper headed into the engine room and found the engines running hot, making the place an inferno.

"Gotta shut 'em down," Mangione yelled over the growl and hiss of the engines and hydraulics.

He rushed to the control panel and it was a simple procedure all controlled by a single shut-down switch. They needed to confirm their decision, and then the mighty beast of a machine seemed to sigh, and then settle to silence.

They looked around – the engine office, control room, and even maintenance bays which should have been a hive of activity with dozens of shipmen, engineers and maintenance workers, was empty.

"I don't get it. Where are they all?" Bella said. "Where do you hide around five hundred people?"

"You don't," Mangione replied. "They're still here, somewhere."

He lifted a wrench, heavy, and big at around two feet long, that was discarded on the ground. He looked at it for a moment, and then walked to one of the large steel support girders.

"Let's see what we got." He banged three times on the girder, and it reverberated right throughout the ship.

They waited as the echo within the steel raced away.

He lifted the wrench to do it again.

"Wait." Bella held up a hand.

He froze mid swing.

She had her head tilted. "Listen."

They all stopped and even held their breath. At first there was nothing, but then there was the faint sound.

"Is that…crying?" Allen Harper asked.

Mangione turned about and then after a moment frowned, and got down on his knees and then leaned forward to place his ear against the floor. He straightened.

"Whatever it is, it's coming from below – the ballast and storage areas." He got back to his feet.

Suddenly they all cringed as Benny's voice blared out in a ship wide communication to everyone on board, calling them all to come out and meet up on top deck.

"Give me a heart attack, Benny, why don't you?" Mangione grinned. "But maybe we should have thought of doing that first."

He went to the console and lifted the mic. "Seeing he's on comms."

He opened the comms line. "This is Salvatore Mangione, down in the engine room, over."

"I hear you, Salvatore, Benny here. What've you got?"

"We hear something coming from the lower deck. Sounds like it might be voices, over." Mangione turned to Bella who nodded.

"Good," Benny replied. "I'll pick up Mike and meet you. Wait for me where you are. Over."

Mangione replaced the hand set. "And now for some answers."

***

Benny picked up Mike at the elevators and the young man stepped in. He pressed the button for the engine room level.

"Find anything?" Benny asked.

"Are you kidding? After you left I hid in one of the room closets." Mike grinned.

Benny laughed.

"But no, nothing. Most cabins are either empty or locked. Nobody home," Mike said.

"Well, looks like Mangione has a few clues for us to follow," Benny said.

"Clues?" Mike asked.

"Yeah, he thinks they heard voices." Benny nodded. "From down at the bottom level."

"The bottom level," Mike snorted softly. "Why can't the voices he hears be coming from the pool deck?"

Benny scoffed. "Buddy, you've gotta be six foot four and carrying a gun. Stop making me nervous."

The door opened and Mangione, Bella and Allen Harper stepped in.

"Going down, ladieswear, soft furnishing, and people crying," Benny said as he pressed the button for the lowest level.

The elevator slowed and the doors opened to a muted light.

"Power must have gone out." Mangione frowned. "Shouldn't have. This is emergency lighting," he said. "I could probably fix it if you want to wait."

"How long?" Benny asked.

Mangione shrugged. "Might take me five minutes or…"

"Forget it," Benny said. "We're here now. In five minutes we'll know what's what. Let's get this over with."

"Smells funny," Bella said. "I was expecting brine, oil, and perhaps some metallic corrosion, but this smells like… over ripe mushrooms or something."

Benny felt a chill on his neck, and didn't like it. "Mr. Harper, you lead us on. Mike, you bring up the rear. We stay tight."

The lights were an orange hued bar every fifty feet and left a lot of shadow. This area was mainly for storage, and bulkhead protection. There was no reason for anyone to be down here other than routine periodic inspections.

Bella had an electronic tablet in her hands that had the ship schematic. "Up ahead, second door on the left leads to the main tank area."

"Got it." Benny wiped his brow.

"Hot as Hell down here," Allen Harper complained.

"It'll cool down quickly now the engines are off. In a few more hours it'll be as cold as the Hudson River."

They came to the door and Harper leaned closer to the steel putting his ear to it. After a moment he shrugged.

"Something, I think." He turned, waiting.

Benny looked at each of his team. "On three, two, one..." He nodded.

Harper turned the door lever and shouldered the heavy steel door open.

Miasmic. The smell was like a physical force and made the air so thick it felt like it coated their nostrils and the inside of their mouths.

Bella gagged.

"Hold it together, people," Benny said.

He suddenly didn't think they were going to find anyone alive.

The team lifted powerful flashlights as they were in a pitch dark steel corridor that ended in a weak light about fifty feet ahead.

"Main flotation bulkhead area up ahead," Bella said as it sounded like she was trying to stop breathing through her nose.

"How big?" Benny asked.

"This one coming is seven hundred by five hundred feet," she said.

"Enough room for all of them," Mike replied.

"Yeah, but why?" Benny nodded forward. "Nice and easy."

"What the fuck?" Harper, leading them, stopped beside an alcove.

On the outer wall was a sign informing them of an emergency phone that would now never be used. But tucked into the alcove in its darkest depths was something that was about eight feet long and looked like a weird, wrapped sandwich. It was glistening brown and yellow in their lights, tapering at each end. Sticky fibers glued it upright to the wall.

"Fucking gross." Benny turned to Bella. "What is that thing?"

"You're asking me?" Her mouth turned down. "I've never seen anything like that before. And I'll tell you right now, it isn't part of this ship. Or any ship," she said.

"Check it out," Benny said to Harper.

The older man turned to look at him, his expression one of disbelief in the glare of all their flashlights.

"Really?" His forehead creased.

"Yeah, sure, just see what it is. Get a closer look." Benny shooed him forward. "Go on."

Harper muttered as he went in closer, keeping his flashlight up, and one hand on his firearm.

The last few steps, he shuffled sideways, taking baby steps.

He stood staring at it for a while holding his light directly on it. He frowned. It seemed to have ribbing all the way from the top to the bottom, and he slowly reached out.

"*Careful,*" Benny said sharply, making the older man jump.

"Jesus, man. Shup up," Harper exhaled through bared teeth.

Benny grinned. "Sorry. Just, be careful."

Harper carefully laid a hand on the thing.

"It's warm. Hard." He knocked on it. "It's like some sort of shell," he said.

Harper knocked on it again, and in the glare of his lights they saw the shell was sort of translucent and something wriggled inside.

Harper pulled his hand back. "Fuck this, there's something alive in there."

"Okay, let's leave that for the Health guys," Benny said. "Continue."

"Up ahead." Bella's face was lit by the glow of her computer tablet.

They came to the end of the corridor and then out onto a steel gangplank that looked down a few steps to the huge open area that was the bowels of the North Star liner.

There was no light, but even their footfalls echoed, giving the impression of a large open space.

They shone their lights out over the massive void.

And then they saw.

"Oh my god," Harper croaked as he backed up.

Benny's lips clasped together.

There were bodies. Hundreds and hundreds of bodies.

There was a low lying mist hugging them and maybe that was the greasy odor of corruption that was so laden with decomposition gases it was laying heavy in the air.

Whatever it was, Benny was just glad they couldn't smell it.

"This is where they all came. Where they all ended up," Benny said in a whisper.

He didn't know why he whispered, he just felt the need to be cautious and quiet right now.

"Why?" Mangione asked. "Why did they come here? How did they die?"

Bella craned forward. "I think there's something on them."

They focused their lights and saw beneath the layer of greenish mist that where the bodies had shirts pulled open or dresses hiked up, and anywhere else there was exposed flesh, there seemed to be things that looked like bottles stuck to them. They were milky white, wet-looking and stacked in rows.

As they looked along the mass of people they saw that nearly all of their bodies had them.

"I don't know what I'm looking at here. But I don't like it." Mike turned. "Maybe now we can call in the authorities."

"Yeah, yeah." Benny nodded, transfixed.

"You hear that?" Bella asked.

***

Back along the corridor, the huge cocoon wriggled and bulged.

And then a split unzipped the tough casing starting from the center and then moving up and down its length. Something muscular started to swell from within.

The casing cracked and more of the muscular thing bulged outwards. Then came a crescent-shaped claw that gripped the edge on one side. And another came to grip the other's side of the split. They levered it open further and a dark limb with bristling hairs began to fully emerge.

Falling from the bottom of the casing was a glutinous liquid and in amongst it were half-eaten human limbs – a meal to assist in its transformation – the head of the creature came next, part massive blowfly, and part human being.

It had sensed the humans passing by, and knew now they had arrived at their destination. It was time.

It sent its signal to the brood.

And they began to emerge.

***

"I hear it." Benny frowned.

From down amongst the bodies there was a sound of popping and cracking, and then the soft sound of movement. Then what might have been frantic buzzing, but deeper, more powerful, like that of tiny machines starting up.

"Look. Those bottle things are moving." Harper pointed, and then began to back toward the doorway.

As the group watched they saw the wet-looking bottles begin to wriggle and then bulge. They found out then where the popping and cracking sounds were coming from as they split and opened.

"*They're fucking eggs!*" Mike shouted. "*Goddamn big eggs*."

In seconds more the first of them burst open and things crawled free, big as a man's fist, and stayed there shivering as their wings filled with blood and power.

"Fuck that." Harper turned to run.

"Back up, everyone," Benny said.

In the cavernous lower hold of the cruise liner the air was filled with the hum of strengthening wings. Then as if a signal had been given they took flight, and headed straight for the only exit – the one with the people standing in its mouth.

***

Allen Harper ran with head down and shoulders hiked. He knew he was being a coward. But even though he worked as a security guard he had never really confronted anyone or anything in his life, and certainly wasn't going to take on a plague of mutant blowflies. No siree.

Behind him he heard his team yelling and the rise of a buzzing sound that rose to that of a jet engine revving up.

He turned to look over his shoulder to gauge pursuit, saw nothing, and dared to hope.

"I'll call for help!" he yelled back down the corridor.

Just as he turned back to the dark corridor ahead he smacked into something that shouldn't have been there. The thing blocked the passageway completely, and in the gloom of the emergency lights in the dank corridor he could make out the form of a bug as big as a grizzly bear.

He was on the ground looking up, and saw on the wall the yellow warning sign and knew exactly where he was – right where that massive cocoon thing was that wriggled when he touched it.

Like it was about to hatch.

And now it had.

"*Fuck!*" Harper went to scuttle backwards but the massive thing fell on him. In the twilight gloom he smelled its stink of corruption and sourness, and saw the abomination up close.

It had the fucking face of a man, or at least the top half as the bottom was one of those hairy pad-like mouthparts of a real fly.

Harper screamed and screamed until his throat rasped and he tasted blood. The thing bent forward and vomited something onto his face.

Immediately he felt the sensation of an excruciating burning. And then he remembered how flies fed – they extruded part of their stomach acid to predigest the food so they could suck it up.

The agony was like nothing he had ever felt in his life, and he screamed and screamed until his tongue and mouth were gone. And then the monstrous fly bent forward to feed.

***

"*Ru-uuun!*" Benny screamed.

The four people turned and sprinted, but were immediately struck from behind by a wave of the huge blowflies. They smacked into the people, and Benny felt the nips of sharp little mouths as pieces of their exposed skin was bitten away by the flies.

They were in a maelstrom of buzzing, zooming spiky-haired bodies so thick it shut out the illumination from the already weak emergency lighting overhead.

Benny heard Bella screaming somewhere – it might have been six feet away, or it might have been ten times that. But it sounded like it was getting farther away and for some reason he imagined her being carried off into the air by hundreds of flies.

Suddenly a gun was fired, once, twice, three times, and he knew it was Mike going mad just firing wildly while his team members were too close to him – panic did that, Benny knew.

Benny put his hands over his head and tried to slog through the storm of bristling fast moving bodies, but his foot struck something, and he went down hard.

He reached down and felt the body. Opening his eyes to slits he saw Mangione, dead, god he hoped he was dead, because his skin was near stripped from his face and there were dozens of monstrous flies burrowing their heads into his body and working furiously at the exposed flesh.

That'll be me soon, Benny whimpered.

He began to crawl towards the way out.

The pain was excruciating as it felt like he was being cut by a thousand razor blades and stuck with needles.

He struggled to his knees. He felt wet all over and knew that most of his clothing and then skin had been stripped away. The nerve endings were raw, and he began to weep.

"*Not like this,*" he cried.

The gun shots sounded again, as Mike called out, firing his last rounds into the swarm, at the walls, and at anything.

Benny heard the last shot and felt the impact of the bullet strike him in the chest. Suddenly all the pain went away, and he flopped to the ground.

Thank God, he thought, as everything went mercifully black.

CHAPTER 18

Italy, Rome, Vatican City, the Vatican Library

"New York has been quarantined." Marco looked up from the computer screen. "They're calling it another flu virus, but, we know it's not."

Isabella paced. "It will break out in every corner of the world now." She rubbed her brow. "And so far we can do nothing about it."

Marco folded his arms. "The human race will be brought low, scattered. And when we are at our weakest, *He* will rise."

Isabella groaned loudly. "Give me some good news. Someone. Anyone."

Leonidas sat back. "I have news, and not sure if it's good, bad, or nothing yet."

Isabella turned. "Well?"

Leonidas read from his screen. "I've been researching any other occurrences in history of the twisted humans like we encountered in our journey to Hell. And I found one, a picture from the 1960s of something pulled from the water in the North Atlantic," he said and turned the screen around.

Isabella and Marco approached and looked down at the image. It was of one of the dog people, severely rotted from a long time in seawater, but the flattened features and deformed legs were unmistakable.

Isabella folded her arms and narrowed her eyes. "They found one floating near the Devil's Peak because there was an entrance to Hell there. But this thing is thousands of miles away from there – too far to drift, so…"

Leonidas raised his eyebrows. "So, there might be another portal."

"Yes, *yes*." Isabella stepped closer. "Where exactly was it found?"

Marco checked the coordinates. "Of course." He began to laugh softly. "Within the Devil's Triangle, where else?"

***

Isabella snorted. "But where exactly?"

"The supposed triangle, the Devil's Triangle, is another name for the Bermuda Triangle, an area bounded by Florida, Bermuda, and Puerto Rico, in the North Atlantic Ocean. It's gigantic, millions of square miles." Marco flat smiled. "Hundreds of planes and ships have disappeared there for centuries."

"The lost bomber squadron," Leonidas said. "I remember, most occurrences date back to the forties to sixties. But there are ancient stories of galleons vanishing there."

Marco typed in some more details. "The Hell beast was found drifting closer to Florida."

"Has anyone who vanished ever returned?" Isabella asked.

Marco typed some more. "Yes." He brought up a picture from the fifties of a young man in a pilot's uniform. "Lieutenant Mack Abrams, recon pilot. He was pulled from the water in 1962." He looked up at his pair of Knights. "He vanished in 1955."

"So where did he say he was for seven years?" Isabella asked softly.

"I think we know," Marco said. "And he told us. Hell."

"How did he get back?" Isabella began to pace.

"Mr. Mackenzie J. Abrams, retired colonel." Marco swung in his seat. "He's alive, 95-years old now and still living in Florida."

Isabella headed for the door. "Find him. Then we're going to talk to him. If he can get out of Hell, we can go there and get out too."

"You're going for Drake." Marco smiled.

Leonidas gave a small laugh and looked up at Marco. "Here we go again."

CHAPTER 19

United States, Florida, Sarasota

Isabella, Marco, and Leonidas turned the car onto Proctor Road and slowed outside the huge villa.

"This is it," Isabella said.

They then pulled into Aravilla retirement villa that was a huge edifice of a resort-style group of buildings that would have done a four star hotel proud – it was well lit, well kept, Roman-style columns out front and smart dressed people moving about, gardening, cleaning, and through one of the fences they saw the glint of a swimming pool.

Marco whistled. "When I retire, this is where I want you to put me."

"You'll get your reward in Heaven," Leonidas chuckled in the back seat.

Isabella stepped out. All three were dressed in sharp business suits with their fake military IDs. They headed to the front desk.

The young man looked up and smiled, but then got a little intimidated by the three formidable looking people in front of him.

"We're expected." Isabella gave him her winning smile and held up her ID. "We're here to see one of our retired servicemen, Colonel Mackenzie Abrams."

"Um, um…" He quickly consulted notes, then his computer. He began to nod vigorously. "Yes, here it is." He peered at the three IDs. "Ah, Captain Montague, and Lieutenants Reardon and Carter." He looked up. "Let me show you the way."

"No thank you," Isabella said. "Just tell us where to go, and you can carry on."

He seemed a little disappointed, and perhaps was hoping for something more interesting to do than occupy the front desk for the afternoon. He told them where Mackenzie, 'Mack', was and the trio headed off briskly.

They found him easily. Mack was in a small villa room that overlooked the rose gardens. Isabella slowed as she saw a man sitting there in blue pajamas looking out over massed rose bushes, all in bloom. He smiled as he tossed bread crumbs to several eager sparrows with one hand while keeping the other tightly rolled into a fist.

"Wait here," she whispered to Marco and Leonidas and then slowly approached. "Beautiful roses," she said.

"It's the manure. And the dry sunny climate," Mack said as he kept his eyes on the birds for a moment more before turning to her. "You can tell your friends to come out now."

Isabella grunted and turned to Marco and Leonidas and motioned them over.

Isabella approached a little more and stopped a few feet away. "Can we speak to you, Colonel?"

"Colonel?" He raised an eyebrow. "Haven't been called that for nearly fifty years. Just Mack will do these days."

"Mack, it is." Isabella came and held out her hand. "My name is Isabella. With me are my friends Leonidas and Marco."

"You FEDs?" Mack asked. "You're dressed like FEDs."

"No, and we told them that we were military to get in and speak to you without someone trying to oversee us. May I?" She pointed at the chair next to him.

"Of course. But there's only one so your friends will have to stand." He turned to the men, looking them up and down with rheumy eyes. "So, not FEDs and not military. Why do you want to speak to me? And no, I'm not reenlisting." He cackled for a moment.

"You know why," Leonidas said. "It's something that happened to you sixty-five years ago. Something nobody believed you about. But we do."

Mack stared for a moment and then turned away. "I don't talk about that." His gaze took on a faraway look as he stared out at the grass lawn for a while. "I learned to keep my mouth shut. Otherwise they were going to kick me out of the armed forces. Or lock me in the loony bin."

"You were missing for seven years. What did you tell them? What did they say?"

Mack begun to chuckle. "They said that I must have washed up years ago. With amnesia. And was living a different life somewhere for seven years." He bobbed his head. "Might have happened. And in the end I sort of agreed."

"But that's not what happened, was it?" Marco pressed. "You went somewhere. Somewhere else."

Mack's mouth turned down. "Somewhere else. Yes, yes, you might say that."

Isabella decided to give him a push, perhaps to bring it all back. "You went to Hell, didn't you, Colonel Mackenzie? The actual Hell, the place."

His eyes lifted to her, and the gaze seemed as old as time itself. After a moment he nodded.

She reached out a hand and laid it on his forearm. "We believe you."

His gaze lifted to her. "Why?"

She stared into his age-drooped eyes. "Because we've been there too." Her mouth curved into a half smile. "And we need to go back."

"Why would you…" He scoffed softly. "Of course. You left someone behind, didn't you?"

She nodded.

"So you want to know how I went there and how I got back." He shook his head. "Please don't go there. It's a bad place. If you went there before you would know that. I saw things that would drive you mad, and maybe it sent me mad, scrambled my brain, and I wandered around as a mad thing for seven years before regaining my senses." He smiled ruefully. "Maybe it was all a dream. I mean, nightmare."

"No dream, Mack." She squeezed his arm. "This is as real as it gets."

"Just making me think about it… I feel sick." He squeezed his eyes shut. "I can't."

"You must," Marco pressed. "The Hell plague is out and already ravaging the land. While we search for a cure, we need all our warriors."

"Captain Drake Stoker, US Special Forces, Reaper squad is trapped there. Help us get him home," she pleaded.

"No one left behind." His eyes slowly opened. "No one left behind."

"That's right," she said. "Leave no one behind. We want him back."

Marco closed in a little more. "Tell us, sir, tell us what happened. Take us back there to the night you disappeared."

Mack sat looking shrunken in his chair for a moment, before reaching across to lift a cup of tea and sip from it. He seemed to draw strength from the milky brew and he straightened a little.

He clasped one papery-skinned hand over the other that was still a tight fist. "It was 1955, and I was on a standard test flight of the new F100 Super Sabre. Beautiful little silver plane that cut the air like a knife. They even put a little picture of Jayne Mansfield in a bikini on the side. She was the biggest blonde bombshell in the 50s. Beautiful," He chuckled. "Noisy though. Like sitting on the front end of a damn rocket ship.

"The Vietnam War was just getting started and we knew we were going to be deployed there. I was cruising over the Atlantic…"

"The Devil's Triangle?" Isabella inserted.

He nodded. "Florida, yeah. Some called it that. One minute I had clear sky, the next there were these swirling purple clouds. I'd never seen anything like it. I tried to turn around, but those damn clouds overtook me, swallowed me. Day became night, and there was thunder outside, even louder than my jet engine."

He shut his eyes. "I remember I was so scared."

"I know, I know," Isabella said softly. "Go on."

"My radio went dead, then all my instruments just went crazy. Nothing worked. Last thing I remember was the engine simply stopped, and I was falling out of the sky." He shook his head. "I was only around a thousand feet in the air. I could sit there and wait to hit the water. Or eject. I ejected.

"The canopy burst open and I was shot out. Thank the lord the parachute opened and even though the wind threw me about like a leaf I floated down.

"The clouds cleared a little and I saw the ocean. I was worried about sharks." He began to laugh sadly. "Was I ever wrong about that."

"Did you splash down?" Marco asked.

"No, the ocean was gone. There was just a huge black hole. Like space, but with no stars in it. I fell into it." He quavered. "I fell and fell and fell. There was no light, no up and down, no left or right. Nothing. But then I heard, *something* – a low moaning, deep, sad, and it made me feel sick to my stomach. It sounded, *felt*, so wrong." He trailed off, wincing as if in pain.

Isabella gave him a few moments and then pressed him again. "And then…?"

"I landed on…shit. Dark and stinking. Miles and miles of it. Like a shore line, but I couldn't see any water." He shook his head.

"But you saw something?" Leonidas asked.

Mack nodded. "Things. Beasts. Some huge and others scurrying like rats. Everything was revoltingly deformed. I ran away."

"But how did you know it was Hell?" Marco asked. "What made you think that?"

Mack stared off at nothing, his gaze unfocussed. "I saw… a man there. I knew him. He died when I was young. Jack Vaughn was his name. He was a bad man, a rapist. He lived close to us when I was a kid and my parents used to tell me to avoid him. They said he was one destined for hell." He scoffed softly. "And then he died, beaten to death by persons unknown. Police never found out who did it. But I don't think they really wanted to. The whole street was happy."

"But you saw him?" Isabella asked.

After a few seconds Mack nodded, and his mouth turned down. "Yes. I saw him. Or some of him. I saw this thing that looked like a big crab or spider on the black shore eating the remnants of some rotting piece of flesh that was stuck in the sea of excrement. I went to walk around it, but it must have seen me and scuttled closer. I froze."

He sobbed. "It was Jack Vaughn's head with legs sticking out each side of it. Damn thing grinned at me and winked." He looked up at her, his eyes watering. "Where else could I have been?"

He held his head in both hands and rocked forward. "I don't know. Maybe I was wrong. When I was picked up I spent years talking to shrinks, and then eventually a priest. He told me I was just imagining everything as no one can come back from Hell."

Mack looked up and saw each of the three people staring at him. "But they can, can't they?"

"Your priest is wrong," Isabella said. "It is true in our faith that escape from Hell is not possible after death. Because Hell is a permanent state of separation from God, and once a soul is there, there is no way to leave. But the key thing here is that the words *after death*, are important." She smiled. "You never died, Mack. You were never meant to be there in the first place."

Mack began to cry. "I knew I wasn't imagining it."

Isabella gave him a few moments to gather himself and he wiped his eyes with his pajama sleeve and sat back.

"So, why are you here?" He gave them a crumbing smile.

"I've also been to Hell, and escaped. But we went through another gateway," Isabella said. "We closed it, but some of our people got left behind. I'd like to try and rescue them."

Isabella reached out a hand again. "We know where you vanished, and when. But the important thing is for us to find out how you escaped."

Mack began to nod. "Of course, of course." His brows drew together. "So strange." He looked at each of them. "I've spent years trying to forget. I've had dozens of people tell me I was wrong or just imagining things. And now, I have someone telling me it's real and I need to remember it all again."

"It's important. Very important," Marco said.

"Gather your thoughts," Isabella said. "Every tiny detail will be important to us."

"Oh god, you really want to go there." Mack's eyes widened.

"We have to," Isabella said. "Help us."

Mack drew in a deep breath and let it out as a long sigh. He clasped his hands together in front of himself and stared at them as he began to speak.

"When I was there, I couldn't tell how long I was there – days, weeks, years, I had no idea. There is no night, day, sunrise or sunset. No moon or stars, nothing. I was always scurrying, always hiding, trying not to be seen by things. I saw some of them so big they were like battleships walking on stilt legs and sucking up things they found in the endless miles of shit-mud." He rubbed his temples. "And others that were like waves of vermin, covering me, crawling in my nose, ears, and even my asshole." He squeezed his eyes shut. "They tore at my sanity. I screamed for hours, and there were screams everywhere all the time. Even the damn rocks screamed, and when I looked down at them, they were people's faces, heads, stuck in the shit mud to their chins."

Isabella felt for the old man and was sorry they had to torture him by making him remember and relive what was the worst time in his life. But she had no choice – she had to know.

"But you found a way out?" she whispered to him.

Mack nodded.

"I saw a dot of light. Far away and high up." He sat back wearily.

"Like a star?" Isabella asked.

"At first that's what I thought," Mack said. "It drew me towards it. Just looking at it made me feel a little less… despairing." He swallowed noisily. "It took me so long, days…" He shrugged. "I have no idea about the passage of time, but soon, I could see the dot was blue colored, and it was floating in the sky. I kept going."

He growled deep in his chest. "Things tried to stop me. Came outta the mud and grabbed my ankles, or dragged at my clothing. They scratched and bit me. I found a stick, or a piece of bone, and fought them. I figured the only way out of Hell, is to fight your way out."

"Good man." Marco smiled.

Mack had a coughing fit for a few seconds and they waited for him to get his breath back.

"Do you need some water?" Isabella asked.

He shook his head and took a big sip of his tea before going on.

"I followed the blue dot. And taking shape below it was a narrow peak, like a shard of stone or growth. It must have been a mile high."

"You climbed it?" Marco said.

"I had to. I felt I had no choice. The color, the blue, it was so clean and attractive compared to the dismal stink and slime I had been living in for I don't know how long."

"Years," Leonidas said.

"Yes, years," Mack agreed.

"I'm not a rock climber. And I had nothing but my bare hands and feet. But I started up. It was easy at first. The first few hundred feet. But then it got steeper, and it was slimy, but nothing was going to stop me. I figured if I fell I would just keep trying. And if I fell and died, then so what? I had nothing to lose. I climbed forever, and with each foot I rose above the stinking plain I felt better and stronger. I began to hope." He scoffed. "Until I got attacked."

"Something, someone, attacked you?" Marco asked.

"Flew out of the darkness, like a giant bat. Look see here." He unbuttoned his thick pajama shirt and leaned forward. He turned slightly as the shirt slid from his withered shoulder.

"I see," Isabella said softly.

There was a raking scar on his old, withered skin, three lines of purple rent flesh.

"It fucking hurt." He laughed darkly, pulled his shirt closed and sat back. "Do you know what the shrinks said when I showed it to them?" His mouth turned down momentarily. "They said I must have done that to myself when I ejected from the cockpit."

"But you didn't," Isabella said. "What happened then?"

"I fought them. Kicked at them as I climbed. I couldn't see them coming at me from the filthy darkness, but they could see me. I don't know how as they didn't have eyes. Or ears. Or a nose. Just a big mouth full of sharp teeth."

"You kept going?" Marco said.

"Had to. No choice now as I was so far up I wasn't about to give up." Mack drew in a breath, swelling his chest and then let it out. "You see, I was getting stronger the higher I went. I don't know why or what it was, but that light drew me on. And gave me strength."

He smiled as he stared at something from his memory of over half a century ago. "Then as I started to reach the top of the peak, one of the weird bat things flew through the beam of light – saw it fully then – monster. But the thing was, when the light hit it, it sizzled, burned, like someone had thrown acid on it. The bastard screamed and flapped away like an old wet sail. They left me alone then. It was like they knew then they couldn't come too close to the light."

Mack rubbed his grizzled chin. "But I had a problem. The blue light was a hole, leading to something shimmering. But it was about five or six feet above the absolute top of the peak. I sat there looking at it for hours. I wished I had a rope, or a ladder, or I was damn taller." He chuckled, and then began to wheeze and cough again.

Isabella knew he was winding down. "It's okay, take it easy." Isabella handed him his cold tea again. Mack sipped and winced.

"*Bah*." He put it down.

Isabella, Leonidas, and Marco waited, and Isabella didn't want to force him, but she felt they were so close to knowing now, she was never going to let him end it there.

"Please go on," she urged.

He nodded. "I looked down. I knew I was high up, but strangely, where I could see up the giant peak, I couldn't see down. It was like I was only a dozen or so feet up, but I know I had climbed at least a mile. But that made me less dizzy, and I climbed the last few feet, and began to stand. Yep, stand like those acrobats in the circus standing on the other guy's shoulders. I reached up, swaying, and then got on my toes.

"I didn't care if I fell, I was so close, I could almost reach it – it was beautiful – blue, shimmering and I knew the light was sunlight, cleansing, warm sunlight. There was nothing to grab onto, but something inside me told me that I had to touch it. So I stretched just that extra inch.

"And I did."

"And as soon as my fingertips touched it I was falling. But upwards – the air got thick, cold, and then that thickness became wet. I sucked in a last huge breath and shut my mouth, because then it turned into water. I was underwater, and swimming upwards towards the blue light.

"All the shit was being washed from me. My back hurt like hell from the flying monsters' scratches, but I didn't care. I knew it was scouring all the bad shit out of the wounds.

"I knew I was deep as my ears hurt, but I'm a good swimmer and not afraid of the water. I swam upwards, and then in the next few seconds, my lungs being about to burst, I breached."

Isabella saw the tears running down the old man's cheeks.

"I can't describe the feeling." He sniffed wetly. "I knew I was miles from shore and probably in shark infested waters, but I didn't care. I tilted my head back and let the sun warm my face. I knew I was free of the nightmare. I was free from Hell."

"Where?" Marco pressed. "Where were you?"

"I floated all day, but the water was warm and turquoise, so I had guessed I was somewhere close to Florida. Just as the sun was starting to sink I saw a boat. And more importantly it saw me. Turns out I was close to Exuma – do you know where that is?" Mack asked.

The trio shook their heads.

"It's part of The Bahamas, lots of little islands close together. The largest of them is Great Exuma. Beautiful place." He scoffed softly. "But I would have thought anywhere was a beautiful place after what I'd endured and where I'd been." He shrugged. "I was there in their little hospital for a week getting my strength. And then the army came and got me."

He looked up with a crooked smile. "No one believed me. They thought I was mad. So, they gave me backpay for all those years I was missing. A small fortune. Plus an honorary promotion to Colonel, and then they quietly pushed me out the door."

"Do you remember anything, any landmarks when you surfaced?" Marco asked.

Mack thought for a moment. "I remember the reef, it was breaking waves, and was too dangerous to approach. I didn't want to cut myself being out there alone. Sharks love blood in the water."

"I know." Isabella smiled. "Thank you, Mack. You've been very helpful."

Leonidas and Marco bowed slightly and left. Mack watched them go for a moment and then turned to Isabella.

"So who are you guys?" Mack's brows had drawn together as he scrutinized her. "You said you're not FEDs, and I don't think you're military, at least not ours. And not police. So who?"

She smiled. "We're from an ancient order dispatched by the Vatican. We're known as Templar Knights, and have been in existence fighting evil for thousands of years." She held out a hand. "And evil is coming, Colonel Mackenzie. And we intend to stop it."

He took her hand and held it for a moment. Finally he opened his other hand, the clenched fist, and she saw what he had been holding tight the entire time – it was rosary beads, with a tiny silver cross on the end. He had held it so long, there was a permanent shape of a cross in his flesh.

He gave her a crumbling smile. "I never used to be a religious man," he said. "But I now know there's a Hell and a Devil. And I think it was the other guy that showed me the way and pulled me out of there." Mack let her hand go. "Good luck. I don't envy you. But I guess it is your duty."

Isabella nodded. "It is what I was made for."

She bowed and left the old man in the sunshine. The sparrows immediately returned to sit at his feet.

CHAPTER 20

Somewhere, sometime, at the seventh Circle of Hell

There was no wind on the Black Sea. There might have been tides, but Drake couldn't tell as there was no shoreline to gauge it by now. There were also no stars, no sun or moon, and with zero landmarks, therefore no navigation points.

With no working engines, and no wind for the sails, he and Benson were on either side of the boat, on their knees, and bending to use the paddles from one of the dinghies to stroke forward, perhaps moving a few feet with each stroke.

They travelled in a direction they just felt was right without any logic behind it. From time to time they bumped up over things in the water, or unseen things bumped up at them. Once Drake felt the oar be tugged hard and he nearly lost his grip on it.

"What the fuck?" He stared down into the primordial ink and saw rising up the side of the boat a long tentacle, but at its end was a human-like hand with long rubbery fingers, and he could see suckers on the palms.

It quested forward, feeling for him. Drake lifted the paddle over his head, waited until it came close, and then brought it down in what he expected was a bone crushing smack on its top.

It was like hitting a rubber tire as there didn't seem to be any bones, but the thing obviously got the message as it withdrew back over the side.

"Watch your oars, Clive. Got something here trying to take them from us."

"Got it," the big man replied.

After another few hours, the pair sat back to take a break and drifted past what looked like an island. It was comprised of little more than a steep muddy hill at its center. They saw people, men and women, naked and emaciated, pushing huge stones up one side of the hill.

They strained and pushed and tugged, many times falling to their knees. Drake lifted his binoculars and focused on them – he saw they were covered in scars, some still bleeding, and he was sure they were carved in with sharp blades and spelling out words. Maybe they told of their sins, or were just cries for help.

He lowered the glasses. He watched as they finally got their stones to the top. They pushed them over the other side of the hill, where they rolled and bounced down onto a pile. Then they ambled down, picked up their rocks, and began to push them back around to the start of the hill to do it all over again.

"Shit," Benson said softly.

"Yeah, and I bet they'll be doing that for eternity," Drake said.

He dipped his paddle into the water again. "Let's get away from here."

He began to stroke and heard Benson doing the same.

Get away from here, he thought.

But to where? Maybe their punishment was to be eternally looking for a way out, day in day out, year upon year, century upon century. And never finding it.

Stop it, he demanded of himself.

Every problem has a solution, he thought.

But Hell is both the problem and the solution, a tiny voice whispered back. And then: *kill yourself, and end your suffering.*

Drake looked around, not seeing anyone or anything. All he heard was his friend pulling the water back on the other side of the boat.

He smiled. *So that's what it wants. Us to kill ourselves.*

"Because we're not dead," he said out loud.

"Damn right," Benson shouted back.

"We're not dead," he repeated and went back to paddling.

In another hour the stillness was broken by Benson's shout. "Hey, check it out."

Drake raised his head and looked to his friend. Benson was pointing at something in the far distance.

Drake turned and saw it – there was a dot, floating in the sky. It was a point of light.

"Is that a star?" Drake asked.

"I don't know. And I don't care. But it's something." Benson turned.

"What say we take a look?" Drake grinned.

"Long way, I think," Benson said.

"You got something better to do?" Drake asked.

"No sir. But I think we now have a destination." Benson knelt back down. "So heave ho."

The men used some new found energy to drag the water back behind them, over and over again.

CHAPTER 21

Right across Europe the quarantine camps were set up, but as soon as they were established, they were filled and then overrun.

France, England, Germany, Hungary, Romania, Spain, every country voted for them at the United Nations emergency meetings that seemed to be held every few days now. It was just that when the situation seemed as bad as it could get, the next day revealed even more new horrors.

It was Russia who first quarantined an entire city called Kazan with a population of one point three million souls. It used to be a beautiful and ancient place in southwest Russia, on the banks of the Volga and Kazanka Rivers.

But they soon found that the infection, caused by an unheard of blood disorder that turned out to be a significant and rapid mutagen, meant what they were quarantining wasn't human. And the limitations of human physical behavior and control didn't apply to what the people had now become.

Then they quarantined the city of Grozny, the capital city of Chechnya. It had a population of over three hundred thousand people, and it was a tightly packed urban area. The population here were even more far gone down the path of monstrous savagery.

And then the first bomb dropped.

It was a MOAB, Mother of All Bombs, the largest non-nuclear weapon in many of the larger nation's arsenals. The MOAB bomb was a thermobaric weapon, meaning it uses atmospheric oxygen to create a massive explosion. Its devastating destructive power came from releasing a large cloud of explosive powder that mixes with the air and then ignites, creating a powerful blast wave with the intensity of the sun.

Of course it was Russia who dropped it. And it was dropped onto Grozny, first, perhaps as a test.

It was detonated in the air above the city with catastrophic results for the population. But satisfying results for the government.

Or so they thought.

The new aggressive program of containment, quarantine, and then total cleansing, only ever kept pace with the rate of infection. Doing nothing meant the plague was burning through the countryside, spread by contact such as a bite or any sort of fluid exchange.

The saving grace seemed to be that the micro-parasite wasn't airborne. But then came the new species of insect vector – massive blowflies the size of rats, that were also spreading the horrifying disease.

And it wasn't just confined to the human population – livestock, domestic animals, and wildlife were also at risk. The body morphing mutagen had no preference for a species. It wanted all species. It just wanted flesh.

France was the first country to take their defensive program to the next level. Law and order was breaking down and instead the law of the jungle was coming back. Gangs of marauders formed on the premise of restoring order and repelling the infected, basically robbed and looted.

But, while gold and precious metals and stones still held value, money was rapidly losing ground. A barter system was returning. And one of the biggest services in demand was security. Armed security. And the better armed and more forceful the better.

War lords and small fiefdoms sprang up. Communes became walled off. Food and bullets were currency.

That semblance of order lasted until the walls were breached. Fires burned everywhere, and the mutated monstrosities now roamed in packs, searching out other communities or the few stragglers who remained behind sheltering in basements.

None would survive.

The French president gave the order to drop a medium single kiloton weapon on July 1st. The target would be on the most grossly overrun city in the country.

The device exploded with the power of 1,000 tons of TNT and obliterated three square miles to melted steel and rubble. And within the next three miles beyond that there was wholesale damage.

Satellite images and then flyovers soon afterward gave an estimated kill rate of ninety percent, and some two million infected were vaporized. And another million more left in a debilitated state.

But as for the infection, it was still there, and all they had done was bought themselves some time before the horde eventually got to them.

***

In the offices of the World Health Organization, Nandra Singh rubbed her eyes with the heels of her hands and sighed loudly. She was relieved that at last they had finally given up on trying to find a culprit for the release of the parasitic infection and now they were focused on a global eradication plan.

Though mistrust still abounded they worked together on finding a cure, a preventative, or a vaccine. They had no choice but to continue the bombing campaign to slow down the infection numbers. It was lamentably agreed that once infected, people were not coming back to any form of health normalcy and so the euthanasia plan was permitted.

Singh looked at the electronic spread map on the wall – it was like fighting an army that didn't sleep, didn't tire, moved at high speed, and recruited new numbers at a geometric rate.

The digital map looked like a slow burning piece of fabric as it estimated the rate of spread, with a counter showing the now billions of people infected – the last few numbers moved so quickly they were just a blur.

The global balance hadn't tipped just yet, but based on the aggressive spread and its speed, the projection was they had just two years before the human race passed a tipping point of more infected than non-infected. And then another year after that when healthy humans might cease to exist entirely.

Nandra looked at the report before her for the third time. "What are you? Where did you come from?"

She flipped a page and read some of the data on country infection rates. Some were doing worse than others. The spread started in the big cities, she guessed because it was transmitted from the international airports. The rural areas were as yet the least infected.

And the reports of the giant flies. They were suspected of also being a prime vector. But there was one place that had next to zero infection rates. The Vatican.

Nandra flipped the pages to that walled city, and looked at the aerial photographs – she had been to the Vatican when she was a girl. And she noticed something new added. All around its perimeter were huge crucifixes, a hundred feet high.

She sat back and crossed her arms. "Yes, perhaps it is time to pray."

CHAPTER 22

Ethan Stoker stood in his living room and stared at the massive grotesque fly thing that was on the wooden table before him.

The creature was about eight feet long, and must have weighed five hundred pounds. What made it all the more grotesque was the half human face of Octavius Conti, staring back at him.

Ethan wasn't human anymore. The thing inside him wore his skin like a suit and was as old as time itself. It did the bidding of the Lord of the Underworld, as well as the Conti fly. It was now one of the lowly execrable servants of the Dark Lord, and was tasked with aiding Ethan in his abominable plan.

The fly reported on information it had gleaned – the bombing runs were slowing down the spread of the Hell plague. Something must be done to speed it up.

Ethan already knew what must be done and stepped forward. The huge fly's probiscis reached out to touch his lips and Ethan opened his mouth and drank deeply of the corrupted plague-filled glutinous liquid that was pumped into him.

In seconds it was done.

Ethan then grabbed the car keys – he had a long way to go, over five hundred miles, all the way to Louisiana, and he needed to be there before the next bombing run.

The massive fly took off and went out through the open double doors like a miniature airplane. Ethan headed for his car.

CHAPTER 23

United States, Atlanta, CDC Clifton Road Campus

General Charles Chuck Carter walked fast up the few steps of the twelve-story block. He looked up at the concrete and glass edifice – the CDC's Royal Campus facility was the largest disease control laboratory within the country.

It housed the agency's premier BioSafety laboratory – Level 4 – the highest level of biological safety in existence. It was well known for containing the high-containment bio organisms, chemicals, and threats.

He was due to attend a demonstration and obtain an update on progress. The Commander in Chief was waiting on his report. What he told the President would dictate their next steps.

He was expected and met in the hallway by one of the scientists he had been communicating with. Gary Worthens was young at thirty-eight to hold such a senior position, but he earned it through hard work, and pure brilliance, and the general was glad they had him.

Worthens smiled grimly. "General Carter, glad you could make it so quickly."

Carter nodded. "This is the priority of the entire country right now. We're under attack from an aggressive parasitic enemy. And so far, we're not winning," Carter said gruffly. "Coming here is not optional."

"Of course, sorry," Worthens replied.

Carter's expression softened as he realized he was being an asshole. He gripped the young doctor's outstretched hand for a brief shake. "Good to see you, Doctor Worthens. Looking forward to seeing what you've got for me."

"Not much good so far." Worthens exhaled and placed his hands on his lab coat pockets as they headed for the elevator.

He turned and looked over the top of his glasses. "I have to put it on record, that myself and all the staff are not happy with the resources, *ah*, test subjects, you have supplied."

Carter grunted. "Neither am I. But so far, I have been told we could be looking at an extinction level event for the human race. And perhaps even for every species on Earth." He flat smiled. "The time for squeamishness is at an end."

Worthens nodded. "I understand the gravity of what is happening. Perhaps better than most. And though I, we, disapprove, we know what sacrifices need to be made."

The elevator doors slid open.

"If we could think of a better way to test it we'd use it." He walked into the elevator and Carter followed. He pressed the sub level 4 button and the doors smoothly and silently slid shut. "But, we can't, so that's why we're all still here."

The elevator smoothly dropped the several hundred floors to the secured laboratories, and the doors opened onto a gleaming white corridor.

Doctor Worthens directed him to the left corridor and Carter walked beside the young man.

Worthens turned. "How bad is it out there?" he asked.

General Carter grunted softly. "One of the last times we spoke you told me that we needed to find some way to stop or at least slow the spread of the parasitic infection; if not the end results could be catastrophic. Well, we haven't been able to stop or slow it. So frankly, it's as bad out there as it could get." Carter turned away. "Time is also our enemy now."

"Do you have any plans?" Worthens asked softly. "I mean other than relying on us?"

"We do, but they're ugly plans. You gotta give us something to work with, Doc. Or those ugly plans become the new reality."

Worthens led him to a pair of doors. One looked fortified, the other smaller. He pointed to the smaller door.

"That's the viewing room. It's sealed and you won't need protective clothing or breathing apparatus. I'll be joining the team in the more fortified room. We'll have the comms open so we can communicate, and you can observe our next experiments."

Worthens gave Carter a single finger salute and headed into the sealed room. Carter watched the door shut behind him and then went to the smaller observation room. Once inside he saw it was elevated, looking down on a huge laboratory. Inside, around half a dozen men and women worked inside bulky Hazmat gear with their own breathing tanks, and huge glass shields over their faces. Worthens hadn't shown up yet, and Carter guessed he was in an antechamber suiting up.

There were other things inside the room, and it was the thing that Worthens and his team had objected to. Or at least said they did.

There were three gurneys in the center of the large white tiled room. On each was a sedated man, a prisoner, and each a convicted murderer.

The men had a life sentence with no chance of parole. But they were told that if they were successful in helping create a cure, their sentences would be reviewed and potentially commuted. All had agreed. Just like the twenty men and women who had come before, and failed. And their bodies ended up in the incinerator.

The downside was the subjects would most likely die. The upside was that if there was a positive outcome, and a potential cure or remission or even a positive immune response, then there would be no need for human trials. Because they were happening right now.

Worthens appeared. "Can you hear me, General?" he said into the throat mic inside his suit.

Carter looked down at the console, and pressed the lit button on the comm set. "Loud and clear. Proceed with the test, Doctor."

The young man nodded.

Worthens motioned toward the prone and unconscious men. "So far the only thing that has had partial success was a full phlebotomy – the total replacement of the blood. However, even this only slowed the infection down, as a single microorganism of the Hell plague, as we have been calling it, means that it starts its rapid replication process all over again, and once it moves beyond the blood stream into the body's cells, well, then it's all over for the patient."

He lowered his arm. "Everything else we have tried, the strongest anti-parasitics like pyrantel pamoate, mebendazole, and albendazole, all had zero effect. We tried interferon, heat treatments, radiation, all too have been unsuccessful."

He nodded to one of his staff. "So, if the existing anti-parasitic drugs have no effect, then we need to create our own."

"I like it," Carter replied.

Worthens stared down at one of the prone subjects. "We have synthesized several variations of a treatment we hope will paralyze, inhibit the growth of, and/or kill the parasites."

Worthens nodded to the scientists waiting behind him and they prepared syringes and went and waited beside each of the patients.

"But first, the men need to be inoculated with the parasite." Worthens stepped back. "Inject," he said.

Each of the three doctors injected the greenish fluid into the men's IV drips.

He faced Carter at the viewing window. "The parasite aggressively splits and grows at an unbelievable and impossible rate," he said. "We're going to try and inhibit it using a combination compound comprising of metronidazole, tinidazole, and trimethoprim sulfamethoxazole. These are specialist drugs used for rare protozoa infections – a tiny, aggressive, and debilitating parasite."

Worthens turned back to the team who seemed frozen, staring at the unconscious men, all the team waiting.

He looked up at the wall clock. "Compounds administered at fifteen hundred hours. Recording." He folded his arms and watched the three patients like a hawk.

Seconds ticked by, and the minutes moved on at an agonizingly slow rate. Heart rate monitors beeped calmy, almost in unison for the three volunteers. It was these devices that gave the first indication there were changes happening.

"Blood pressure increasing," a woman intoned.

Worthens paced along behind each gurney looking down at the prone individuals. Each had a bag of saline fluid being pumped into him, and many different monitors reading his heartbeat, brain waves, and body temperature.

As yet only the heart rate was rising, and not alarmingly.

"What should we expect?" General Carter asked.

Worthens turned toward the glassed in booth. "To begin with, heart rate increase, body temperature rise, production of white blood cells, just like the body is gearing up to fight a fever. I'm sure if the men were conscious, they might say they felt nauseous and had a headache. But other than that not much."

Worthens paced again. "The parasitic intrusion has a one hundred percent infection rate. And a one hundred percent mutation rate. It manifests quickly. Within minutes." He nodded. "And so far there has been nothing to slow it, let alone stop it." He nodded toward the patients. "But this is promising."

Carter leaned forward and frowned. From his high vantage point he thought one of the subjects seemed to be changing color.

He blinked a few times and then focused. And then he was sure of it. The heart rate monitor started to ping fast and loud. And then in the next instant the man's legs seemed to lengthen, all the way past the end of the table.

Carter straightened.

The man's legs, once past the silver bench top, then drooped as if they were boneless and began to head toward the floor.

Then one of the other patients beside the stretching man seemed to swell, and swell, blowing up like a balloon. His gut rose three feet, and the massive pillow-like torso started to fill down past his groin and his arms were also being enveloped.

"Worthens…?" Carter warned into the mic.

"Not now, General." Worthens rushed from one patient to another.

The third man who had been still and silent did the opposite of the balloon guy, and began to deflate. His robust body of just seconds ago started to collapse in on itself. The face was the worst as it flattened, then shrunk back into the skull. Same as the chest and gut cavity. His muscular thighs and legs began to sag, and then the body glistened as if there was oil covering him.

Carter's jaws clenched as he watched the third guy dissolve into a large puddle of grey mush and then fall in great dollops from the table.

The massive gut of the man next to him started to shiver and veins showed on the drum-skin tight flesh. Carter knew exactly what was going to happen.

"Get back!" he yelled into the mic.

Too late – the man exploded, and Carter heard it right through the thickened safety glass in front of him that became coated in a red and black mush. He stepped closer and saw that within it, things wriggled and squirmed.

"There you are, you little bastards," he growled as he stared at the tiny things. "And now you're out."

He peered through the glass at the doctors covered in the revolting remnants of the exploded human being, and just as he'd thought he'd seen enough, he saw the elongating man twitch.

Carter frowned, and peered through the gobbets of bloody flesh stuck to the window. He saw that the man's arms and legs were around twenty feet long now, and even his neck extended off the table to hang upside down a few inches from the floor.

The boneless limbs twitched, and then Carter saw the head turn on the end of the long rubbery neck.

The arm moved snake-like across the floor until it got to one of the doctors at a bench wiping the remains of the bloated guy from his glass visor. The hand didn't grip his leg, but continued around it, coiling for a moment, before suddenly tightening.

The man yelled and looked down. He tried to dance away, but the coiled tentacle arm hung on. Not only that but his other arms and legs were whipping around trying to find more victims.

Carter stared and if that wasn't enough to test his sanity, the belly of the elongated guy split open, and what he at first thought was a massive open wound lined with broken ribs, was in fact a long mouth lined with triangular teeth. And he knew exactly where those tentacles were going to try and drag the captured doctors into.

Carter sighed, and opened the mic. "This is General Charles Carter, in observation room 12, overlooking the laboratory. It has been overrun, and we need an extreme prejudice cleanup crew ASAP."

He signed off and turned away. "Looks like no one is getting their parole after all."

He headed out, and only paused to smack his hand over the locking mechanism of the laboratory room door. He now knew what their course of action was to be.

He headed to the command room to organize the military response.

EPISODE 09

In every man sleeps a monster. But in some it wakes.

CHAPTER 24

Barksdale Air Force Base, Louisiana

The Barksdale bomber base was home to the 2nd Bomb Wing and the 307th Bomb Wing. It had over six thousand seven hundred active duty military and reservists and twenty-four hundred civilian workers, with many strike planes and bombers in fortified underground hangars. By any metric it was one of the largest bomber bases in the country.

The order had come down that there was to be a bomb run, internal, to cauterize an infection site on the mainland.

The job fell to Patricia Danvers, known as the 'Ice Maiden'. Danvers was in her early forties and had over twenty years' experience in various military aircraft. She had nerves of steel, and appreciated the gravity of what she was being asked to do – bombing your own country was crap, but she knew what was going on out in the world, and if they could slow the infected down by a few weeks then that was a good thing.

Danvers checked her wristwatch – one hour to go. She would be taking a B-52H Stratofortress bomber with a crew of just three counting herself as pilot, plus copilot and bomb master. But it was her that would ultimately release and detonate the device.

She wore a sidearm as was usual and had on the one piece flying suit. She was ready.

As she went to join her crew, there came a knock on the door.

***

Ethan sped to his rendezvous – night and day without taking a break. He didn't sleep, drink, eat, or even stop to piss. He didn't care about this vessel, this suit of skin he wore, because if it wore out, he would simply get another one.

He arrived at the Barksdale base with little more than an hour to spare. He still had his high level security Special Forces ID, and was able to enter unchallenged. He headed straight to the bomber pilot barracks.

The flies had told him what was being planned, and who would lead the mission. He just needed to find them.

The barracks always had armed guards so close to mission time and

Ethan pulled out his ID and waved.

The soldiers scrutinized it. "What's your business here, Lieutenant?"

"I'm a family friend of the Ice Maiden. Come to send my regards and wishes for luck on her mission." Ethan smiled benignly.

The soldier stared back. "I'm sorry, sir, you're not on any approved list."

"I know that." Ethan shrugged. "It's supposed to be a surprise. Can't you just let me see her for five minutes? I'll come straight back out."

The two broad young men refused to budge an inch. One of them motioned to a large building off to the side. "Go and have a coffee and some pie in the canteen and catch up when she gets back."

Ethan shot both hands out and grabbed each man by the front of their shirts. He dragged them forward and together, opened his mouth and vomited a sticky black slime over both their faces.

The men only screamed for a second as their tongues and jaws rotted away. Ethan held them for a moment more, quickly looking over his shoulder. He saw no one around so dragged both bodies to a line of flowering bushes outside the barracks.

He dropped them like sacks of garbage. "Should have let me in."

He reached down and unclipped a pass card that was stuck to one of the soldier's belts and then headed to the barrack's door. He swiped it and the door buzzed and clicked and he went in fast.

Ethan had been in pilot's barracks before and knew there was a central chill-out area, a small chapel, washrooms, showers, and a few officer's rooms. He bet Patricia Danvers was in one of the rooms, and even though her tag was the Ice Maiden, he bet she was as jumpy as a rabbit.

Ethan walked along the rooms in the corridor, his palm up to them as he sensed for her. At one door he stopped, smiled, knocked once, and pushed the door open.

Pat Danvers wasn't there, but he saw she had been as there was a coffee on the table top. He heard a toilet flush and Ethan waited.

In seconds more she came out of the washroom, and stopped cold.

"Who the hell are you?" She frowned. "This is off limits."

"Captain Danvers." He saluted. "I have some last minute instructions."

"What?" Her frown deepened. "Bullshit. We'll see about this." She headed for the phone.

"Wait." Ethan grinned.

Danvers turned, scowling.

"Please allow me to introduce myself." His grin widened.

"No." She began to snatch up the phone.

Ethan moved quickly. As she reached for the phone, he grabbed her wrist and pulled her to him. She struggled, but was no match for his titanic strength. He pulled her in tight to him, his eyes on hers, and pressed her body against his.

"Fuck off!" she yelled and punched the side of his head with her free arm.

Ethan didn't flinch but leaned his head forward, and she turned her head away. He then grabbed the back of her hair and kept her head still. In the next seconds he clamped his mouth over hers.

Her eyes went wide, and Ethan's neck pumped as the vile liquid came up from his belly and into hers.

Some of the black goo started to leak from her nose and she seemed to swoon as her eyes rolled back in her head. Ethan released her and let her slide to the floor.

He went into the washroom, picked up a hand towel and returned, kneeling beside her and gently wiped her nose and mouth.

"Much better," he said.

Pat Danvers' eyes opened. She got to her feet.

She looked at him and nodded.

Ethan saluted gain. "Good luck."

He left the room.

***

Pat Danvers carried her helmet and walked to the huge Strato bomber flanked by her two mission buddies, Red Hargraves and Derek Coleman.

Danvers was the mission commander, Hargraves, the elder, was the copilot, and Coleman was the weapons system officer, the bomb master. Both were competent and each knew the gravity of the mission ahead.

None of them wanted to be dropping bombs on their own soil. But the alternative was the country might be totally overrun by the infected.

The massive bomber was already out of the hangar and on the runway, and the trio used the gangway steps to enter the belly of the plane.

Danvers stopped to look back into the hold – there in its cradle was the device – fifteen feet long and weighing five thousand pounds, it was a thing of beauty and a technological marvel.

Danvers turned away, unlike Coleman and Hargraves who took a few moments to regard the massive device. They'd never actually done a run with live ordinance of this capacity.

The trio did a quick site check and then took their seats in the cockpit which was a hi-tech command center bristling with technology and sensors.

Danvers and Hargraves took the pilot seats, and Coleman took the third chair at a small console.

After another ten minutes they were given the green light and the base commander's voice was directed into the earphones – he told them they were saving their country, and to go with God.

Danvers' lips curved down a little and instead of the usual *roger that* and a small *thank you*, she instead, just gave a curt 'roger.' And closed the comms.

"Ready, gentlemen?" she asked.

"All green, Chief," Hargraves said.

"Good to go," Coleman added.

The massive turbine engines whined up in power and the leviathan craft began to move silently forward.

Two fighters would escort them as was mandatory, and as the huge dark craft picked up speed, Danvers tilted the flaps, and with enough thrust to lift a small building skyward, the Strato bomber lifted into the air.

Danvers half turned to Coleman. "Coleman, enter the PALs."

"Now?" he asked.

The Permissive Action Links (PALs) were security devices installed on nuclear weapons to prevent unauthorized use. They function as electronic locks that require a specific code to be entered before the weapon can be armed or launched. They were rarely engaged before the target was in sight, and Coleman knew it.

"Danvers, we're still a ways out," he said. "Maybe we should…"

"That's an order, Mr. Coleman," Danvers said. "You're the weapons system officer and I want the weapon to be ready."

Red Hargraves turned in his seat and met Derek Coleman's eyes. He shrugged and nodded briefly. Bottom line, Pat Danvers was the mission commander, and they were there to follow her orders.

Coleman entered a string of commands and green lights came on his console and also at the nose of the weapon. Seeing this she turned to her copilot.

"Enter your codes, Hargraves." She stared with dead eyes.

Hargraves turned and his brows snapped together. "What?"

They all knew that US nuclear weapons have several fail safes designed to prevent unauthorized or accidental use. These include physical security measures, like Permissive Action Links (PALs), and procedural protocols such as the two-person rule and the command structure with dual passcodes.

There was no self-destruct, as it could be compromised by enemies.

Once all codes were entered, then control of the detonation was in the hands of the bomber pilots. Usually, they were altitude determined. But not always.

"We're miles away," Hargraves said. "We can wait until we're a little closer."

"Hargraves, don't make me order you as well." She gave him the same dead stare again.

"Okay." Hargraves sighed and entered the code. "This is highly irregular. And I must inform you I'll be putting it in my report when we return to base."

He entered the code, and then turned. "Package is armed and ready for…"

Danvers had her gun pointed at him.

Hargraves just stared in confusion.

She fired. The sound was loud in the cockpit.

"*Jesus!*" Derek Coleman yelled from behind them.

Pat Danvers turned, pointed her gun.

"Don't." He held up his hands.

She fired again, hitting him in the chest dead center.

Once done, she gripped the wheel and began to turn the huge craft in the air.

The smaller escort fighters stayed with her, and she heard their rushed questions into her earpiece. She took them off.

Pat Danvers brought the bomber around, and lifted her altitude. She knew that by now the base commander would be screaming into her headpiece, and her time was running out.

She accelerated, trying to beat the inevitable and when the Barksdale bomber base was showing up on her radar, she began to drop. It would only be minutes before she was in range.

She didn't even need to hit it as she knew that if she detonated the payload anywhere within half a mile it would be obliterated, and even beyond that another mile of destruction.

There would be no more bombers taking off from Barksdale. Ever again.

Her eyes were wide, and a black thick substance started to dribble from her lips and coated her teeth.

Pat Danvers, or whatever it was that occupied the shell of Danvers, entered the final code. Both codes entered meant the command of the detonation was now hers alone.

"Hail the Father of Flies," she screamed as her hand hovered over the detonation command button.

***

Base Commander Bill Megan was a man not known for hesitation. The bomber had come around, and was on a heading back toward the base. All communications had ceased.

Something was wrong. And with the payload the Strato bomber carried there was no time to find out what. In a blink he decided.

"Fighters, attack is authorized."

The two fighters came in at the bomber, easily matching its speed, and fired two AIM9X sidewinders. The small and fast air-to-air missiles crossed the air space in seconds, and didn't miss.

The huge bomber was blasted in the guts and in the center of the flaming maelstrom it broke apart midair, with the pieces falling to the ground as a hundred flaming comets.

In the split seconds after the hit with the huge fireball hanging in the air, both attack pilots saw something take shape – a huge horned beast roared its fury and frustration and then dissipated. Neither man would ever mention it to anyone.

Strike successful. Returning to base, came the robotic voice of the lead strike fighter pilot.

Commander Megan drew in a deep breath and let it out slow through his nose. He turned. "Find out what went wrong. All surveillance, all communication Danvers, Coleman, and Hargraves had going back for a week."

Catastrophic destruction had been averted. This time. But until Megan knew what happened, they'd ground all planes and pilots.

***

Ethan Stoker stood on the hill ten miles from the base and watched through high-powered binoculars. He had seen the bomber be destroyed.

He lowered the glasses and snorted softly. The detonation was a long shot, but it didn't matter. There would be no more missions leaving Barksdale, and other bases until they carried out an investigation. Even if that only took a few days, it gave them time to advance the horde.

He whistled as he walked back to his car.

There was a lot to do, and the Master needed to rise soon.

CHAPTER 25

North Atlantic Ocean, the Devil's Triangle, off the coast of Florida

Isabella, Marco, and Leonidas had rented the large sailing boat, and headed as close to where Mack thought he had surfaced as they could determine. The destination was only approximate, and could be off by several miles. They hoped it wouldn't make a difference.

Isabella had taken note of the way Drake had mounted a cannon to the deck of his boat, and had done the same this time. They'd throw it overboard when they went back and just pay for the rivet holes in the deck.

She wasn't sure what to expect, but having a formidable weapon made her feel better about where they were going and what might be there waiting for them.

Twenty miles back they had cut the engines and just relied on the sails, but now the wind had stopped and they just drifted.

"We could be miles away or right over it," Marco said.

The three Knights were dressed in combat outfits and had a range of weapons already packed, holstered, and sheathed as well as their ancient swords. They also had backpacks with climbing equipment, ropes, and supplies for many days.

The trio had no idea what they were looking for or what might be waiting for them if they went through, but wanted to be ready in the event that whatever they came up against they'd be ready for it.

Isabella had her hands on her hips and walked to the boat's railing. "I'm not sure what we should be looking for."

She glanced up at the sky – pristine blue and cloudless from horizon to horizon. The wind had dropped away, and the only sounds came from their footsteps and quiet conversation.

"Nothing above water, so…" Isabella turned, "… drop the aqua phone, and we'll let the drone camera out as well."

"Good idea," Leonidas said.

He brought up the aqua phone which was basically a waterproof microphone that he lowered over the side about fifty feet and turned it on.

They listened intently, searching for something, anything, out of the ordinary. But all that came back was the usual pops, squeaks, and sound of fish feeding on the bottom. After thirty minutes, Isabella straightened.

"Put the drone over. Let's keep the phone down, just in case."

Marco brought up the drone, a three foot long torpedo-shaped device with two wings on each side complete with flaps for navigation. It was water jet propelled, and its front was a glass dome housing a powerful light and camera.

There was also five hundred feet of cable to keep feeding it power and it sent its images back to them.

"It's two hundred and fifty feet deep here," Marco said. "Want to check the bottom first?" he asked.

She shook her head. "Remember what Mack told us? When he entered the water, it was blue. That means he was well within the sunlight layer. And if he had appeared two hundred and fifty feet down, he might never have made it to the surface."

"So he appeared mid water, or close to the surface. Got it." Marco locked the cable to the socket in the drone's rear.

He lifted the heavy object and walked to the side of the boat and lowered it over. "You're free, little one. Or free for at least five hundred feet."

The drone bobbed in the water, until he went back to the command console that was inside a suitcase.

He flipped it open and checked the flaps, camera image, light and jets. When he was sure he had full control, he pushed it forward and then turned it in the water to face them.

The twelve inch screen showed Isabella and Leonidas standing on deck, and just the top of Marco's head where he was seated.

He turned it around. "I'm going to do growing circles. Then I'll let it run on auto and set it to trigger an alarm if it sees something interesting." He checked his wristwatch. "Once we exhaust this top-to-bottom hemisphere, we'll have to move to get insight into the next five hundred foot hemisphere."

The trio stood on deck just watching the water, the horizon, and now and then, the sky. The languorous warmth of the sun was comforting, but lulled them into somnolence.

After twenty minutes Marco turned from watching the water. "Did anyone bring any fishing rods?"

Leonidas chuckled. "You wouldn't know what to do if you caught one."

Marco grinned. "I've seen pictures. And besides, I hear you can kiss them and throw them back."

"Stay focused." Isabella lifted the binoculars to her eyes again. "I just feel… we're close."

Both men went back to staring at the tiny screen.

"We need to find it, or it needs to find us." She paced to the stern and after a while slowly shook her head. "But this could take weeks, months. Time we don't have." She turned. "Let's try something. Target practice." She reached to her belt where there were half a dozen small vials of water, holy water, and extracted three.

"On my count – Marco port side, Leo, starboard, and I'll take the stern." She held the three vials ready. "Three two, one…" She tossed the small bottles over each side far and high into the air.

The small things travelled fast, and she pulled her gun. When the bottle had finished its arc, she fired. Marco and Leonidas did the same.

All three bottles were struck and obliterated, and the small amount of holy water dispersed as a fine mist over a few dozen feet as it settled on the water around the boat.

There was nothing at first, but the boat rocked as if a wave had struck it. A breeze lifted gently, but oddly there was no smell of sea salt, but something else.

"*Phew*, that stinks," she said. "Like…" she turned.

"Yes, like the underworld," Marco said. He went to the drone screen. "Nothing down there."

"Leo, I suggest we suit up," Isabella said softly

Only Leonidas and Isabella rushed to pull on wetsuits, as Marco was going to stay on the surface. Hopefully to find them when they returned.

The pair scrambled to pull wetsuits over the battle clothing, and also placed flattened rebreathers over their backs. Their boots fit into the fin ends, and they held their masks ready.

The boat rocked again.

Suddenly the drone's proximity alarms screamed and the cord that was attached to their underwater drone started to reel out at phenomenal speed.

Marco raced to it, but couldn't grab it in time before it yanked the screen and controller from the deck and it vanished over the side.

"Either we got something's attention, or I think Moby Dick just ate our drone," he said as he scanned the sea surface.

The three Knights took up positions on the rear deck, each facing the water with their guns up. Clouds began to gather overhead, and the revolting smell got stronger. Then the boat began to move.

"Looks like we've just found the current," Leonidas said.

"Or we have company," Isabella replied.

Something rammed the boat hard enough to throw the three of them to the deck. Isabella was first up as something rose from the water at the stern.

At first she thought it was a tentacle, but then the end opened in a mouth and she saw it was like a giant snake or long necked dinosaur.

Her two companions were up beside her, and she shot at the thing piercing the neck. It pulled back below the water.

Silence and stillness followed.

"That was too easy," Marco said, aiming out at the water.

For several more seconds they stayed in formation, until the boat started to turn.

"You were saying?" Leonidas scoffed.

From the starboard side the head reemerged, and lashed out at Marco who dived out of the way. They fired again, and once more the thing pulled back.

"Notice something?" Isabella asked. "There was no wound on it. Either it healed real quick or…"

From all three sides heads on long necks emerged and Isabella was first to pull her sword, lashing out and slashing at the beast.

More heads on long necks appeared, each at least three feet long and with mouths filled with backward-curving tusk-like teeth.

The boat lifted in the water, and then tilted.

Isabella was slammed into the gunwale and gripped it with both hands. She looked over the side and saw then what they were fighting – it was like a hydra, a huge body of massive proportions, a mottled grey, and from one end a dozen serpentine necks sprouted.

She guessed it was one of the things responsible for a lot of missing ships in the area, and also bet it had risen from the underworld.

"Hold it off!" she yelled and struggled her way to the front deck.

Marco and Leonidas battled the beast, keeping its attention on them while Isabella went for the deck cannon. Beside it was a case and she quickly knelt, flipped it open, and took out the special shells – each had a tungsten head tip, but behind that was a hardened glass casing containing holy water.

She loaded one of the ten inch shells, locked it down, and then swung the barrel around.

Something that big was impossible to miss, and Isabella didn't hesitate, firing immediately. The shell impacted with the massive body and penetrated deeply into its mottled flesh.

The responding scream from the dozen mouths hurt her ears as a black ichor spilled from the huge wound in its side. With an explosion of water it pulled away from the ship and immediately started to surge away.

"Follow it!" Isabella yelled.

Marco went for the command deck and started up the engines. He brought the boat around, pushed the throttle forward, and took off after the beast.

They kept it in sight for another half hour before its stubby tail lifted in the air and it went down.

They found the spot and circled, looking down over the side.

"Anyone want to guess what's down there?" Leonidas asked with a half grin.

"Somewhere we don't want to go, but have to go," Isabella sighed.

She walked up to Leonidas. "Leo, this is my personal mission. Not something you need to accompany me on."

He smiled down at her. "Do you believe Drake can help us?"

"Yes, I do," she replied.

"Then by helping us, he is helping the world." He crossed himself. "And that is why I will go."

They clasped hands firmly and she nodded and smiled up at him. "To Hell and back."

Marco stood before them with a small leather pouch. Isabella and Leonidas knew what it was and opened their wetsuit vests and combat outfits underneath exposing their chests.

Marco said a few soft prayers, dipped his finger into the powdered rib bone of Paul the Apostle and firstly created a cross on Isabella's chest and then Leonidas. The crosses stayed on their skin for a moment and then it was as if they were absorbed into their bodies.

"Come back safely," Marco said. "I'll be waiting."

The pair walked to the stern railing and stepped through onto the transom. Each affixed the fin ends to their boots, and pulled their masks down.

Isabella turned to bump fists with Leonidas, and then jumped in. Leonidas followed.

The first thing Isabella noticed was the water was moving, and they were picked up in a current and pulled along and slightly downwards. On the way down Isabella hoped that the sea beast had truly gone – fighting it on the boat was hard, fighting it underwater would have been the end of them.

They gathered speed, moving along and down and she suddenly realized they were in a vortex. She checked her wrist depth gauge, and it said fifty feet already. So far she didn't feel undue pressure, maybe because of the water's agitation, but she knew they weren't equipped to go to two hundred feet if that's where the current was trying to take them.

The current seemed to increase and their movement in the current became faster as something was drawing them in. Soon they would reach the nadir, the lowest point, and just as she was wondering what and when that would be, she saw it.

"Up ahead," she said into the mask's microphone.

"I see it," Leonidas replied.

There was a dark smudge. Even though the light was diminishing at their depths this stood out as a shadow hanging in the water. She could tell it wasn't solid, but it was there, and just looking at it made her feel miserable and depressed. It had to be what they sought.

"This has got to be it," Isabella said as they were being drawn towards it.

There was no turning back or avoiding it as the current was too strong. Fifty feet, thirty, twenty – there was still nothing to see inside the smudge, as it seemed as cold and lightless as the dark void of space.

Isabella pulled the inflatable buoy from her vest and tied a rope to it. She turned the valve and the round red buoy inflated, and the buoyancy took it from her hands. She let the rope reel out.

The buoy's desire to float matched the drag of the vortex's current and the red balloon-type inflatable hung in the water, stationary, as if it had a perfectly balanced buoyancy.

"Our trail of breadcrumbs. I hope," she said.

"Here we go," Leonidas said they were drawn to the smudge.

And then in.

The transition was mind boggling as they went from the thickness of water, to an intermediate stage of a misty mushiness, and then into dark air. And they were falling.

"Grab on," Leonidas yelled.

Isabella threw her arms wide and the pair of Knights landed on top of a dark peak. It was only the well-toned reflexes of the fit young people that saved them as they grabbed on, and even then Isabella slid twenty feet to the slick rock, and luckily the wetsuits and gloves stopped her being abraded by the dark slimy stone.

Her slide stopped and she looked up. Leonidas was above her watching intently. And over his head was a rope, dangling from what looked like a misty blue window.

"Just like Mack described," she said and pulled off her face mask.

Leonidas did the same, and the pair clung to the dark pinnacle and looked out over the nothingness. They couldn't even see how far up the mount was as its base was lost in darkness. But if this sea mount was what Mack told them about, then they were perhaps a thousand feet up.

Leonidas looked up at the shimmering window. "If Drake is anywhere close by, he should see this." He looked down at her. "What do you want to do?"

"Climb down to the base." She looked out into the darkness. "Mack said there's a black sea down there and this is an island. Then we work out how to find him, or he us."

A sudden gust of wind ruffled her hair.

Leonidas looked up. "He also said there were flying things that attacked him." He unzipped his wetsuit so he had access to his weapons.

"Yep, I can feel them," she replied.

She also unzipped her wetsuit and drew out a hand gun. She stared out into the darkness.

"The flying beasts that attacked Mack." She looked up at Leonidas a few feet above her. "We're too exposed up here."

Just as she turned back to the darkness, there was an impact above her, and she turned in time to see something large and leathery flapping away and Leonidas falling. She flung out an arm, and he caught her hand.

He was far too heavy to stop his fall, and all she would have done is drag herself off the peak as well. But the athletic man only needed enough tension, slowing of velocity, and direction so he could swing back to the peak and he let go quickly to once again cling to the rock.

He drew in a couple of deep breaths, and looked up at her. "Thanks." He nodded. "Yeah, too exposed – we better get lower."

The spike of dark stone reminded her of a smaller version of the Devil's Peak that had started all this less than a year back. Maybe these things were created for a reason, or were relics from some past dark age that was swallowed up beneath the Earth before humans walked upright.

It took them nearly an hour to reach the base of the peak and they found themselves on a small decrepit island with little more than a giant up-thrusting of dark rock at its center.

Isabella looked up to see the dot of blue high in the black sky, or roof, or whatever was up there. It looked like a guiding star, and she hoped wherever Drake was he saw it up there and it was drawing him to it.

The pair removed their wetsuits and stood in their fighting outfits. They placed headband lights on and also had wrist flashlights. However, they only had food for a few days and water for a little longer. After that, she had no plans.

Isabella turned slowly looking at their dismal surroundings. The shoreline was a patch of stinking, slimy mud only about fifty feet wide all around the monolithic, dark peak. It made for a small island in the middle of an ink black sea. And she could tell by the way the water swirled and bubbled that there were things below the surface that could probably see her without her seeing them.

As there was no debris on the island there was no chance of making a raft, and not even she was foolish enough to try and swim out into the darkness.

"What now?" Leonidas asked.

"Now?" She placed her hands on her hips and slowly turned. "Now, we try and draw Drake to us."

She reached into a thigh pouch and pulled out the flare gun. She loaded one of the incendiary plugs into its squat chamber, lifted her arm straight up and fired.

The red flare shot away from them, reached a height of about five hundred feet and bloomed into a large glowing red flower that ever so slowly fell back towards them.

"Good a plan as any." Leonidas turned to her. "Let's hope it's only Drake that is drawn to us."

"And before we run out of flares," she replied softly as she stared into the darkness.

CHAPTER 26

"Hey, did you see that?" Drake stopped paddling.

"See what?" Benson lifted his head. "No, what was it?"

"I thought I saw a flash of light. Red," Drake said, still up on his knees.

The boat drifted to a stop. It had been laborious work, as the seventy foot boat under the power of just two men was barely being propelled forward. From time to time they were set upon by creatures large and small, and Drake knew both his and Benson's ammunition was rapidly running low and soon they would need to resort to defensive postures using only knives or their oars, not ideal, as some of the things that attacked them were as large and fearsome as sharks, but sharks bulging with tentacles or even hands.

"Red, you say?" Benson turned to him. "Is that good?"

"If it was a flare, then yes," Drake replied.

"Where exactly?" Benson asked.

Drake pointed flat handed. "One o'clock, give or take a degree."

Just then, seeming miles away, a red streak shot into the air. It rose for a few seconds and them bloomed in a huge red flower.

"Yes sir, we have ourselves a 37mm long range parachute flare." Benson put his oar down to clap once. "Well, what are we waiting for? Let's paddle until our assess fall off."

Benson began to dig his paddle in and pull it backwards. Drake did the same and the two big fit men began to drag the boat forward, foot by foot. Impatience was the mind killer now, as they probably travelled at little less than a walking speed of about three knots.

Drake thought the flare was about two miles away, and at their rate of closure, he estimated about an hour at least. And that was if they didn't have anything ambushing them on their way.

Drake's oar hit something below the surface and he cursed softly. The water stayed unbroken save for his paddling, but the atmospheric darkness and ink black water didn't help his gut feeling that they were being trailed by something looking up at them just down there.

"Who do you think it is?" Benson asked.

"Ethan probably, and maybe Addison. And Isabella too," Drake replied.

"Yeah, Ethan, he's come to give a bit of payback for you rescuing him – the twins got each other's back," Benson chuckled.

Drake scoffed. "To tell you the truth, I don't really want my little brother down here again. If he gets lost one more time, then nobody but nobody is going to come looking for him."

"Bullshit, man." Benson laughed. "His big dumb brother would. Brotherly love overrides sanity." Benson stood for a moment and looked into the distance. "Hey, maybe we should let them know we're coming."

"Good idea," Drake said. "Tie your flashlight to the bow. It might run out, but maybe they'll spot it. I don't want them moving off as we're closing in."

Benson did as asked, and Drake called him back to resume his rowing. The pair reached and pulled, reached and pulled, faster this time, and over and over like a pair of machines.

After twenty minutes, Drake could feel the fatigue starting in his shoulders which were both burning from the strain. Drake pulled on the oar again, and hit something solid. He hoped it was just debris, but when he went to pull the paddle out for the next backstroke, the oar was heavier.

He pulled it up and looked at it. There was something coiled around it, like a colorless pipe.

He shook it, but it clung on. "*Get the fuck off!*" he growled.

But the thing hung on. He flicked his light at it, and saw it was probably as thick as his forearm, pale and white, and like a pipe of muscle coiled up around the oar. He would have estimated it was about four feet in length, and he could see it had its head tucked down tight against the wood. But then again, the other end looked the same.

Drake smacked it down on the water, and then against the side of the boat and it still clung there. He didn't want to lose the oar as they had no spares, and if that happened, the idea of having to paddle by hand when this monstrosity was proof of what was down there.

"What's going on over there?" Benson yelled.

"Got a hitchhiker," Drake shouted back.

He held the oar in his lead hand and reached for his blade. If he couldn't shake the bastard off, he'd cut it off.

He drew the oar closer, and placed the blade near to where he thought the head was – big mistake – the other end whipped around and latched onto his arm. It was like a remora in that there was no discernable head or eyes, just the blunt ending to the pipe opened from a dot to a round sucker mouth that suctioned onto him.

"*Fuck!*" Drake still held the oar and battered it, but the thing might as well have been made of the same substance they make truck tires from and its muscular boneless body didn't seem bothered by his attack.

The sucker mouth then began to hurt as if the suction had turned to teeth.

"*Arrggh*!" Drake gritted his teeth and bashed his arm with the coiled monster up against the side of the boat. Once again it didn't seem bothered at all.

"*Benson, little help here!*" he yelled.

In seconds the big man was beside him and grabbed it, but the muscular pipe wasn't going to release him.

Benson wrenched Drake's arm up against the gunwale, and drew his own blade. The big man leaned into it as he cut the muscular flesh, and finally there was a spurt of black blood.

Maybe feeling the damage, it released Drake and sprung around to try and latch onto Benson.

"Not today, asshole," he yelled, and swung around and then flung the thing fifty feet out into the darkness.

Drake had a hand over the wound on his arm and took it away to look at it.

"Bit you?" Benson asked.

Drake could see that the skin was sort of dissolved or worn away, and just pink flesh showed.

"Hell yeah, it did. Wore a hole in me." He reached into his pocket for the med pack, brought it out and quickly found the small bottle of iodine. He splashed some on, creating another whole level of agony for himself. Then he placed a bandage on and taped it down.

He looked at Benson. "Thanks buddy. I think it was going to eat right through my arm."

Benson smiled. "Can't let it do that; we need those arms."

Drake grinned. "Back to paddling, right?"

"You got it." Benson went back to his paddling station.

Drake looked out into the forward distance – there were no more flares to guide them. He thought they must have travelled half way by now.

"Come on guys. Show us we're on the right track," he whispered.

He stared for a moment more, and then went back to the pull and drag of paddling.

***

It was a few hours since she had launched her last flare and Isabella paced around the small island – it was only a few hundred feet around so circling it only took minutes until she was back with Leonidas.

The man stood with arms folded, staring out into the darkness. They both tried to stay away from the water as from time to time things stirred the surface and splashed out there, and given the denizens of the upper caves they had encountered, they had no hesitation in believing that some monstrous beast could launch itself from the inky water to attack them at any moment.

She came abreast of Leonidas. "We're not even sure what direction they might come in on. If they come in."

He nodded. "They could be hours away." He turned. "Or days, or weeks, or…"

"Years. Or never." She sighed. "I know."

"How long do we give it?" he asked.

"At least a few days. I have two flares left, and you have four." She grimaced. "I wish we could light a signal fire…" She looked around at the disgusting melted stuff that had washed ashore, "… but there's nothing here that'll burn."

Leonidas pulled his own flare gun, loaded a plug and fired it into the air. "One more for the road."

It sped away, climbing quickly, and in seconds more bloomed into the giant red flower that would light the landscape for the several seconds it took to float back to the water.

They looked around at their dismal surroundings – the black spike of towering rock was at their backs, but all around was an oily looking sea that had probably never seen a breath of wind in all of its existence.

When the flaring ball of red light was just about twenty feet from the water she turned to see a huge lump had breached the surface, and worse a pair of totally white bulging eyes were fixed on her and Leonidas.

"Contact. Eleven-o-clock," she said, as she pulled her weapon and backed up.

"I see it," he said. "Big." He exhaled. "And not much damn cover here."

She looked over her shoulder. "You know, I think we'd be less vulnerable if we were a little higher."

"I agree." He pulled his rifle from over his shoulder. "You start to climb while I cover you. When you're up fifty feet, you cover me."

"On it." She turned, holstered her weapon, and began to nimbly climb the dark stone. The athletic woman scaled the first fifty feet in a few minutes.

"Your turn," she yelled.

Leonidas turned from the water, pushed his gun over his shoulder and went for the wall.

The thing surged from the dark water.

"Incoming!" Isabella yelled and began firing.

Leonidas must have known he was too low to avoid the attack, so had no choice but to turn and fight.

It came up on the muddy shore coming straight for Leonidas at the base of the rock wall. The thing reminded Isabella of a dinosaur-sized salamander, as it had a flattened shovel-shaped head that was nearly all mouth. Two small totally white eyes sat high on top and down the center of its back were thick bristles or perhaps spines.

The pair of Knights fired into the huge slimy-looking body, as it left the water on squat, powerful legs.

The bullets smacked into the dead corpse flesh and didn't slow it at all. Instead, the thing that was probably fifty feet from blunt head to paddle-shaped tail, began to open a mouth that was half its entire head.

Rows and rows of nail-like teeth were displayed. Anything that got hooked on those wasn't getting out of that mouth ever again.

Leonidas had his back against the wall. High above him, Isabella got ready to jump and land on the thing's back. But Leonidas crouched, pulled his flare gun and quickly jammed a plug in with shaking hands.

The monstrous beast opened a mouth big enough to easily swallow him whole and he turned in one motion and pointed it down the gullet. And fired.

The flare went down the throat and ignited as it went, also illuminating thick ribs on its way.

The amphibious beast slammed its mouth shut, and seemed to think on what it had just been fed for a second or two as its two tiny white eyes bulged. And then it opened its mouth and red smoke billowed out, and deep inside the flare had now exploded, the incendiary heat must have been agonizing.

It turned, heading back to the dark water, and in seconds vanished beneath the stinking dark liquid.

Leonidas slumped and exhaled. He turned and looked up with a half grin. "Heartburn."

"Good thinking," Isabella said. "Now get your ass up here."

Leonidas went up fast and in moments was clinging to a shard of rock beside her. He looked out over the water.

He shook his head. "How are they ever going to make it? I mean, we can't even stay close to the water for an hour, and we're expecting that somehow Drake is going to come across it."

She snorted softly as she stared out into the darkness. "If anyone can do it, that guy can."

He half smiled. "I think you lionize him."

"I admire him." She lifted her chin. "And I have faith in him." She then raised her arm and pointed. "Like I said, if anyone could do it, he could."

Leonidas turned to where she motioned. Out in the darkness there was a tiny pinprick of white light.

He saw it and began to chuckle. "You're kidding me."

"He is magnificent," she smiled. "Let's bring them in."

She reached for her flare gun, loaded it, and fired into the air. The flare rose and exploded in its red bloom above them.

***

Drake saw the flare. This time it was closer and for a few brief seconds, he saw the huge peak.

"There's some sort of mountain. On an island, I think," he said and pulled on his paddle.

"Please be people," Benson muttered. "Normal people."

They pulled hard on the paddles, and every stroke brought them closer. From somewhere out in the darkness, there was the sound of water dripping as if from something in the sky. Drake turned for a moment, and thought he saw the glint of something shining wetly but high up.

There was a deep splash and it was gone. A small wave sloshed up against their boat.

"I think something is following us," Drake said.

"Then it's a race," Benson said. "Last lap, Captain Stoker, let's make it count. *Yehaa*!"

Benson dug in and pulled hard on his paddle, over and over.

Drake snorted softly. No one had called him Captain for many years now, but Benson was right; this was the time to throw it all in. If that was a rescue party, they had a chance of being free. If not, they were being drawn to their doom. All or nothing.

Stay confident, he thought.

There was another splash, and the sound of something heavy lifting from the water out in the darkness. Whatever was behind them was keeping them in sight, but staying out of sight itself.

Benson was right – it was a race – and he just hoped they made it to that island before that thing decided to take them on.

***

Leonidas fired the last of his flares, this time in the direction of the tiny light coming towards them.

One of the reasons was he was concerned that it might not be a light, but instead the single luminous eye of some sort of sea beast.

The red flare burst into its usual furious light and color and sank slowly toward the water.

Thankfully he was wrong.

"It's a boat." He grinned. "Those crazy Americans did it."

"I can't see anyone onboard." Isabella squinted.

"One each side, paddlers," Leonidas replied.

The light illuminated the mid-sized boat and about a hundred feet of water all around it.

"Bad news," Leonidas growled. "Behind them."

Isabella shifted her gaze and saw the huge lump following the boat. From time to time a long neck would lift. And then another. And another.

"Dammit, I think it's the thing that attacked us on the surface." She pulled her gun.

"I don't think they know," Leonidas said.

"Let's give them some cover." Isabella began to rapidly climb down. "It's all in now."

She began to slide and climb down. Leonidas did the same. When they jumped down the last six feet, Isabella pulled her flare gun and fired her last plug into the air.

It went straight up, burst and bloomed, and lit the dark spike and the surrounding water.

Leonidas and Isabella spread apart, guns up. But so far the beast was staying directly behind the boat and keeping pace with it, and so they had no clear shot.

Isabella could make out the fading flashlight they had stuck at the bow, and saw the two men paddling. She couldn't help feeling the bloom of happiness in her stomach as she spotted the form of Drake, and on the other side his big friend Benson.

"Should we tell them?" Leonidas asked.

"No, we keep 'em focused on getting to us," she said. "If it looks like it's going to attack, we might get a clearer shot as they get closer."

The pair of Knights kept their guns trained on the boat and the massive beast right behind it. Isabella saw Drake lift an arm and wave, and in the red illumination of the flare she thought she might have seen the glint of his teeth, in a broad smile.

Come in, Drake, faster, she prayed.

"Why isn't it attacking them?" Leonidas asked.

Isabella shook her head. "Maybe it wants them on the island. Or wants us all together – a few tasty morsels of meat stuck on this outcrop."

Drake stopped paddling to wave again. Benson called and also waved.

"*Drake!*" Isabella yelled. "Keep paddling, faster."

Benson and Drake went back to stroking rhythmically but slowly, eating up the yards to the island. In another five minutes, they were so close, Isabella could clearly see their grime-covered faces.

Behind them as the water shallowed the huge beast began to emerge.

"Spread out," she said and she and Leonidas went to either side of the approaching bow of the boat.

"Are we ever glad to see you," Drake yelled through his broad smile as the prow of the boat slowed to a stop as it began to dig into the soft mud.

In response, Isabella and Leonidas started firing. The noise was near ear splitting in the dark silence and Drake and Benson ducked, but turned. And it was only then they saw the leviathan beast with the multiple heads on long necks right behind them.

Both men jumped into the water and began to wade towards the beach. Behind them the beast went down under the onslaught of bullets.

The pair staggered up onto shore, and Isabella kept her gun trained on the dark water where the beast had just submerged.

She saw that both men were ragged and ruined from their ordeal, and needed food, water, and about a week's rest – and right now they probably weren't going to get them.

"*Run!*" she yelled.

***

Drake and Benson staggered up the slimy beach to the peak wall. Isabella and Leonidas backed away from the water, keeping their guns trained on the swirling dark surface.

Drake had propped himself up against the wall, breathing hard. "You came," he said.

She went to him and threw her arms around him, looking into his face. "Of course. You thought I wouldn't?"

"No, because it's madness." He grinned and took the water bottle she offered.

Benson also took one and the pair also wolfed down a few energy bars.

"You would have come for me," Isabella said. "Just as you came for your brother."

"Ethan." Drake nodded. "How is he? And Addison?"

"I have not seen them," she said. "We've had other priorities. The Hell plague is out, and we need to stop it or cure it."

Drake held her shoulder and nodded. He turned to the water. "What the hell was that thing?"

"I don't know." She turned back to the water. "It was trailing you all the way here, but not attacking for some reason."

Drake also looked out at the dark sea surface and stepped forward. "It's still out there; I can feel it."

"Me too," Isabella replied and grabbed his arm to pull him back.

Drake turned to her. "So, how? How did you get here? I thought we destroyed the entrance at the Devil's Peak."

"We did," she said and craned her neck far back to look upwards. "But we now know there are other entrances around the world. Some hidden in plain sight."

He followed her gaze. "You followed a guiding star."

"You might say that." She smiled. "It's the way we came in. And our way out." Her brows snapped together. "*Hey*, it's gone."

"What was up there?" Benson asked.

There was nothing there now. The blue dot of light was missing.

"There's a portal. Or was," Isabella said. "We came through it. Swam down and went through it." She scoffed softly. "We left a rope dangling there – right at the top. We need to climb."

"How high?" Benson asked.

"About a thousand feet, give or take," Leonidas replied.

Benson groaned.

"Yes, it's high, but manageable," Isabella said. "If that portal is still there, you're going home. How's that for motivation?"

Benson chuckled. "Lady, I will grow wings and fly up this little bump in Hell's ocean."

The four of them turned and selected outcrops for handholds and steps, and began their climb. Almost immediately behind them the water boiled and surged.

"Something is pissed that we are trying to leave." Benson looked back over his shoulder.

"We climb, we take turns to stop and shoot, and then climb some more," Drake said and leaned back to sight his big friend. "Clive, last lap."

"On it." Benson started up.

When they were no more than a hundred feet up the massive beast surged up onto the small black beach. Its massive mottled grey body lumped up behind it, and from where they perched, Drake saw that the creature reminded him of a sea going dinosaur, except the paddle flippers ended in claws.

"Dammit," he cursed as the long serpentine necks immediately rose to try and snatch at the humans.

The four of them did as suggested. Drake and Benson only had handguns and a few rounds remaining, but Isabella and Leonidas threw them each a spare clip. The Knights had rifles and handguns, and from time to time, one of them would stop their climb and fire back down at the massive car-sized heads.

Though they had little chance of killing the beast, they could do enough to distract, slow it, or maybe puncture one of the eyes. Although the strange thing was he couldn't see any eyes on the heads.

It certainly didn't stop the thing at all, but it slowed it as each time it was fired upon, it stopped its climb to hug the dark stone.

Drake finished, then Leonidas took up the turn and shoot task. Then Benson, followed by Isabella. They were still only about five hundred feet up by now, but their strategy worked in that it kept them ahead of the beast.

Behind them the rock started to crumble and the black tower of stone shuddered as the massive weight of the monster was brought to bear on it.

"The peak is narrowing. If it gets much higher, it might snap it off," Isabella said.

"With us on it," Drake yelled as it was his turn to fire again. "We can't stop it. We just need to stay in front of it."

This time he managed to strike one of the many heads dead center, and it hissed like a steam train, and the damaged head pulled back a little as it stopped its climb. But there were so many more.

Drake then turned to scale higher, and move as fast as his screaming, already fatigued muscles could carry him.

Isabella led the group, constantly looking upwards trying to find the shimmering blue portal window. But there was still nothing there.

She saw they had only around three hundred more feet to climb – she wondered what would happen if she reached the top and there was nowhere else to go.

And the thing was still coming.

It was no place to conduct warfare as even though it was the high ground it was exposed and precarious. Plus their ammunition would soon be exhausted.

"Come on, be there," she whispered.

Behind her Drake came next, then Leonidas on the opposite side, and falling back was the huge form of Benson.

Isabella turned to fire down again at the thing. Its massive whale-sized body clung to the dark stone, and its many heads snaked forward.

The heads were gaining on them, and when she turned this time, she frowned in confusion – it was then she saw the thing a little more clearly – the individual heads had no eyes, and were just mouths on long muscular pipes.

When she followed them back to the body, they didn't join to some multi-pronged neck as she had thought, instead they emanated from within a wide mouth – these things were acting like extended feeding apparatus, and she bet that if they got hold of one of them, they would be fed back into that cavernous maw.

And the worst thing of all, the massive beast raised huge flipper-type appendages that had spiked ends, gripped the rock fifty feet higher and levered itself up even further.

Benson was being run down and his breathing was ragged and his movements slower. She knew that the hardships he and Drake had endured had drained them both. And the big man was enormously strong, but with the size and strength came an Achilles heel of fatiguing more quickly.

"Climb, Benson," she shouted.

"Don't wait for me," he yelled back.

"Don't make me come back and carry you," Drake yelled.

"Don't you dare stop, Drake." Benson scowled and dragged himself up another few feet.

Leonidas was first to make it to the top of the peak, and balanced there, looking around. Isabella came next, perching just below him.

"Anything?" she asked.

Drake came up to a few feet behind the pair of Knights, but there was nowhere for him to climb further as the narrow peak could only fit two people.

"Are we done?" he asked, and turned to fire another two shots.

"The blue window was here. Just here…*somewhere,*" she lamented.

The peak shuddered as the beast climbed higher and then lurched a few feet to the left before coming back. They hung on, but Drake slipped a few feet.

"This spike of stone isn't going to hold much longer." He climbed back up. "Got any flares left?" he asked.

"One," she replied.

"Now or never," he said.

She loaded the plug, pointed the squat gun straight upwards and fired.

The flare shot straight up into the black atmosphere. It exploded and then began to sink slowly back to them.

But there was nothing – no blue window, no portal, just black on blackness.

"Oh no," she whispered. "It's gone."

The flare drifted lower.

"There." Leonidas pointed.

Hanging in the air, almost invisible, and nearly right above them was about twenty feet of rope, hanging there, seemingly coming from nowhere. But as the flare went below it, they saw it actually fed into a dark circle.

"The portal." Isabella grinned, feeling her spirits soar. She turned back to Drake, grinning madly. "I'm a dummy. It makes sense now, of course. It was daytime when we came down, but must be night up there now."

"Night, day, summer, winter, I don't care. Let's get out of here." Drake grinned and looked over his shoulder. "Okay, big guy, we are leaving."

Drake saw then that Benson seemed stuck as the leviathan beast dragged itself up another fifty feet. But then it didn't stop and instead it came on another fifty, making it almost within reach of Benson.

Soon it would be on all of them – *or* – the pinnacle they perched on was creaking and swaying, and Drake knew that the ancient rock could not take it anymore. In his mind's eye he saw a hundred foot of the top peak break away, and carry them all to the dark mud a thousand feet below.

Isabella must have had the same thought as she turned to Leonidas. "You go first," she ordered. "Tell Marco to be ready. If he's still there."

"He will be." Leonidas turned to Drake and pointed. "Do *not* get left behind. We came a long way to get you."

The Knight then looked up at the rope dangling about five feet above him. He had to slow his breathing, readying himself for the insane jump into the blackness to grab a sliver of rope hanging in nothing.

He kept his light on the rope, but it still moved in and out of visibility. He slowly crouched, coiling his muscles as he seemed to count down, and then *leapt*.

Drake's mouth dropped open as the man seemed to snatch at nothing, but he caught the rope's end and hung on. Then hand over hand he ascended, and like a magician's trick, he vanished into a black hole.

Isabella turned. "Drake, you're next."

"No, you're next," Drake said. "You're too short to leap up and grab the rope."

"You're right, I am," she replied. "Thats why you're going to jump up, grab on, and then I'm going to climb up your body."

"Not without Benson," he said and turned back. "Give him another…"

There came a massive creaking and popping and then the massive rock peak started to tilt.

"Go, go!" Benson yelled.

Benson looked down at the approaching leviathan. The snake-like heads coiled and thrashed, and some had wrapped themselves around the peak, perhaps to give the massive creature extra stability. But directly below him the massive mouth hung open, waiting.

"Climb, my friend." Drake held out an arm. "You're coming with us. We've come too far…"

Benson shook his head slowly. "No man, I'm done. Those worms are all in me." He smiled up at Drake. "You were the best captain and boss I ever had. Thank you."

"Don't you fucking dare." Drake scowled. "I'm coming down."

The peak moved again, and Drake glanced upwards. He saw that they were now not in alignment with the rope and it was an extra foot up and away from them.

"We're going to miss it. It'll be out of reach soon. *Come on…*" Isabella yelled. "We need to go, *now*."

The massive peak made a noise like a gunshot, and a crack ran right up its center. And then as if that wasn't enough, the beast dragged itself up another dozen feet.

"I'm coming," Drake said, and took a step down.

"Stop." Benson held up a hand. "I can do this. Besides, I'm the one with the secret weapon."

"What?" Drake paused.

Benson opened his fist and showed Drake the grenade. He grinned darkly. "Show time."

He pulled the pin.

The big man kept the rueful smile on his face and his eyes on Drake as he let go of the pinnacle and fell backwards.

"No-*ooo*!" Drake screamed.

The two hundred and fifty pound man hurtled down the rock face, and the monstrous creature opened its mouth to accept him.

No sooner had the moth snapped shut, then there was a muffled *thump*, and the mouth burst open as flesh and some of the tentacle tongues or whatever they were, were blown free in a gout of flame.

The creature screamed, and in its rage, shook the dark spike of rock even more.

"Drake, *we are leaving!*" Isabella shouted even louder than the beast.

Drake then snapped out of it as the shard of rock shook back and forth and pieces of the dark stone fell from all around him. He began to climb fast.

When he was at the apex and balanced beside Isabella, she pointed.

"It's up there, can you see it?" she asked.

He could only just make out the rope dangling down. It was now six feet up, and not directly over the peak. It meant if he leapt for it and missed, then he wouldn't come back down on the rock summit and instead would plummet a thousand feet to the ground, or into the beast's damn mouth.

"You need to grab it, wrap it around your wrist and hang on, waiting for me." She held his arm. "I'm going to leap for you, and climb up your body. You must be ready."

"I'm ready now." He turned to her. "Give me a spring."

She nodded, crouched, and meshed her fingers together into a saddle.

"Count of three." She smiled. "Eyes on the prize."

"You're the prize," he said, and felt his cheeks flush at the dumb pass, and the timing of it.

"Not now, Romeo. Focus," she said, but smiled nonetheless. "Ready?"

Drake looked upward and focused on nothing but the end of the rope and her voice.

"Three, two, one…"

As she reached the top of her lift, he leapt.

The rope wasn't there, but the combined power of his thighs and her throw up, meant he was able to take a second grab – the first he grabbed at nothing but air, but then he found it as her light beam hit it, and he grabbed on. It was wet, but his hand didn't slip.

As she requested he wrapped it around his arm, and dangled there right at its end. He turned to her, his free arm outstretched and his hand open.

His wingspan meant he was now only about three feet from her, but the dark peak began to teeter back and forth.

He knew she had seconds before the colossal spike of stone toppled like a massive, petrified redwood to crash back to the dark water.

Isabella crouched, her face a mask of pure concentration. The peak began to shift away from him and she didn't wait, and leapt.

She sailed towards him as the thousand foot high spike of dark rock fell away from beneath her. There was nowhere to land now and there would be no second chance.

Drake stretched out, and their arms came together and he gripped her wrist as she did to his.

"Got you," he said.

She hung on, dangling there, and breathing hard.

From out of the darkness, a huge bat-like creature slammed into her and clung on. In the spinning light of their headlamps and flashlights, he saw the revoltingly familiar face of one of the deformed things that were once people.

Isabella cursed and fought it with her free arm, but the extra weight and jerking made Drake's hand slip a foot down the wet rope.

Isabella punched and beat at it, but it kept moving and its long claws gripped her as it moved around onto her back.

Drake could see what it was getting ready to do – bite deeply into the back of her neck. He could do nothing but grit his teeth and stare.

The thing was on her back now and the female Templar Knight swung her head back trying to headbutt it. She also drew a dagger she repeatedly stabbed behind her. But the abomination was too fast and avoided each of her strikes. It bared its teeth.

"*Please, no.*" Drake gritted his teeth from the strain.

The gunshot split the air, the bullet hitting the thing between the eyes. It peeled off Isabella and fell away into the darkness.

Drake and Isabella looked up to see a soaking wet Leonidas had slid back down the rope and was aiming his gun. He holstered it.

"Can we go now?" He smiled roguishly.

Drake grinned and then had to turn back to concentrate on pulling Isabella up so she could grab onto the rope herself. He felt more tired than he had ever felt in his life, but knew this might be the last time before rest. And as he had said to his lost friend, Benson, now was the time to put it all in.

He pulled her up and she swung her other arm up and grabbed the bottom of the rope. She held it and looked up at him and smiled.

"Thank you," she said.

"Piece of cake," he said and then looked upwards.

Leonidas was waiting for them. "Drake, it gets thicker, and you'll know when to hold your breath as we'll be in water. We'll need to swim to the surface – about fifty to sixty feet, got it?"

Drake nodded. "I'm ready…for anything."

The trio began to climb.

***

Drake followed Leonidas up the rope and from time to time he looked back down at Isabella coming up after him.

After all the horrors he had endured, and all he had lost, he felt strangely elated. And that was down to the woman who had jumped back into Hell to pull him out. No one had ever done something like that for him, and he doubted no one ever would again. Maybe Ethan, but he was blood.

He couldn't wait to see his brother again. And Addison, and the sunlight. And he couldn't wait to spend some more time with Isabella.

He grinned as he climbed. This was the first time he ever felt something more than just a groin-led attraction for a woman. This time he felt something deeper. He suddenly wondered whether she felt the same. Maybe she just came back out of a sense of duty.

He sucked in a deep breath, summoning his last ergs of energy and continued the slow agonizing climb up the rope. It was hard going as the rope was slick with water, and he could smell the salt water on it. Up ahead he saw Leonidas' headlamp light grow dimmer as he entered some sort of darker place as if he were climbing into a thick cloud.

As he followed the man, he found the air becoming thicker, moister, and he struggled to draw in breaths.

He slowed his climb and looked down and saw Isabella looking up at him.

"Get ready to suck in a big deep breath, and I mean big, and then hold it. Then climb real fast. You gotta swim up about fifty feet," she said.

He did as asked and in the next few feet, he knew the air was moving beyond being breathable and water was running down his face. He drew in a breath all the way to the bottom of his lungs, and then Drake climbed fast.

His muscles screamed from the pain and fatigue, but then suddenly the miasmic heat of where he had been was replaced by coldness, and wetness, and the pressure of quite deep water. After the sensation of being dragged back down by gravity he was now buoyed and being lifted.

He let the rope go and kicked off, swimming upwards in the inky black water. But this water wasn't the decrepit stinking vileness from below, but clear seawater that washed away the blood and gore, mud, and excrement.

He kept his eyes open, and saw the glimmer of something up ahead. He swum towards it, feeling the pressure lighten and knew he was coming to the surface. His lungs could barely contain the air anymore, and as he started to see pops of light from a growing dizziness, he breached the surface.

Drake threw his head back and gasped. And then coughed up the water-laden air from his last big deep breath. He grinned, and then laughed out loud – nothing had ever smelled so sweet. And that glimmer he had seen? It was a half-moon, silver, and shining like the most beautiful gemstone he had beheld in his life.

Beside him, Isabella came to the surface. "*Yes!*" she yelled.

Not far away, they saw Leonidas stroking toward a boat, and a man onboard had a flashlight shining at them.

"Ahoy," he yelled.

Isabella swam to Drake and put a hand on his shoulder. "We made it." She wiped the hair from his face.

"How long? How long was I down there?" he asked. "It seems like I was trapped there for years."

"Time means nothing down in the land of dark eternity," she replied. "But you were only gone two weeks." She tugged him towards the boat and started to swim backwards, keeping her eyes on him. "Come on, much has changed. And there is much you need to catch up on."

"I'd follow you anywhere," he said and swam after her.

CHAPTER 27

Italy, Rome, Vatican City, Vatican Library – the scroll room

The discovered scroll was tugged out a fingernail's width more, sprayed with a fine mist of a hydrating and softening solution, then paused, waiting for a full minute to let it soak in and then dry.

The newly released scroll section was then passed under a special blue light that brought out the dyes and inks, and though it could never bring them back to their full radiance, it made them readable. And then the process was repeated for another minuscule tug.

Father Francesco Magnoli was one of the dedicated archivists whose role was to oversee the care and security of the fragment. Stationed with him was a Templar Knight. After the intrusion of a few months back no more chances were to be taken. There was too much at stake now.

Fixed above the treatment cabinet was a camera recording everything. But Magnoli was impatient to read every scrap that was newly revealed. And when he read, his eyes went wide.

He rushed to the camera and printed off the last few images.

"You have something?" the Knight asked.

"I think so. Something fantastic," Magnoli said. "I must tell the Holy Father. Wait here."

He rushed from the basement archive room and headed for the ancient stone steps, running up them until he came to the huge and ornate ground floor. From there he headed to a special elevator, entered his passcode, and the door slid open. It would take him directly to the Holy Father's residence.

Magnoli inhaled; inside it smelled of expensive incenses and fine silks, and he drew it in deeply, believing it might be the essence of the Pope.

Once the elevator opened he rushed to the double oak doors, and the Knights barred his way.

"I have urgent news for his eminence," he begged.

A green light went on beside them on the wall, as the security camera had granted him access.

Magnoli rushed in where several cardinals were flanking the Pope. He went down on his knees.

"You have found something?" The Pope leaned forward. "A cure to this hellish plague?"

Magnoli shook his head. "The cure is not yet revealed," he said. "But where it can be found *is* revealed."

The Pope closed his eyes and nodded. "By the grace of God." He opened weary, red-rimmed eyes and leaned forward. "And, *where* is it?"

Magnoli lifted his eyes. "The Garden of Eden."

CHAPTER 28

China, Changsha, Hunan Province

The cattle farm was large for China with over ten thousand head of free grazing Huaxi cattle. The weather was benign, the grass thick, and they spent their days eating and snoozing.

When the sun went down many just formed into groups and knelt or folded themselves to the ground, close enough to enjoy the herd's communal warmth, but far enough apart to not be stifled by the methane gas belching stomachs.

When it became full dark, the massive fly landed amongst them. In the moonless darkness it moved silently from animal to animal biting each, and inoculating them with a tiny bit of its saliva. Its touch was light and before dawn it was gone.

***

Hung Sen, owner and head chef of the massive West Lake Restaurant always chose the cattle from the herd personally. He liked a good muscle tone, youth, and a hint of fat around the middle.

The West Lake Restaurant was the largest upmarket restaurant in China, and indeed the world, as it boasted a seating capacity of five thousand guests in two large communal dining areas, and with over one hundred private rooms.

Hung Sen had been overseeing the multiple kitchens at the West Lake Restaurant for five years. He had been greeted personally by the premier, and he was known for providing the best of everything. In return, it was making him a very wealthy and respected man.

The cattle were loaded and his instructions given. The several thousand pounds of meat would go to his restaurant's personal abattoir, and be stripped down and carved into dozens of different cuts of meat. It would then be delivered to the kitchen's loading area by 2pm that very day.

Hung Sen jumped into his Mercedes S65 AMG that was the size of a small liner, and turned on the air-conditioning – he changed the vents to internal. Frankly he couldn't stand the smell of farm livestock. Give him an already skinned carcass any day over a smelly, hairy animal with all that shit between its cloven toes.

***

The sun began to set, and the restaurant managers knew the first of the guests would arrive soon – usually the families with children were first in to enjoy a meal, and then be gone before the small one's youthful patience ran out.

That night was a special night for the West Lake Restaurant as they had one of the largest private rooms booked out by the premier and his most trusted officials. Plus all their families. There would be one hundred and twenty people, all expecting a memorable banquet. And Hung Sen wanted to deliver.

It would start with the traditional mix of meat dishes – beef, pork, chicken, and fish. Then once the guests' bellies were starting to fill, he'd bring out the delicacies – the small dishes of panda meat, baby vaquita fillets – it was the world's smallest dolphin and very rare. There would also be tiger meat for vitality. All this course's dishes were of highly endangered species, highly priced, and therefore highly valued by the elite guests.

The annoying thing was he would be expected to gift the meal to the premier. It grated on him, as he was supplying millions of yuan of his best produce and meat. But he would be rewarded with the friendship of the premier, and for as long as the man was in power, Hung Sen would be untouchable. And that would be satisfactory compensation.

***

Hung Sen moved between kitchens, testing, tasting, and barking shrill orders. His teams worked like machines and now by 8pm, the dining rooms were at near capacity. He knew that guests came from hundreds of miles to sample the fare at the West Lake Restaurant.

He saw the dishes being prepared for the premier and approved. They would take them in soon, and his waiters were all dressed in red silk outfits, and he too wore a red silk jacket – the color of luck and power. He would be master of ceremonies, and he wanted them all to see who was in charge of their feast. He wanted them all to remember him, and remember this grand night.

The time came and the massive platters were lifted onto red silk shoulders and carried to the elevators. The waiters would all wait until the entire serving team army had arrived to enhance the spectacle, announced by the clap of a gong.

Hung Sen walked along the line of fifty servers. This was only going to be the first of many, many dishes and servings. Added to his team here, the wine and beer pourers would never stop refilling glasses.

Satisfied, he picked up the gong, and entered the stage area above the large private room. He smiled as he observed the loud, happy voices, laughter, fine clothing, and red faces from the champagne.

He drew in a deep breath and with a bang of the gong, the room silenced, and the guests turned.

He smiled down at the elite, the wealthy, the powerful, and the dangerous. Through the haze of cigarette smoke he saw all their round faces shined and flushed from the alcohol. The powdered faces of the wives and mistresses were like perfumed, porcelain dolls.

Hung Sen held his arms wide – they would all remember this night forever.

He bowed deeply, and when he rose, clapped his hands once. "Ladies and gentlemen, esteemed guests, and great premier." He held out an arm towards the large double doors. "I present, *the banquet*."

It began.

***

With military precision, the food went out to tables. The army of attendants strived to get the first course dishes onto every table at the same time.

The first course began with bird's nest soup, followed by Peking duck. Various seafood dishes came next, all with a variety of crispy fried or lightly sauteed lobster, king crab, shrimp, and a range of shellfish.

Then came the beef dishes. First up, he served *Shui Zhu Niurou* – it was a Sichuan specialty, and featured wafer thin sliced beef strips that were poached in an oyster and duck brain broth, often with a generous amount of chili oil.

Then came one of his personal favorites, the Black Pepper Beef, a Cantonese delicacy. The dish featured tender beef stir-fried with black pepper, onions, and bell peppers, creating a mouthwatering flavor with a little punch.

Hung Sen was delighted to see plates cleared, and laughter ringing out. The night was going extremely well, he thought.

He headed back to the kitchens, as they would be preparing for the dessert round soon. There would be many small, sweet and savory things to choose from, and they even had a dessert chef that had mastered French pastries.

But the crowning glory would be his famous, and exclusive, Shangri-La's pudding – dusted with 24-karat gold and priced at around thirty-six hundred Yuan or five hundred US dollars per serving.

He went through the door from the stage and headed for the elevator.

He nodded and smiled at some of the waiters still taking out food and returning laden with trays of empty plates.

He could afford to be good humored with them as they had done their jobs masterfully. Each would get a small bonus for their work tonight because he knew the sweetest melodies weren't just because the orchestra had a great conductor, but because the musicians were on note as well.

Hung Sen sighed contentedly and lifted his arm to press the elevator's call button, and heard the plates crash to the ground just behind him.

Hung Sen froze, his shoulders hiked – his teeth were gritted in trepidation as he turned and immediately started heading toward the sound. He prayed the plates had fallen in the corridors to or from the dining area. If they had fallen in amongst the guests, there would be embarrassment and his entire evening's work could be ruined.

He had a knot forming in his stomach as he couldn't get the image of the plates having fallen *on* a guest, an important one, and that is all that would be remembered from the evening.

Hung Sen reentered the stage area and looked out over the crowd – his brows snapped together – it was chaos and impossible for him to even try and understand what was happening.

People were grabbing at their necks, writhing on the floor, and screaming. But the more he looked the more he saw, and the worse it got.

There was blood, so much blood. One woman had climbed onto the lap of a large man, and was biting his face, ripping bits of flesh from him as he flayed uselessly, and she was swallowing the gobbets with relish.

Another man was pulling at his hair, then his cheeks, then ears, and then he reached into each side of his mouth and pulled, and pulled harder, stretching the flesh, and finally ripping it.

Hung Sen's teeth gritted in a rictus of fear as the man pulled the skin back from his own head, and the bloody skull emerged, not dead, but snapping at the air, with lidless, bulging eyes rolling madly. But if that wasn't enough to tear at Hung Sen's sanity, the man's entire skeleton started to pull itself up and out of the torn and sagging bag of skin.

"*Stop, please stop*!" Hung Sen put his hands to his head and backed up.

No one would have heard him as the sounds coming from inside the private room was the chorus of Hell – the wails, screams, and unearthly grunts and growls of things not of this world.

On the ground just ahead of him, two men looked like they were melting together, and they writhed and wriggled for a moment as the flesh from one flowed over the other like melted candle wax. Their clothing simply melted into the flesh, and in the next moment, the combined thing rose up on all eight limbs, the two heads dangled underneath it on boneless necks, and from the large, joined chest, a mouth ripped open with a wet, sticky noise.

That was enough. Hung Sen turned and ran then, heading out of the room and directly to the elevator. His phone was continually ringing, and he snatched it out, answered it but before he could even speak, he heard people shouting about a madness coming over the other dining areas – it wasn't just the VIP room, but the entire restaurant.

He disconnected the call and began to run. He didn't want to wait and see the result of five thousand guests going mad or turning into some sort of horrors from a madman's nightmare.

It was a disease. Had to be. He had read there was something affecting some of the European nations, and now it had found its way here.

He went straight to the car park, ran to his car, jumped in, and in seconds more he was speeding away into the night.

He began to weep. But then even through his tears he began to laugh, wildly. He had been right; this was going to be a night every one of them would remember.

Just not for the reasons he hoped.

EPISODE 10

To fight evil, first know the darkness.

CHAPTER 29

Florida, Citrus Park, Alvina Street

The Knights had rented a small house in a quiet suburb as yet untouched by the plague and only intended to be there a day or so, giving Drake a little time to recover.

Drake sat out on the back deck on a folding chair just in his shorts and let the glorious sunshine warm his face and body.

Inside the house Marco and Leonidas were already packing their bags and checking weapons. They always seemed to be preparing for their next mission.

Drake's sixth sense told him he was being watched and he inhaled, smelling Isabella's sporty deodorant. He bet she was standing at the sliding doors behind him. He knew she had already sent out for some replacement clothing as even his boxer shorts looked like they belonged to a hobo.

He half turned and smiled when he saw her.

"Did it really happen?" he asked.

She came and sat beside him in the next chair. "Unfortunately, yes," she said.

In her hands she had a computer tablet, and held it out to him.

"It's not over. And perhaps it has only just begun. The Hell plague is out now, the minions are preparing for the Great Beast's return." He took the tablet from her and she sighed. "But first they need to bring the human race low."

Drake looked at the tablet screen where she had lined up some images and short movies of what was happening around the world – there were images he recognized from his time in Hell, but now they were occurring on the surface world – mutated abominations, monstrosities that stretched the mind into disbelief, and the ground and buildings covered in red veins as though they were sucking the blood from the very Earth and cities.

He frowned down at one image. It showed a giant, a hundred feet high. The massive, deformed thing swatted at planes, attacking like a distorted version of King Kong. But as the vision panned in on it he could see that the enormous being was actually made of hundreds or thousands of people all somehow glued together, and like bristling hairs the arms and legs, hands and feet, stuck out as well as faces pressed into the body, with eyes and tiny mouths open as though screaming in pain or terror.

Drake dropped the tablet into his lap and closed his eyes. "This is a nightmare," he sighed. "What can we do?"

Isabella leaned back in the chair. She tilted her face and also closed her eyes, letting the sun warm her face. "We fight, of course." She half smiled. "We fight, we push back, we slow it down." She sat forward and reached out a hand to lay it on his huge bicep. "We're in a race, Drake. The beast wants to rise, but the Earth isn't quite ready yet. We have to make sure it's never ready."

Drake rubbed his face with both hands and also sat forward. "How do you convince people to fight against a being many don't even believe exists?"

"Haven't you heard?" She half smiled. "The Devil's greatest trick was convincing the world he doesn't exist." She exhaled. "But if they had seen what we've seen…"

Drake chuckled. "People think it's some guy painted red with horns. But it's not. It is the most monstrous thing you can ever imagine." He pushed his dark hair back, and groaned. "It's still in my head."

She rubbed his arm. "You're out now. You're free."

"Free." He placed his hand over hers, and nodded. "I hope this is real, and not a trick. Because if I close my eyes and reopen them this time and find myself back there, I'll go mad."

"This is real." Her fingers meshed with his. "Tomorrow morning, first thing, we leave." She leaned forward and lowered her voice. "But tonight is ours. And tonight will be real."

She stood, keeping hold of his hand. He rose with her, and she pulled him and he followed her to her room.

Inside he frowned. "I thought, ah, I thought, being with the Vatican, you were not allowed…?"

She smiled, her dark eyes smoldering up at him. "I am not a nun, Drake Stoker." She put her hands on his bare chest, feeling the slabs of hard muscle.

Drake grabbed her, running his hand up the smooth curve of her back. The skin was still sun warmed. "I've dreamed about this for so long," he whispered.

"Tonight there is just us." She reached into the front of his pants, gripping him, and pulling him out. He reared up, so hard he felt like the skin was going to split.

"Oh god," he said. "I mean, sorry."

She laughed. "The pleasure of loving is one of our greatest gifts."

She pushed his pants down, and as she did she sank to her knees in front of him.

***

It was three hours later that Isabella and Drake reappeared. Drake felt happier and more alive than he had in weeks, months, maybe ever.

"Oh boy." He grinned as he saw the pizza boxes.

On the counter top was stacked four pizzas and the smell was delicious. He looked up at Marco and Leonidas, who were opening a bottle of red wine.

"Please tell me you guys didn't order yourself two pizzas each?"

Leonidas laughed as the cork popped. "Why, you need to refuel for some reason?" He raised an eyebrow, but then leaned forward as he grew serious. "She is like a sister to us. Remember that."

Drake nodded and raised a hand. "Good intentions only. She's a good woman." He turned to the sound of the washroom door opening. "Probably the best I've ever known."

"Good, we agree," Marco said.

He pointed to the boxes. "One of each type. They say they're authentic Italian pizzas, but they always put too much topping on them." He snorted. "And one of them even had pineapple on it. Blasphemy, I say."

Drake stood. "Well, lucky for me my favorite is all kinds, so I'll take any one of them."

Leonidas handed him a generous red wine, and Drake took two and turned to hand one to Isabella.

She took it, and leaned into him. She raised her glass. "To fighting, and winning. And for the sun to shine on the world once more."

The four of them drank wine, ate pizza, laughed, and talked about things they'd done and seen in days gone by, and all of them had nothing to do with Hell, the Devil, or evil.

Finally when the food was done, they sank into a few of the sofas. It was getting late, and Drake felt a drowsiness coming over him.

"What now? Where to?" he asked.

"We leave tomorrow morning." Leonidas stared into his near empty wine glass. "We have been recalled to the Vatican. There has been some new information that may help us."

"You?" Marco asked.

"I need to go home, and see my brother," he said. "Tell him I'm okay. Also check on Addison. She went through a lot." He looked across at each of them. "Did anyone hear from either of them?"

"Yes and no," Isabella said. "I got a message from Addison, and missed it. I tried to call her back several times, but got no answer. Then I was sidetracked to try and find you. I forgot to follow up. Sorry."

Drake half smiled. "I'm kinda glad you got sidetracked."

"You two were close?" Marco asked.

"Ethan and I? Sure were. We were twins," Drake replied.

Leonidas stood and walked to the small open kitchen. "When he went missing, you went looking for him. You sacrificed a lot. Nearly everything for him."

"He'd do the same…" Drake began. "Well, he was sick, and has been through a lot."

Drake turned to Isabella and saw her share a glance with her fellow Knights.

"What?" he asked.

"I'm coming with you," Isabella said.

"No, you need to check in back home. I don't need a babysitter." He held up a hand and waved her down. "He's been sick, and remember, he and Addison are engaged, so they…"

She tossed him her phone. "Call him."

He sighed. "Fine."

He entered the number, and held the phone to his ear. The recorded message answered.

He didn't leave a message and then tried Addison's number. He waited and then once again he got a recorded message.

"Not there, either." He tossed the phone back to her. "I'll be there tomorrow anyway."

"*We'll* be there tomorrow," Isabella said. "Besides, I'm dying to see this Stoker Ranch you have been boasting about."

"No boasting needed." Drake smiled.

He sunk back into the chair. He should have been feeling mellow, but instead there was nothing but disquiet beginning to bloom in his belly.

CHAPTER 30

The United States, the Pentagon headquarters for the Department of Defense

General Charles Chuck Carter had just left a Joint Chiefs meeting and he had been tasked with the rural eradication of the infected population.

One of his compatriots would be dealing with the urban eradication, which was a far trickier job as there were still uninfected populations in those cities so the fighting would be almost hand to hand, building to building, one damn monstrosity at a time.

Carter's jaw was set as he was ordered to carry out his battle pan; basically their military assets were going to be turned inwards. There were no real external threats right now, as every country in the world was dealing with the same problem – people were becoming infected. And if they didn't die, they changed into all manner of horrors. And then infected more people, or fucking ate them.

He ground his teeth as he remembered some of the creatures they had captured for study. They were animated, but not really alive. They had no functioning organs, or flowing blood. They could be taken down with a head shot, but unless you blew every arm and leg off them, and since some of these things had six or eight limbs, then they just kept coming at you.

But fire also worked. Fire burned them and hurt them.

So fire it would be.

The waiting chopper took him directly back to his base of command, and from there, he brought in his senior officers to brief him on any latest developments. And then he delivered his orders.

Carter listened as Colonel Hartford got him up to speed on the different quadrants out in the field – so far they had pulled a few remaining families from roof tops, but from what they could tell, the area was overrun. The hordes moved in massive packs or herds. Thousands of skinless-looking things swarming over hillsides and through valleys, eating anything flesh and blood in their path. And if they caught some stray people, well, they were either torn apart, or assimilated.

He was shown images from drones, and his mouth turned down in revulsion – there were the familiar dog-ape looking things that were naked and looked skinless and glistening wet.

They had flattened faces and long snouts ringed with needle teeth. He hated them all. He had no pity for them as he knew their humanity had left them, and what was moving them now wasn't a person, but something evil, something that needed to be eradicated.

But the new development was when they moved through the heavier forested areas. They said there were giant things moving from tree to tree – flying. It seemed some of them had taken to the sky.

That was on top of the multi legged beasts like giant crabs that were when two, three, or more beings seemed melted together as a single entity. It seemed the horrors never ended.

Once his team had finished briefing him, it was his turn and he laid out the battle plans – they would enact multiple high speed bombing runs and use the latest thermobaric weapons. The plan was to incinerate anything moving out there.

He looked at each of the men and women before continuing. "Without this plan, we estimate that worst case scenario we will soon be fighting hand to hand. We don't want that. So, we need to slow these things down. Thin the herd, so to speak."

"Sir, we aren't a hundred percent certain that there aren't living people still stuck out there," Captain Marine Henandez said. "Can we deploy rapid evac choppers in the event we locate non-infected, sir?"

Carter turned. "I wish we could. But that would slow us down, cause us to be selective in our targeting. Right now, their side is growing by hundreds or thousands a day. When I said hand-to-hand fighting, you can read that as *we would be overrun in a day*. I don't want that to happen, do you?"

Henandez shook her head. "No sir."

Carter nodded to her. Fact is, he felt the same as she and probably all of them did. There were some poor saps trapped out there waiting for a rescue that was never going to come.

"We have a job to do. A dirty one. Clear your minds, and just focus on saving the United States." He straightened. "The fightback starts here. Understood?"

The group all came to attention. "Sir, yes sir."

"*I can't hear you!*" General Carter barked.

His officers roared like first year cadets.

He nodded. *Good*, he thought. There were some long and damned dirty days ahead. Motivation matters.

"Prepare your pilots, and let's get that munitions loaded." Carter saluted sharply and left the room.

As Carter strode down the corridor he thought through their strategy and what they had learned from previous events.

Following the devastating internal breach that led to their own bomber pilot trying to turn back on the base, each pilot now had to undergo an optic scan – one of the things they found with the 'changed' monstrosities, was they had a little something extra in their eye. It was a new growth, just like in nocturnal animals that gave them the 'shining' effect seen in the back of their eyes. They had grown a reflective layer just like the tapetum lucidum in wolves, bats, big cats, and other night beasts. In effect, it gave the monsters night vision.

The mission before them was simple – the drones would seek out the large moving herds of the Orcs, as the crews were calling them now, and then they would use F-22 and F-35 stealth fighter jets, chosen as they can carry weapons internally in weapons bays, and big enough for loading the larger thermobaric weapons.

The thermobaric devices were also known as fuel-air explosives or vacuum bombs, and were a type of explosive that consumed atmospheric oxygen to sustain combustion, creating a powerful blast wave and high-temperature fireball. They covered larger areas, were less impactful on buildings or surroundings, but devastating on softer targets – like people, Orcs, or anything else that couldn't get out of the kill zone.

General Carter took to the main control and observation room to watch the mission. The current monitoring technology was a combination of satellite imagery and drone eyes-in-the-sky that meant everything was like a video game. It was all up on screen from multiple angles.

"Jesus," he said softly, when one of the larger Orc herds was spotted.

Carter exhaled slowly. There must have been thousands of them, tens of thousands, moving over the countryside in a dark wave. It was hard for him to get his head around that not long ago these were normal human beings, people just living their lives.

He also noticed out in front of the monstrous wave a herd of deer, rabbits, and other critters tried to stay ahead of them. It seemed that human beings weren't the only thing on the Orcs' menu.

"Target acquired," came the monotone voice over the speaker from the first of the fighters.

The sleek fighter came in fast, low, and released its payload.

Pickle away, the pilot said, and then banked hard.

The device didn't need to impact with the ground to explode, as they were designed for an air, or atmospheric detonation.

The bomb detonated, inhaled oxygen, and then the pyroclastic-style blast heated up the air and ground beneath it for hundreds of feet in all directions.

Carter squinted as the bomb's blinding flash whited out screens for a second or two, and then when they came back, he saw it exhale its dragon's breath over the landscape.

After a few seconds, the second plane dropped its payload over another area, and the same for the third. Half a mile of the ground covered in countless thousands of beasts was obliterated.

"Returning to base," came the final words from the lead pilot.

Carter stood, and folded his arms. He watched as everything burned, and the cloud and dust began to settle. The ground was scorched black, and he knew the surface would be melted to glass down there.

There would also be a sooty, greasy residue – the remnants of tens of thousands of pounds of flesh that was near vaporized.

He narrowed his eyes. It looked like a good result. But he couldn't say mission accomplished just yet. They would be performing these types of bomb runs night and day for as long as it took. There were millions of these things out there now, and each one of them through a single bite spread the parasitic infection and had the ability to make more of themselves.

They could not be reasoned or bargained with; they could only be killed. Or they would kill or convert us, he knew there was nothing in between.

The dust and smoke started to settle and the drones came back like a swarm of mosquitos to hover overhead and begin photographing everything. There was a ground zero for a thousand feet across charred black and nothing was left standing in there – not a stick of a tree, blade of grass, or living being. Then outside of that there were charred bodies, and just beyond that a few moving creatures that were significantly mobility degraded.

Beyond that the herd was moving away, scattering. He estimated they must have taken out tens of thousands of them. He knew that soon the dispersed herd would coalesce again. And then they would strike again.

Carter nodded his satisfaction as he looked back at the amplified images of ground zero point again where the ground looked like black glass. He was about to turn away when he thought he saw movement.

He concentrated, and his brows slowly came together.

Then it was confirmed.

"*Movement!*" one of the controllers said.

Carter walked closer to the huge screen. "How? How does anything living survive that?"

Colonel Rennie came and stood beside him. "How do you kill

something that wasn't alive to begin with?"

From various areas tiny eruptions of red began to appear. There was something pushing up through the glass-like ground and rising up.

"Amplify that!" Carter ordered.

The camera zoomed in.

It looked like a questing tendril or tree root. But it was blood red.

"Take the drones in lower," he said.

Several of the drones dropped to within fifty feet of the ground.

"Surface temperature is still at over two-fifty degrees," intoned one of the operators.

"Nothing can live in that. I mean, nothing that was there before." Carter folded his arms. "What the hell is that stuff?"

The red tendrils got to about five feet in height, looking like a forest of them now, and then they collapsed to the earth. They quested along the ground, branching, and covering it in a red mesh, like some sort of gigantic branching mold.

"Those things we just fried," Colonel Rennie said, "their bodies were incinerated and turned to dust. But it seems that debris has worked itself into the soil and is somehow growing like seeds."

"This is not fucking possible," Carter seethed and paced away.

"What do you want to do?" Rennie asked.

Carter turned. "Suggestions?"

Rennie looked up. "Hit it again."

Carter pointed to the mission controller. "Another bomb run, on the same coordinates, ASAP. Whatever that shit is, I do not want it spreading over God's green earth on my watch."

The men watched as the mission parameters were relayed and another jet armed and scrambled. It took just fifteen minutes before the plane was on its way, and by then the red mesh, looking like blood filled veins, covered the earth.

The pilot didn't hesitate, and the target was clear. The thermobaric weapon detonated over the site and the drones had pulled well back. Their screens whited-out again for several moments but then when they cleared the group watched and waited in silence for the outcome.

Carter paced.

"Visuals up," a voice said from behind him and the General turned.

Once again the ground was blackened glass, and there was no sign of the red veins.

Carter held his breath.

But then the word he dreaded.

"*Movement.*"

He stared, his brows drawn together so sharply, he was giving himself a headache.

Sure enough, a tiny red tendril was coming up.

He exhaled and shook his head. "We have a problem."

CHAPTER 31

USA, Texas, the Stoker Ranch

Drake sat in the huge SUV at the front gates to his massive property. Beside him Isabella stared out the front window.

"This is weird." He frowned. "There's usually a small army of people that work here."

"Maybe Ethan let them all go," Isabella suggested.

Drake shook his head. "No way; some of those workers have been with us for years. They worked for my dad and were practically family. There's no way he'd fire anyone."

"Well then, where is everyone?" Isabella asked.

"Let's find out." Drake headed in through the already open iron gates. The wrought iron above them on an arch spelled out 'STOKER' in iron-worked calligraphy.

The driveway was long leading up to the main homestead house, a large two-story building with huge front and back porch, lots of sandstone and wooden beams.

As he came close he saw that there was a designated place for his employees' vehicles to park, and they were all there.

"I don't get it. Seems everyone is here for duty, but nobody is coming out." Drake stopped the car and his hand hovered over the horn getting ready to give it a double toot as he normally did to let people know he was home.

His hand hung there for a moment and he lowered it. For some reason, his former Special Forces senses were coming to the fore, and they were telling him that stealth might be the better option right now.

"Front door is open," Isabella said.

"I see it," he said.

He turned to her. "You should…"

"Come with you? I sure am." She opened the door. "I came here to support you. Not be a passenger."

Drake nodded. He needed to override his urge to protect Isabella and remember that she was as highly skilled as he was. He'd be thankful for the backup.

He opened the glove compartment and took out the gun. Isabella reached into the backseat and grabbed her sword and scabbard and once out of the car slid the harness onto her back.

He led Isabella up the steps and, holding his gun in his right hand, used the left to ease the door open wider. Drake peered around and saw an empty room.

He turned to her and used his hand to motion left, and for her to go right, and then went in fast. They spread each side of the door and quickly ascertained the large receiving room was empty. There was no sign of a problem and everything was in order.

A large grandfather clock ticked in the corner and there was a single coffee mug on a table top. He turned to her and pointed to the stairs for her, then to himself and to the rear rooms.

Isabella immediately went up the steps – the second floor held the bedrooms and she quickly went from room to room, finding mostly unmade beds. In some of the bathrooms she noted that the shower stalls, baths, and sinks were all dry indicating no one had used them for several days.

She came to a railing looking down as Drake came out of one of the front sitting rooms and he looked up.

She shook her head and shrugged.

He waved her down.

Drake then led them to a front library – one of his favorite rooms. It was huge, filled with books and heavy leather furniture, and his grandfather's desk, a huge Mahogony and leather-covered beast that took four men to lift.

He gripped the door handle, turned it, and then jerked his hand back. He looked at it in disgust and then showed Isabella – it was covered in something like petroleum jelly.

She looked up into his face and mouthed: *be careful.*

Drake wiped his hand on his pants and then pushed the door open.

"*Ah*, shit," he whispered.

The large multi-paned window was smashed outward, and inside the room it looked like a tornado had blasted through it. The huge desk was splintered, as well as the oak swivel chair. Paintings weren't just ripped from walls, but ripped to shreds, and every book from the shelves was destroyed.

But it wasn't those things that caught Drake's attention, or the missing people; instead it was what was left behind – torn clothing – some of it bloody, others covered in the same slime that coated the door handle.

"Drake, we've seen this before," Isabella said.

"Yeah, we have, dammit," he sighed. "They've been turned."

Drake picked up a few items and kicked aside some piles of others.

"Can't see anything that belonged to Ethan or Addison." He turned to her. "Maybe they got away when they realized what was happening."

"And didn't bother trying to warn you? Or contact you? Or me?" She tilted her head. "Be on guard, Drake Stoker."

He nodded and the pair walked to the window, and saw a few more remnants of the torn clothing leaving a trail to the barn.

"We need to check that out," she said.

"When we're finished here," he replied.

They continued with their search, and Drake headed for somewhere that was his own inner sanctum – his office, and the one where he had originally planned this misadventure all that time ago. Ethan never really went in there, but maybe he thought his older brother was gone for good.

Drake pushed the door open, and the smell assailed him: death, corruption, and something he was readily familiar with.

Isabella grabbed his arm and they waited. There was a soft sound, a low hum and a clicking like hundreds of knitting needles working furiously.

He held his gun up and Isabella drew her sword. The lights were out and the thick curtains drawn making it shadowy inside. First thing he did was head quickly and quietly to the large windows, grab the heavy drapes and yank them back.

The sunlight caused an immediate reaction. There was a body, and sitting upon it were dozens of large blowflies, each the size of a puppy.

They took to the air, and Isabella kicked the door shut behind her. In a flash of blue shining steel, she swept her sword back and forth through the air with unnerving skill and accuracy, and in seconds the giant insects were all cleaved in two and they fell with soft thuds to the ground.

Drake approached the body, and slowly crouched on one knee beside it. "No, no…"

Isabella sheathed her sword and lowered her head.

He reached out to the young woman's body. Addison's face was mottled and bloated, and they could both see that her neck was severely broken and had flopped bonelessly to the side.

"I'm so sorry, Addison," he whispered.

"At least she wasn't turned. A small blessing," Isabella said softly.

He nodded and screwed his eyes shut tight for a few moments.

"But you have a bigger problem," she suggested. "Ethan."

He looked up. "Maybe he got away."

She stared back at him.

"We have to find him. He might be in trouble," Drake said.

"Drake, you have to face the possibility that…" She drew in a deep breath, "…that maybe he never left Hell." She straightened. "Maybe what we brought out of there wasn't Ethan at all."

Drake covered his face with his hands. "When we were in Hell, Benson and I thought we heard his voice, calling to us." He shook his head. "Oh no, what have I done?"

"We were all tricked by the Father of Flies," she said. "He used us to sneak a demon from Hell into our world."

Drake ran both hands up through his short cropped black hair, and shook his head. "Nope." He stood. "Until I know differently, I assume Ethan is still Ethan." He turned away. "We continue to look."

They searched the rest of the house and found nothing or no one. But there was one place left to check.

"The barn," he said. "We always kept the horses there. Just a few for riding."

They went out front and around the side, crossing the path to one of the larger out buildings. The barn was huge, and its broad double front doors still closed tight. But the side door was swinging open. Drake drew his gun, and Isabella still held the sword in her hand.

Drake came up against the barn and slid along to the open side door, pulled it open wider and peered inside – he saw nothing and went in, quickly followed by Isabella.

He recoiled – once again the stench of death assailed them, but this time it was a hundred times worse. They also walked into a wave of humidity, and the ever present buzzing of flies. But this time just normal blowflies, thousands of them all crawling over and zooming around a small mountain of meat.

Drake only recognized some of the horses by their heads, all ripped from their bodies. Every other part of the animals had been torn to shreds, as if a giant had been taking apart cooked chickens.

"Why?" He lowered his gun and staggered forward. "They're not eaten, just massacred."

"It was a message," Isabella said softly.

He turned to her. "But why do this brutality to the horses?"

"Did you love the horses?" she asked.

He nodded. "Of course I did."

"Then that's why," she replied softly and laid a hand on his shoulder. "This is an evil that doesn't want to just consume you. It wants to break you. Break you down, both physically and psychologically until there is nothing left but despair. Perhaps even to the point of suicide."

"Addison, Ethan, my workers, the horses." He wiped his eyes with a forearm. "All gone."

Isabella led him outside the barn, where the air was much thinner, cooler, and cleaner.

"Drake, it will try and take everything from you until there is nothing left," she said. "And at this point, some men, even strong men, would fold. But you must be as strong as I know you are. You must guard yourself for battle, Captain Drake Stoker, because this is what we are in now. More than just jumping out of a helicopter to make war in some far away land. This time we fight for your sanity, and the entire human race."

Drake drew in a deep lung filling breath. "I can do it."

"You *have* to do it." She came around in front of him and held each side of his face. "And I'll be there with you every step of the way."

He bent his head forward and kissed her lips.

She pulled back, brushed his hair back and smiled. "I know it's hard."

"So I guess we try and track down Ethan," he said.

She shook her head. "More than likely he'll find you. We have other work to do. We are losing our war, and need to fight on every front," she said. "But now, we need to return to base, and I want you to come with me."

"Home base?" he asked.

"The Vatican," she replied.

He raised his eyebrows.

She half smiled. "Don't worry. They already know all about you."

Behind them on the roof of the barn, the fist-sized fly squatted, watching them, listening. After they left, it sped away in the air – heading for Texas.

CHAPTER 32

USA, Texas – South Texas Nuclear Generating Station

Ethan Stoker stood on the car hood and used a powerful pair of binoculars to look out at the South Texas Nuclear Generating Station. It was one of the largest in the country, and produced around twenty two thousand gigawatts of power and supplied energy to millions of Texan homes and businesses.

Ethan knew that power production kept the lights coming on, provided services to a million appliances, and kept hospitals and other life-saving services in operation. It was one of the major demarcation lines between the modern and the archaic, between order and chaos, and you take away the power, and soon, the population devolves back into a form of primitive tribalism. And that primitivism is ripe for subjugation.

He had parked several miles away from the station because he knew that the facility was heavily surveilled and protected. Not only that, but the fortifications were also extreme. There was no way anyone was going to attempt to break in there without attracting a formidable response.

But he had other plans. He didn't expect to storm the facility himself. He was going to rot it from within.

There was a thump from behind him and the car jerked a little. He turned to see the five hundred pound fly on the trunk.

He scoffed at the ridiculous obscenity of it; the part human face on the massive blowfly was ripped with obedience and pain – the man, Octavius Conti, who had dreams of being king was brought low to being the vermin of the world and a slave to the Father of Flies.

The massive Conti fly reported in what he had found. There was a man, Percival Hanbridge, who was the facility manager and had access to all areas who was just finishing his shift and would be leaving soon.

Ethan nodded. Percival would be their way in. He called the fly forward and it lifted its probiscis, gently touching Ethan's face. It emptied its stomach.

Ethan drank deeply of the vile brew that he would deliver to Percival.

Texas would be the first, then he would make his way all across the country doing the same to other power generating stations. It wouldn't be long until the country was dragged back into the Stone Age.

And then, the time of the Father would be here.
Ethan slid back into the front seat and started the car.

***

Percival Hanbridge exited the station's car park, and passed through two gates before he was out on the first of the roads leading to the outer perimeter fence of the station.

Already his mind was on what he'd order in for takeout that evening. Living alone meant he was master of his own destiny, and given he didn't know how to even boil an egg or make toast, meant take out and the online menus of the dozens of restaurants in the town were his best friends.

"Tacos," he said and he mulled over the crispy shell variety with the salty beef, chilis, shredded lettuce, and salsa, with plenty of cheese. He could almost taste them. But then, "Egg noodles with duck and plenty of plum sauce."

He sped along the highway, humming a tune, and doing seventy. As the sun still had a few more hours until sundown, the highway was his. It would only take him half an hour to get home to the large modern apartment he had in Bay City that overlooked the park.

It had all the mod cons he could want and a gaming system that he would have killed for as a kid. It was expensive, but as he was paid well at the station and he only had himself to spend his money on, he decided to treat himself.

He flicked his eyes to the rearview mirror and saw the SUV coming up fast behind him. His brows came together – he was doing seventy so to be run down so fast, that fool must have been doing at least a hundred.

Hanbridge slowed and pulled to the side a little. *Best let this guy get to wherever he's going,* he thought.

The driver shot past, veered in front of him, but then put on the brakes.

"*What the fuck*?" Percival slammed on his own brakes.

He was effectively stopped dead and then the guy got out. He was big, fit, and he turned to wave. He grinned broadly and looked friendly enough, and Percival thought maybe he was going to tell him he had a broken light, or low tire pressure, or something like that.

He waved and though Percival's first instinct would have been to put the car in reverse and not let the guy get too close, this time he waited for him to walk up to the side of the car. He knocked once on the window. Percival pressed the button for the window to scroll down, just half way.

But it was enough as the man's huge arm came in the window. The guy's big hand wrapped around the back of Percival's neck.

All Percival could think was how strong this guy was as he dragged Percival's head forward, while at the same time he lowered his face to the window.

He's going to try and kiss me, Percival thought and tried to pull back.

But the guy was far too strong, and sure enough, when their faces were close, the man fixed his mouth over Percival's, and used a tongue that was more like a thick, dry, strong finger to lever his teeth open.

And then to Percival's absolute horror a thick torrent of the vilest substance he had ever tasted was poured into his throat. It both burned and revolted him, but when his stomach tried to eject it, something else fought back and kept it down in his belly.

The man released him, and Percival coughed and gagged for a moment.

"*What the fuck, you creep!*" Percival screamed.

But then he heard the voice.

And then everything changed.

Percival fully opened the window and the man handed him a large black bag. He took it and placed it on the seat beside himself.

And then turned around and headed back to the station.

***

He passed through all the security checks as normal, smiling and nodding at the armed guards who commented about him forgetting something.

In the underground car park, he grabbed the bag and headed up to the main control room. It was always operated by two technicians. Outside there were more, and also a seated guard at the desk.

The guard, Tony, a fifty-something guy with white hair and large stomach waved. "Hi Percy, what are you…?"

Percival reached into the black bag for the gun, drew it out, and in one smooth motion fired point blank into Tony's face.

He then brought the gun around and shot the two external technicians.

The glass surrounding the main control room was soundproof and he smiled as he saw the two remaining internal technicians had not even noticed what had transpired just outside their work space.

They soon would.

He used his pass code to enter the sealed room, and shot them dead without drawing a breath. From there he had two more objectives.

He went to the panel, seeing all the green lights for energy production. There were several ways to shut down a nuclear facility. But to do it manually, he needed to initiate the '*scram*' button to initiate an emergency shutdown.

That would trigger a control rod insertion, where rods are forced into the reactor arena that would absorb neutrons in the core immediately stopping the nuclear chain reactions that fueled the energy production process.

He did so quickly, overriding any alarms and second level authentication requests. In seconds more all the lights across the board went red. He had shut down the plant. But this was only temporary. Unless…

He went back to his bag and drew out the second thing that the man had given him. Without ever seeing the object before he knew what it was and what he was to do with it – the powerful charge had enough plastic explosives to totally destroy the control room.

It would take them years to rebuild. If at all.

He set the charges along the panel top, inserted the detonator, and then didn't bother with a timer. He had no plans to try and get to safety.

This was why he was chosen. This was his job.

"*Hail the Father of Flies!*" he yelled, and pressed the detonator.

The room exploded in a fireball that burned through the room, and shot several hundred feet into the air.

All across Texas lights started to go out.

***

Ethan smiled as he stood on the trunk and watched the fireball lift into the air. He then jumped down preparing to head to the next power station.

But just then a fist-sized fly came and landed on his shoulder. It buzzed furiously for a moment, and he turned his head listening to it.

"A cure?" He frowned. "No, that will not do."

He leapt into the SUV and headed to the airport.

CHAPTER 33

Rome, Vatican City – the Marble Room

Drake looked around and was in awe of the scale and opulence of the room let alone the city. Isabella had been right when she said they were expected, as they were met at the plane door, taken out a side entrance of the airport without passing through customs or immigration, and whisked to a waiting car that was like a long black ship. And then green lit all the way to the Vatican City.

The resident who met them, Cardinal Tommasini, was tall, craggy faced, but friendly. And once again, he knew everything about Drake and his background.

They were taken to a separate room and Drake, Isabella, Leonidas and Marco were seated in amongst several dozen other senior members of the city, and also a rank of about eight more powerful and formidable men and women who Drake assumed were more Templar Knights.

It was soon confirmed when they swapped greetings with Isabella, and spoke rapidly to her in Italian, locking him out of the conversation.

There was a small dais at the front of the room, and for all the archaic, old world wealth and history, it seemed it had kept pace with technology, as a presentation was about to begin and it looked to be something he had never experienced before in his life as the images were holographic, and appeared to be floating before them in a three dimensional display.

"*Wow,*" Drake whispered.

Isabella nudged him and smiled. "Yes, we've come a long way from brandishing crucifixes and throwing holy water."

"I still don't know why I'm here," he said.

She squeezed his thigh. "Everything will be explained. I'll be back soon." She left her scat.

Drake turned, beginning to rise. "Hey, where are…"

"You're here for balance, Captain Stoker," Cardinal Tommasini replied, obviously hearing him.

"*Oops*." Drake sat back down.

The room quietened and their focus split between Tommasini and Drake. And he guessed there were many others wondering why an outsider had been brought in as well.

Tommasini motioned to a priest to the side who was working the technology, and an image began to take shape at the front of the room, just hanging in the air. It was of the ancient silver scroll he had encountered in Isabella's possession all that time ago. Now, it was shown stretching and unfurling, and the ancient dyes and inks were visible.

"You are familiar with this object, Captain Stoker?" Tommasini asked.

"I am." Drake held his hands wide. "But I still don't know how I can help. Your Knights are a formidable force, and you have all the intel."

"What is more valuable?" Tommasini began. "An unbeliever who has seen, or a believer who has never seen?" He smiled. "Where you have been, few have ever travelled and even fewer have ever returned." He clasped his hands together. "So, it is really you that has all the intel."

Drake wasn't convinced, but as Isabella wanted him there, he'd play along.

Tommasini then motioned to the image of the scroll. "We are people brought up in our faith to believe in the word of God. But maybe that can blind us sometimes. We need people who are skeptics, but have seen enough so that they retain an open mind. That's you, Captain. And just remember, though you may not believe in God, he believes in you."

Drake nodded.

"There is a mission that is needed. The most vital mission for over two thousand years that we must undertake. There will be a battle, and it is one we cannot afford to lose. One the world cannot afford to lose."

The image changed to a floating picture of Barak, the Knight they lost in the deep caves when he was pulled into a crack in the wall by some abomination from the deep.

Tommasini clasped his hands as if in prayer. "We honor our fallen." More faces appeared and vanished, and Drake guessed they were other Knights that had died recently. *So many*, he thought.

The images faded away.

"And we celebrate the victors." Marco and Leonidas' faces appeared. "The rank of captain of the Templar Knights goes to Leonidas Bianchi and Marco Stromo, for courage, duty and honor."

There was a round of muted applause, and Drake turned and smiled at Leonidas and Marco. The men nodded back.

Then the face of Isabella appeared, but it dissolved away, and when it vanished she stood there coming from somewhere at the back of the room. She had on a deep scarlet cloak, and an attendant came and handed Tommasini a large and long wooden case.

He placed it on the dais as Isabella came and stood before him.

"To Isabella Romano, promotion to the rank of Commander of the Templar Knights." He smiled and waited for the applause to die away. "And with that rank we also bestow upon her the sword of the righteous. It is the cleaver of the dragon's heart wielded by St George, and also known as the piercer of the stone, once called Excalibur."

Drake's mouth dropped open as he stared at the beautiful blade.

Tommasini lifted out the magnificent sword, whose blade shone blue and was fixed with a single huge gem in the pommel.

The cardinal went on to explain how the blade had been blessed by every Pope since the very beginning. Tommasini held the sword out on the palms of both hands. "Use it and wield it with wisdom, strength, and righteousness."

Isabella bowed, and reached to take the sword, holding it up in front of her face for a moment. She then turned it blade down and, gripping the steel, held it aloft again and turned to the room.

The Knights burst into applause and got to their feet. Drake did the same, almost becoming overwhelmed by the spectacle and gravity of the event.

When the room quietened, she gripped the sword by the hilt again and swept it back and forth, testing it, the soft zing of it cutting the air, satisfying to listen to. After another moment she placed it in her scabbard over her back and bowed.

Isabella then left the stage and in minutes more she retook her seat beside Drake.

"Congratulations, Commander." He nudged her. "So now you outrank me." He smiled.

"I always did." She nudged him back.

With the formalities completed, the screen changed again, this time back to images flashing up of the abominations and diseased hordes sweeping over the countryside. It showed the roving herds of the horrors; most of the deformed things Drake was familiar with, but in amongst them were monstrosities that were enormous, some the size of elephants, and some ten times that.

Drake had seen such things in the pit of Hell, and now he saw they were out and walking the Earth. It was clear that in this war the odds were already near insurmountable, and it had only just begun.

"The war is not going well. The Devil prepares to rise as his minions till the earth in preparation for him. There is no cure, and cleansing fire is now also being shown to create even more challenges as the seed of evil infiltrates the very soil."

The images changed to show the red tendrils spreading over the earth, and in some places covering miles, with nothing else living or growing there.

"We prayed for a cure." Tommasini smiled. "And now, there is a chance one might exist."

"What? A cure?" Drake sat forward.

The image resolved into a section of the scroll, and focused in on the ancient words.

From amongst the crowd there was an intake of collective breaths, and expressions of wonder at the revealed words. Drake couldn't understand a bit of it.

He turned to Isabella. "What is it, what does it say?"

"The Garden," she said almost reverently. "It's real."

"What Garden?" He grabbed her arm.

She smiled. "*Gan Eden* – which means, the Garden of Eden."

***

Tommasini quietened the murmurs of animated conversation. "The scroll has told us that the answer to our prayers lies within *Gan Eden*. The Garden of Eden. But we do not know where exactly, or even what it might look like."

The image floating in the air resolved to a high level map that was a satellite image of a dry and mountainous landscape, but had borders and names written upon it.

"The location of the Garden of Eden was never definitively known. However, it is believed to be situated in the Middle East, potentially near the Tigris and Euphrates rivers, in what is now modern-day Iraq."

Tommasini looked across at the map. "The area makes logical sense as the Tigris and Euphrates are two major rivers in Western Asia, defining the historical region of Mesopotamia. They originate in the highlands of eastern Turkey and flow southeast through Syria and Iraq, eventually converging to form the *Shatt al-Arab* waterway before emptying into the Persian Gulf."

He nodded as if seeing the ancient lands in his mind's eye. "These rivers have been crucial for the development of ancient civilizations and in fact, the fertile land between the rivers, known as Mesopotamia, was often referred to as the cradle of civilization."

He meshed his fingers together at his waist. "The rivers have seen the rise and fall of numerous ancient civilizations, including Sumer, the Akkad, Babylonia, and Assyria. And before any of them, there was a garden there, a wonderous place, where everything began."

Tommasini looked across at the map that changed to a physical image of the land, from the dry valleys to the craggy mountain ranges.

"Somewhere there, perhaps hidden, is the place we seek. And one we must find, as the scrolls have foretold that within its wonderous gardens there is a cure to the Hell's plague. And if we can do that then perhaps it is a way to stop the Devil rising." He turned to the group. "We will not rest until we have found it."

"Are there clues?" Isabella asked.

Tommasini turned to her and smiled. "We believe so."

The map changed again to show a mountain range, but this one covered in green.

"Northern Iraq, and just inside Turkey. There are many areas that are forbidden to enter. No one knows why or remembers. But there is a place there the locals call 'the Eye of God', and there is a story that says that the setting sun through the Eye will see the way to Eden."

"To the Garden of Eden?" Drake asked incredulously. "The Adam and Eve, Garden of Eden?"

Tommasini held his hands wide. "This is just a legend on the end of a myth. Maybe it does, maybe it doesn't. Sorry, but it's all we have."

"Where is this mountain range?" Isabella asked.

Tommasini pointed at the map. "There."

The map enlarged, showing a place called *Elbaşi* on the *Solhan* River.

He turned to the group. "If there is a chance that Eden is there, then we must take that chance." He looked down at Isabella. "Isabella, take your strongest team. Leave tonight. Let nothing stand in your way, as soon, the forces of darkness will even overrun us here."

Isabella stood. "It shall be so."

She turned and called out nine names, including Marco, Leonidas, and Drake, plus six other men and women.

"Prepare yourselves," she said. "We leave immediately."

Isabella turned and bowed to Tommasini who made the sign of the cross in the air over her. She then headed for the side doorway, with Drake in tow.

"Guess we're leaving," he said, almost jogging to keep up. "Think we might find it? The Garden of Eden? I mean if its real."

"It's real." She turned and smiled. "And I don't *think* we will, I *know* we will." She held her hands out, palms up. "Can't you feel it?"

He half smiled and shrugged. "I'm the doubter, remember?"

***

The high speed plane took them directly to Ankara where they cleared what could only be loosely defined as customs and immigration. Just like the rest of the world, there was chaos, and few people working.

Still, a lot of money changed hands to allow the ten Templar Knights to pass through the checkpoints as a Vatican diplomatic party without any searches or X-rays of the mountains of baggage they brought with them.

They then had two helicopters take them all the way out to Solhan, a small town that was on the edge of the Solhan River.

Boats were acquired at a greatly inflated price. Where they were going was Kurdish territory, and was not only forbidden for strangers to enter, but was so volatile and dangerous even the Turkish military avoided it.

And that was as far as the helicopter pilots would take them. From there the boats would be taken along a deep and languid river bordered by huge craggy cliffs on each side making it look primordial and secretive.

The water was a deep green and freezing cold. Where they were headed was the mountain region, and even though it was the end of spring, the rivers were still carrying the temperature of the ice melts from the mountainous region higher up.

The boat rides were also a time for Drake to meet his fellow travelers, the other six Knights.

They had a single large boat that fit all of them and their gear. They had packed significant armory, provisions, and both cold weather gear, climbing gear, and even wetsuits and diving gear with air tanks. It seemed they came prepared for everything, as they all knew there would be no going back to restock – it was all bet on this mission.

Drake talked to all of the Knights, assessing the team as he would for any of his own Reaper missions.

With them were two Knight scholars: Matteo, a language and cultural specialist for the Turkish region, and Francesco, who was a biblical scholar who had made it his life's work to look into the existence of lost or hidden places such as the Garden of Eden. He seemed the most electrified by the chance of what they might find. He was also the one who pinpointed their destination – *Elbaşi*.

Further back in the boat were two female Knights, Bianca, and Aria. Both looked competent and as if cut from the same mold as Isabella. They were young, dark eyed, and formidably fit.

Bianca smiled at him, and he nodded and smiled back. Isabella then kicked his foot, and gave him a fiery glance – message received – he looked away from the other women.

Right at the back of the boat were two huge and fearsome-looking men, Rocco and Enzo. Both must have been between six three and six five, and had the square jaws of heavyweight boxers, and hands to match.

He would have put these two guys up against his best Reapers, and he wondered how they'd go against Thor and Benson.

He felt the pang of regret and guilt then; just thinking of his lost team members still cut him deep. Both had fought to the end and were honorable men, and big Benson had given his life to save him. He was more than a colleague and comrade; he was a lost friend.

Drake sucked in a deep breath and stared straight ahead, but his vision had turned inwards. So much had happened to him over the past year, and so far, most of it was shit.

He turned to see Isabella looking up at the cliffs and observed her in profile. The smooth jawline and brown slightly olive skin, with dark hair and even darker eyes to match. She was way too good for him and he couldn't understand what she saw in him. And yet, she had climbed into Hell to pull him out.

He smiled, and guessed that not everything that had happened to him was bad.

The river narrowed as the cliffs seemed to press inwards. Drake watched the tops and from time to time was sure he saw the outline of a head pop up, all the way up there.

"Yes, we're being watched," Francesco said. "They've been following our boat for the last five miles."

Drake scoffed, marveling how he missed it but the Knights were on top of the surveillance.

"Kurds?" he asked.

"Yes, and in this area, very tribal," Francesco replied. "These are the desert Kurds that adhere to ancient customs and dress. And are very distrustful of strangers." He turned to Drake and smiled. "But they love guns and ammunition. That's why we brought extra."

"We pay them to cross their country?" Drake asked.

"We pay them to stay alive." Francesco grinned. "And also, hopefully to hear any secrets or legends they have heard of Eden, and this mysterious Eye of God."

The cliffs narrowed again, and Drake suddenly worried about what would happen if it got too narrow for the boat. He looked at the sheer cliff walls – hundreds of feet straight up. *Be a helluva climb,* he thought.

"Twenty miles," Matteo chimed in.

"Not bad, if push comes to shove, we can walk that," Drake replied.

Francesco shook his head. "Not without the Elbaşi Kurds' approval."

"How many of them do you think there are?" Drake asked.

"About two hundred living in Elbaşi. More living out in the desert. And thousands more spread all over. The best case scenario for us is to get in their good graces, and pick up a guide. I know a lot about this area and the people, but there's nothing like someone who grew up here to show us what and where things are."

"I heard that," Drake said.

"Something coming up," Isabella said.

The narrow gorge-like crack opened up to a large still pond. It was around two hundred feet across and at the far end the river started up again. But cut into the cliff wall was a series of zigzagging steps leading to the top.

And standing there were several men cradling guns.

"Our welcoming reception," Drake said, feeling for his gun.

Isabella put a hand on his arm. "No one is to draw weapons. Yet." She turned to Francesco. "Weave your magic, Francesco."

Francesco stood in the boat, placed a hand on his chest and yelled a Kurdish greeting. He bestowed good luck and fortune on the people, the land, and the village elders, who they had brought gifts for.

He pointed to the team in the boat. "We come just seeking something that is lost and would have some information from you. That is all."

A few of the people watching had disappeared.

"What now?" Isabella asked.

Francesco continued to wave up at the Elbaşi Kurds. "Now, we wait and see if they will allow us to come up. Or they will kill us all and simply take what we have."

They waited on the water for twenty minutes, mostly just watching the cliff rims, and trying hard not to lift their weapons. They were all within reach if they came under attack, but basically, Drake knew, they were in a kill box, and the only cover was to jump over the side of the boat. And then get picked off when they tried to come up for air.

More people appeared at the cliff rim.

"Here we go," Francesco said.

One of the men yelled down at him, and Francesco breathed a sigh of relief.

"We're on. Let's go," he said.

They powered the boat in close to the steps and tied it off. They each took packs and the supplies, with Rocco and Enzo shouldering the largest of them.

The climb up the hundreds of stone steps was steep, and they tried to ignore how old and crumbling they were, and also all the guns pointed at them.

At the top, they saw about two dozen Kurdish fighters in their traditional garb which comprised of small woolen caps, shirts with no buttons and overwrapped with a type of shawl, and voluminous pants.

They also wore multiple swords and knives hanging on large belts. And every man had Kalashnikovs which were pointed at the Knights.

Drake noticed that they had young eyes in old, weathered faces colored a reddish brown from desert living. They were sunbeaten but probably only in the twenties or thirties.

Francesco waved, and reached into his own pack and took out multiple bags of tobacco, an item highly prized out in the wilds.

Each man took a pack enthusiastically, and lowered their weapons to do so.

Drake looked long at each of the Kurdish fighters – he relaxed a little now that they had made it up to the surface, and knew that if the Knights were anywhere near as skilled as Isabella, then they could easily take them all down in the blink of an eye without suffering a single casualty.

Francesco talked to a few of the Kurds and finally, one of the men waved them on, and the Kurds headed off.

Francesco turned. "We're to meet the chieftain. This will determine if they will help." He chuckled. "Or kill us all and rob our bodies."

"That's some tough negotiation you did there," Drake scoffed.

"What will determine if they will or won't?" Isabella asked.

Francesco shrugged. "What we say to them, our gifts, the weather, who knows. But I suggest we keep our eyes open as in all seriousness they're known for being a shoot first ask questions later bunch."

Drake knew they could take down the two dozen they met. But if they were walked into a village where there was about two hundred of them, then the odds shifted, and away from them.

They marched over the baking hard packed earth for an hour, and Drake suddenly missed the river. In the distance, and surrounding them there were tall mountains, most with ice and snow on their shoulders. He bet the temperature dropped at night in these parts as he had learned before coming that this entire area was well above sea level.

The smoke rising just over a hill told him they were approaching the village, and he knew that the Kurds had sent runners ahead, to give the elders and chieftain a heads up of their approach. As they came up and over the hill he saw the scattered houses.

For the most part they were made from clay bricks, were sharp cornered and well maintained. There were pens with goats, chickens, and in the street a few children played games.

But all that stopped when the group entered the compound and the children eased back against the walls to sullenly stare. It seemed distrust was bred into them.

They were taken to the largest house and bade to enter. Only one of the group who brought them came inside, but the rest took up positions at open windows, lounging there with the barrels of their guns pointed inwards.

That distrust again, Drake thought.

Inside there was a boiling pot, several wizened men sitting cross legged on rugs, and one at the center that had a gold chain around his neck.

On the wall behind him, were heads stuck there, many in different states of decay. Drake looked at each of them, and saw hats and helmets that identified them – Russian, Turkish, Iraqi, and he was sure that one was either English or American. He also noted there was plenty more space on the wall for more heads.

They were ordered to sit, and Isabella, Drake and Francesco took to the front, and behind them the other Knights spread out, each watchful and ready for anything.

"My name is Akum Mohammed Ardehi." The old man looked at each of them. "You are warriors," he said, and Francesco translated.

"We are," Francesco replied.

"You seek something amongst us or our lands?" Akum asked, his old eyes lingering on Isabella, then went to Bianca and Aria. But slid back to Isabella sitting out front.

Drake knew that he probably couldn't understand why a woman was given any sort of leadership position. *He may see this as weakness*, Drake thought. And from what he knew of Middle Eastern desert cultures, weakness wasn't something they respected.

"There is a great sickness sweeping the world," Francesco began. "It has not come here yet, but it will. We seek a cure that we believe is in these lands."

"We know of this sickness that makes men into beasts," Akum said.

The chieftain leaned back to speak to one of the men who gathered a few more warriors and they departed briefly to soon return carrying between them something large covered over with a heavy shawl.

It must have been a box or cage and there was something moving around inside. Akum told them to put it down in front of Francesco, Isabella, and Drake, and pull the covers from it.

There were horrified gasps and murmurs from the men around the room. Isabella's eyes narrowed as she stared at the skinless-looking creature with the flat face, viper teeth, and eyes like pools of oil.

"This was a man once," Akum said. "We have tried everything we know, and consulted many mystics, and no one can bring him back from what possesses him."

"And they never will." Isabella saw the sad look on the tough old man's face. "Who was it?"

"My son," Akum said softly without taking his eyes from the thing.

"The most merciful thing you can do is release him," Isabella said. "Kill him." She looked up at the man on his large chair. "I will be honored to do this for you."

Akum seemed to think on this for a while. "No, not you. This is our burden."

She nodded. "I understand. But while he lives he can spread the infection. Releasing him would be what he wants."

The old man's eyes shifted to Isabella. "Tell me of this cure?"

"We think it will stop the spread of the infection. It will stop people turning into these horrors. But it will not bring them back. That is not possible." She shook her head. "I'm sorry."

He stared. "I thought we are far away, and I think this is not just your problem."

"It will eventually make it here. Or the beasts will," Francesco pressed. "Then we will all end like this."

Akum stood, pulled out a long scimitar and walked toward the cage. He had his warriors use spears to force the thing near to the bars closest to him, and when pressed up against them, he reached the blade in, and sawed through the neck. It took an effort, but the head came free, and the thing slumped, its clawed hand falling outside the bars.

Akum reached down and held the long clawed hand for a moment. "You are free of this curse now, my beautiful son." He stood and turned away.

Isabella shot foreword, pulled her dagger, and cut off one of the fingers. She placed it in a jar and tucked it into her pack.

Akum sat and turned to the Knight. "Where is this cure?" he asked.

"In a place that is looked on by something called the Eye of God. Do you know it?" Francesco asked.

After a moment, the old man nodded. "I do. But no one goes there, it is haram. Poison."

Francesco held his hands wide. "We have no choice. Show us the way. That is all we ask."

"For what?" Akum asked.

Here it comes, Drake thought; the bargaining.

The horse trading went on for many hours, in between drinking sweet strong tea and smoking a lot of the gifted tobacco.

Isabella handed over the pistols – a dozen Glock 17s – they were a beautiful weapon; reliable, durable, and used worldwide. The guns were gladly taken and handed out.

Next came the knives, and another dozen – black bladed Col

Moschin desert warfare knives, a durable knife that was razor sharp and made from super hardened steel.

These were also taken with a nod and a sweep of Akum's hand.

Drake was beginning to think they were going to give away all their gifts and still come up short. But Akum's eyes were on something else.

He finally pointed to the jewel pommeled sword over Isabella's back. He asked for it.

Francesco tried to explain why that wasn't for trading, but Akum wanted it. Finally the translating Knight relayed the position to Isabella.

"I see." She smiled and turned back to the old man while speaking to Francesco. "Tell him that if his best swordsman can take it from me, it is his. But if I best him, he will give us a guide and his protection to the Eye of God."

Francesco nodded, and did as she asked.

Akum slapped his knees and rocked backwards for a moment, before speaking quickly to one of the men in attendance. The young man stood, nodded, and sprinted from the large room, while the crowd slapped their thighs and hooted their support and approval.

Francesco laughed softly. "I think he has called for his champion."

In just minutes more a tall young man with a full black beard and fiery eyes entered the communal room. He brought with him a long curved sword tucked into his belt that Drake recognized as a Persian scimitar – a light and deadly weapon.

Akum ordered the room cleared and everyone moved back to the walls. Including the Knights.

Drake stood with Isabella and leaned closer to her to speak softly while continuing to smile. "If he kills you, they're all dead."

"I just hope they don't think the same thing." She smiled up at him. "Maybe my head will hang on their wall."

The man named Beliz took off his robe and shirt displaying a muscled chest, and then drew his sword, taking a few practice swipes in the air. His lips were curved in a smile of pure confidence, as he looked at the small Italian woman about to face him.

Isabella drew the jeweled sword from over her shoulder and the gleaming silver blade made the chieftain smile, probably as he thought it would be in his possession soon.

Drake noticed she didn't need to take any practice swings, and stood patiently, calmy, and waiting for the bout to begin.

Akum raised a hand, and then dropped it.

Beliz began to crab walk to the side holding his sword ready. Isabella tracked him, keeping her eyes on his and not the sword.

And then the first stroke came – Beliz swung down hard and fast, and his blade was met by Isabella's, and he instantly used the recoil to round again with a mid-section strike that would have cut her in half if it struck.

But Isabella was like smoke, and moved so fast, she just wasn't where she was a second ago, and his blade sliced the air instead.

Beliz came back fast, swiping, slicing, and thrusting, but except for the rare clang of steel from a parry, she was just proving too fast for him.

Drake noticed that the smiling confidence of the village elder had now left his lips.

The old man murmured something to the attendant to his side, orders were relayed, and then from the crowd another young man entered the arena, this one also with a sword.

Drake went to draw his gun, but Isabella held a hand up to stop him, and then took them both on.

Drake was in awe of the woman, who took it up another level, and must have been toying with the tall Beliz. This time she pressed her own attack, and several times hit the men's bodies with the flat of her blade, when it could have been a death stroke.

The eyes of the two young men grew furious, as they never found an opportunity to strike a clean blow, and Drake was guessing they would have no qualms at all at running her through if they had the opportunity.

As the two men's fury rose, they became less balanced, and more determined to land a decisive strike. Next time, Isabella parried a blow, but forced her blade ahead to cut the cheek of Beliz, then rounded on the other man, and cut his sword arm's bicep, so that blood ran down onto his sword grip. She did it again and again, until the men were covered in small cuts.

Drake marveled at her constraint as he knew if it was him, he would have beheaded both the men in the first few minutes.

Just as Drake was wondering how they would ever deescalate the bout, the chieftain fired one of the new guns into the air. The sound was loud in the room, and everyone froze, waiting.

Akum swept his hand to the side indicating the contest was over. Just as well, Drake thought, because if Isabella had bested them both, the shame of being beaten by a woman might have been too much for the entire tribe.

She bowed to Akum, and then stuck the sword over her shoulder. She turned and spoke to Francesco, who nodded and went and returned with a spare Vatican Knight sword. This one equally ornate, but without the jewel. Drake found out later it was not blessed and therefore just a weapon.

She handed it over, and Akum looked mollified enough to take it and nod to Isabella. Akum spoke to Francesco again and the Knight smiled and bowed deeply.

"The chieftain says he will allow one of his men to guide us to the Eye of God. It is atop a valley, two days from here. But they will not enter as it is haram. And if we enter, we are not to return to their village."

Isabella nodded and bowed again. "We accept with honor and gratitude." She straightened and spoke to Francesco. "Tell him we would like to leave, now."

***

Drake walked beside Isabella. "Well, that was intense."

She smiled back. "Yes, it was very difficult… trying not to kill them in the first minute."

He grinned. "Talented and modest."

He held binoculars to his eyes. "Two days to the north-east. There are mountains there."

"Makes sense. We're looking for somewhere high that looks down into a valley." Isabella turned and then groaned.

Drake saw why – their guide was to be the tall swordsman she had just bested.

"Beliz. Hope he doesn't hold a grudge." Drake laughed softly.

The group shouldered all of the remaining equipment, a little lighter now that all their gifts had been handed over.

They set out along a foot track more than a road. But after the first hour of walking the track simply turned into a well-trodden path, and then vanished all together.

The air was bone dry because of the altitude so they tried to preserve their water. Beliz had told them that it would take them a day to reach the mountain they searched for. Then another half day to scale to its peak at the rim of the valley. It would take them even more time to enter the valley but he would leave them at the top as he would not enter.

They walked all day as the sun passed overhead, and then when it was beginning to get low they came to the base of the mountain. Or rather range of mountains.

They broke camp and with the setting sun and in the lee of the huge geological upthrusting, it was pleasantly warm, and would stay like that until the sun was fully gone and night had fallen. The group ate their meagre meals, and brewed coffee and tea. Francesco and Rocco talked with Beliz, and though he was still embarrassed about being beaten by a woman, he was keen to find out how she became so good.

Rocco and Francesco, both good with the swords themselves,

worked with him, and basically told him that his arm was good and his movements fluid. But his footwork let him down, leaving him flatfooted, and that is how Isabella was able to dance around him so easily.

Though Drake doubted that the man would ever forgive Isabella, he made new friends and would at least go away mollified and a better swordsman than when he started their hike.

The group posted two night guards on rotating shifts and Drake lay next to Isabella. She kept a little distance between them and he guessed she didn't want the other Knights to see how familiar they had become. That was fine with him, and when no one was looking, she stole a kiss from him as the lights began to go out.

Drake stared up at the most star filled sky he had ever seen. The lack of electric lights anywhere and altitude seemed to magnify their stellar light show and he couldn't help his mind going back to the lightless void he had escaped from.

Bone tiredness eventually dragged him into a troubled sleep, and his imagination took him back to thoughts of Ethan. He thought he had rescued him, but instead, he might have freed something dark into the world. And that meant Ethan was still down there, trapped, perhaps for eternity.

Drake didn't know it, but he wept in his sleep.

CHAPTER 34

Back in the village, the Elbaşi Kurdish men sitting around a small table and drinking dark tea out in the street heard the sound coming out of the darkness.

They glanced at each other, frowning, and then concentrated – it sounded like the buzzing of a machine – they were well aware of the things called drones that could drop from the sky and explode, but this sound seemed deeper than that, heavier.

In minutes more they stood as it sounded like the thing was closer and circling their village, and then in the next moment something landed in the middle of the street. The men stared in confusion as they tried to work out what it was.

"It's not a drone," one said.

"Animal?" the other replied, carefully drawing a sword.

The three men spread slightly, as they saw that the object turned out to be two things as a man stepped from the back of a huge revolting creature – a blowfly – bigger than a horse.

The man walked toward them, smiling. He looked exactly like one of the strangers that had been here the day before.

With his grotesque steed with its ghastly human face waiting in the street he drew up to them and looked down, looking into the eyes of each with amusement.

He spoke in fluid Elbaşi Kurdish. "Where is the group of strangers that was here?"

The men shook their heads, not about to give up any information without some sort of payment.

The man's smile never faltered. "Then let me give you some motivation to jog your memory." The man shot an arm out, and grabbed one of the men by the neck.

He lifted him one handed as though he weighed nothing, and reached out with his other hand to hold the struggling man's shoulder. Then with a twist and jerk, he ripped his head from his body.

He threw the head onto the table, knocking the small cups and tea urn from it.

"We can do this the easy way, or the hard way," he said.

The men scrambled toward the large room, obviously planning to rouse the chieftain and the other fighters.

"The hard way it is then." Ethan followed.

***

In an hour, every man and woman in the village was in ragged and bloody pieces. Halfway through his massacre he had found out what he needed to know, but the thrill of what he started was too intoxicating to stop.

Ethan was coated in sticky blood and gore and stopped to lick his fingers. He then bent to pick up a rag and wipe the blood and viscera from around his mouth, face, and hands.

He waited until the Conti fly had finished sucking at the open gut of a man, and then when done he looked off into the distance in the direction of the mountains and where the sun was just beginning to rise.

"The mountains," he said. "They may beat us there, but what a surprise we'll deliver when we meet again."

He mounted the back of the fly.

"There'll be no cure, and the Master will rise before the next moon is full."

The grotesque monster insect lifted into the air, and headed toward the sunrise.

CHAPTER 35

The shining sliver of moon was falling behind the mountains as the darkness was chased away by the rising sun.

Drake was already up, and had begun stoking up the fire to get some coffee on. They'd need to fuel up as the mountain was going to be an arduous climb and they needed to be at its rim by mid-day to witness what they were told was the vision through the Eye of God, whatever that might be.

Beliz left them there, bidding them good luck. But his face betrayed to them that he didn't expect to see them again.

Following breakfast they packed up and this time it was Rocco and Enzo who led them upwards. Isabella spent some time walking with the other female Knights, Bianca and Aria, and Drake walked with Leonidas and Marco.

They talked about the things they liked to do as hobbies, but avoided talking about Hell, or Ethan, or even the plagues burning over the surface of the world and what that heralded. They just shot the shit about fishing, hunting, and Drake listened contentedly as the pair talked about their favorite Italian soccer clubs, or football as they called it, which was just weird to him.

They stopped several times on the way up when they found flatter ledges. The climb was only about a forty to fifty degree angle, and was surprisingly greener underfoot so wasn't the loose scree that can make even a low-slope climb dangerous.

It was late morning when they finally made it to the mountain peak's crest and the group looked down into a wide green valley. After a desert hike and climb in a near barren landscape, they now saw a flock of birds wending its way over a silver stream far down below. Now and then the stream turned into huge bellies that formed deep ponds that were overhung with trees that draped leafy branches down to the water's surface.

Even on the valley walls there were huge trees, olive and oak, and beeches that looked as old as time and grew right from the stone, and all the way down to a forested valley floor.

"I guess it's good that it's forbidden land." Isabella stared dreamily. "It means this oasis will remain untouched."

"It's beautiful," Drake replied. "I could image building a little cabin down there, and I bet there's fish in that stream and in those deeper belly ponds."

She scoffed and turned to him, grinning. "Maybe come back next year, if, *when*, this is all over."

Drake pointed. "What is that embedded in the walls? Looks like glass."

Francesco smiled. "I know what it is. And it's rare to see so much if it. It's called Zultanite, a reflective gemstone only found in Turkey. It's also known as Diaspore and Csarite. It's a low value gemstone, but thousands of years ago, it was prized for making the most beautiful tiles for the ancient kingdoms in the area until it was mined out." He half smiled. "This might be one of the last places it is close to the surface."

"Magnificent." Isabella then turned to Francesco. "So now, we need to find somewhere that looks like it deserves the name of the Eye of God."

The sun was coming up behind them, and several amongst the group drew forth binoculars and scanned the rim, the walls, and even down at the valley floor.

"The ancient texts say that the noon day sun will catch the Eye of God," Francesco said softly. "We find it today, or we need to wait again until tomorrow."

"Maybe something on the valley rim, that casts a shadow. Or a beam of light that points the way," Drake said.

"Or a distinctive shadow," Isabella added.

They waited as the sun rose.

"Eleven thirty," Francesco announced.

The time seemed to be moving too fast.

"I got nothing." Drake concentrated through the binoculars so hard it was giving him a headache.

"It has to be here. It has to," Isabella said through her gritted teeth.

"Unless they've led us to the wrong valley," Leonidas said.

Isabella sighed. "Don't even think that."

They watched as the sun slowly rose, and the time moved towards midday. The Zultanite caught the light beams making it look like there were lit windows in the stone walls.

"I got nothing," Drake said. He lowered the glasses and checked his wristwatch. "Fifteen minutes until noon."

The sun rose and the ten people scanned along the valley. They stood in silence, just watching.

"Five minutes," Drake said.

"Maybe we're not in the right place." Leonidas turned. "Maybe we're supposed to be down there looking for it."

"One minute to go," Drake said and felt the knot of impatience twist in his gut. If they missed it, they'd have to wait until tomorrow and would have lost an entire day.

He sighed; at least that meant they could spread some of the team out along the opposite cliff and more down in the valley to cover different perspectives.

Their watches hit midday, noon on the dot, and the sun was directly overhead. Everyone held their breath and concentrated.

"*There.*"

One of the embedded sheets of Zultanite started to glow and at its center was a piece of duller stone. The effect of the reflection made it look like a giant glowing eye that cast a strong beam like a search light into the valley.

"The eye," Isabella announced. "Follow its gaze."

The focused beam shone like a massive pipe of light directly down onto one of the largest ponds in the river valley, right at a thick clump of ancient olive trees at its edge.

"That's where we're going." Isabella grinned. "Mount up everyone, we have a destination."

***

It took them several hours to make it to the valley floor, and Drake looked around at the meadow-like quality of the grass. He crouched and pulled some, rolled it between his thumb and fingers, and then smelled it – fresh – and he bet the soil here was rich and fertile. He turned slowly and saw wild flowers, and lush trees, some hanging with olives, and others in fruit blooms.

"Are you sure this isn't the Garden of Eden, right here?" He rose to his feet.

"I'm not sure of anything right now," Isabella replied. "But the Eye pointed the way to the edge of the small lake, and that's where we'll start our search."

In another half hour they came to the large pond that was fed by the stream. It was only about two hundred feet around, and was clear, but by the color was undoubtedly deeper at its center.

Willow-like trees hung over its edges, and dragonflies the size of small birds hung suspended over its glassy surface.

Isabella and Francesco went to the stand of trees right at the pond's edge that seemed to have been illuminated by the Eye's beam. It only took them twenty minutes to search the area for anything that might indicate an entrance, or clue to the whereabouts of the Garden of Eden.

Drake wandered to the edge of the pond. On the way over he had dipped a hand into the stream and felt the cold water that was obviously ice melt from higher up in the mountains. But as he came closer to the water, he felt something unexpected against his facc – warmth.

He dipped a hand into the pond again, and this time felt it was as warm as bathwater. It shouldn't have been, and the only way it could be so was if there was a hot spring somewhere, and he doubted that as this area was geologically very old and stable, so no volcanic activity. And that meant there must be a warm water source coming from somewhere else.

He began to remove his weapons and strip down.

Isabella saw what he was doing and walked towards him, her brows creased but a small smile on her lips.

"And what do you think you're doing?" she asked.

"Maybe what we're looking for isn't on the surface." He pointed. "The pond is warm here. Just here. It shouldn't be. There's warm water coming from somewhere, and I'm going to find out from where."

They had all brought basic diving gear, but for now Drake, just in his boxer shorts, began to wade into the water as it was near crystal clear, with the Knights gathering to watch him.

"Back soon." He dived forward.

Drake swam around to a deeper area close to the trees that were overhanging the pond. It was dark there, but sure enough he felt a current coming at him. He swam slowly along the surface, coming to a deeper area of about nine feet of water, and then dived down – he settled there hanging onto some long pond weeds and immediately saw the cavernous opening hiding under the shelf of stone.

Got you, he thought, and let himself drift back to the surface.

He came back up and sucked in a deep breath. He grinned. "There's a cave, a big one."

Isabella made a fist. "*Yes*. I feel we are almost there."

Drake swam back to the pond's edge and climbed out. "Got to be six feet around with warm water coming out at us. It's dark so couldn't see in," he said. "It might be what we're looking for. Or it could be blocked just inside."

"No, this is it." Isabella turned to the Knights, clapping her hands. "Okay, everyone, this is it. We have a cave dive. Suit up and let's see where it goes."

She pointed at the huge form of Enzo. "Enzo, you get to stay at home base, and guard our rear."

The big man nodded, and stopped undressing. Everyone else quickly shucked off their clothing, pulled on wetsuits with the boots with detachable fin ends. They also pulled out bags to keep their weapons dry.

In minutes more they were ready, the group of nine extremely fit and tall people looking a little like superheroes in their tight wetsuits. They also carried full face masks that covered their faces from forehead to the chin, and allowed communication.

Isabella went to the water's edge. She turned to hold an arm out to Drake and smiled. "Captain Stoker, take us in."

He nodded, pulling his mask down over his face. "Testing, testing…" He turned and got a thumbs up from the group.

He waded in deeper and then dived.

***

The group swam behind Drake. He got to the cave mouth, and waited for them. When the group was ready he switched on his flashlight and headed in.

After just the first dozen feet he found the cobbled stones on the bottom laid down as a path.

"This must have been dry once," he said.

"This entire land was far more arid a few thousand years ago," Francesco said. "Perhaps it was desert then, and the river was only a trickle that sometimes dried up."

In another few feet Drake slowed as he came to the bones. The creature had been huge, maybe nine feet tall, with huge wing bones spread either side of it. But the face must have been a nightmare with jagged-looking teeth and large eye sockets.

"What the hell is this thing?" he asked.

"Fantastic." Francesco swam closer. "I can't be sure, but I think it's a *Cherubim,*" he said breathlessly. "They're an angelic being mentioned in the Bible. They were said to be powerful winged creatures and were the guardians, protectors, and messengers of God."

He lay a hand on the huge skull's forehead and scoffed softly. "We sometimes call them cherubs and paint them as fat little babies with wings. But as you can see, they were fearsome and formidable."

"What's it doing here?" Isabella asked.

"That's the good news." Francesco turned to her. "They guarded the gates of the Garden of Eden." He ran a hand over the huge skeleton. "According to biblical accounts, God placed cherubim and a flaming sword at the eastern gate to prevent Adam and Eve from re-entering after they were expelled."

Francesco floated up from the remains. "We must be close, because they guarded the gate that marked the boundary between the Garden and the rest of the world." He turned. "I guess we should be glad it's expired. This thing would be a challenge to get past."

"Especially under water." Drake turned away. "Keep going."

They continued on, and Drake noticed the incline and also that there was pressure building against his eardrums.

"We're going down," he observed.

In minutes more the small cave they were in opened out into a larger underwater cavern, and just in the beam of their lights was the end of the cave. But its end finished in a set of moss and weed-covered steps.

The group gathered and then carefully swam to their top and one after the other lifted their heads above the water.

"Holy shit," Drake whispered.

There was a huge stone wall. No, two walls, *gates*, each about fifty feet high and that again wide.

They left the water, taking off their face masks and the fin parts of their boots.

"Armor up," Isabella said.

The Knights quickly retrieved all their weapons and fit belts and scabbards over their bodies.

"Notice something?" Drake asked.

The group turned from him to the gates.

"It's open," Francesco said.

Sure enough the massive gates were ajar; only by about three feet but more than enough to pass through.

Leonidas walked forward and looked down. "This was opened recently. The mud is still churned here." He pointed. "Boot prints. From a big man."

Isabella frowned. "And something else."

There were others tracks that were impossible to identify. At first they looked like tiger pug marks as they were big, bigger than a hand-span, but there was only two pads, and what looked like large claws on each side instead of the front.

"I've seen a lot of tracks, but I have no idea what made those," Drake said. "And I'm not sure I want to meet it."

Marco peered in through the gates. "There's something else." He looked back to them with a smile. "There's light inside."

EPISODE 11

And I stood upon the sand, and saw a beast rise up out of the sea, having seven heads and ten horns, and upon his horns ten crowns, and upon his heads the name of blasphemy – King James Bible

CHAPTER 36

Brazil, Rio de Janeiro - atop Corcovado Mountain

The towering statue of Christ the Redeemer that stood ninety-eight feet high with outstretched arms held wide that had watched over Rio for around a hundred years was surrounded with scaffolding, and men worked over it like ants.

But suddenly all across Rio de Janeiro dogs began to howl at the sky and every bird in the city took to the air.

The men stopped work, sensing something was coming. They all stared upwards at the massive statue.

The hairline cracks at the base of both feet, just under where his toes showed below the shawl, began to rain dust.

They looked up to see red liquid running from the eyes.

"*Jesus weeps,*" came the cry and the men dropped their tools and began to climb down and then run from the giant stone statue.

Then with the sound of a cannon boom, the cracks became fissures, and the Redeemer began to fall forward like the mightiest tree that ever existed.

The colossal thing fell and crashed down the mountainside like rolling thunder. Later, one of the men being interviewed said that he was sure he saw the statue try and take a step.

"But that is impossible." He asked, "Right?"

He looked to the other workers, but they all looked away from him.

He never got an answer.

CHAPTER 37

The Devil's Peak, Pacific Ocean, 450 miles east of the Australian coast

The huge black spike jutting from the ocean began to glow. Above it purple clouds swirled and lightning forked in every direction as the fury of the sky was being unleashed in a maelstrom at what was coming.

The black rock glowed red at the top, from the infernal heat emanating from inside it, and finally the top two hundred feet was blown into the sky like a massive bullet to travel a thousand feet into the air.

What it left behind was a smoldering cauldron a hundred feet across that seethed and boiled with magma, steam, and pure hate – hate for the entire human race, and everything that God had created.

In minutes more, the first huge tentacle came up and over the rim.

The beast was rising.

EPISODE 12

In the Center of the world there is a Garden. In the Center of the Garden there is a Tree. And in the Center of the Tree there is a Fruit. But beware its Guardians.

CHAPTER 38

The group entered and spread out.

Francesco held his arms wide and began to laugh, but that soon turned to weeping.

"It's so beautiful," he sobbed.

They were standing on a small rise and still on the ancient, cobbled pathway that led down into the most beautiful garden any of them had ever beheld. Overhead there was a soft green glow, perhaps from a form of bioluminescence, or some other divine cause.

"This place is enormous," Drake said. "Hidden here, forever."

Isabella nodded. "It goes on for miles. A forest, fed by the warm water, and all fed by the green light."

The glow made the tops of the trees shine and they could see some were enormous, reaching hundreds of feet into the air. There were swathes of grass in meadows, reeds bordering ponds, and some plants even with the buds and blooms of flowers.

"And I'm told Adam and Eve turned their back on all this," Drake scoffed. "Bad move."

"Remember who talked them into it." Francesco's eyes were narrowed as he looked about. "We need to be on guard as there may still be evil in here."

"What are we looking for?" Leonidas asked.

Isabella turned slowly. "If I had to guess, I'd say it was an apple. It grew on the tree of life."

"It made them mortal," Francesco replied. "In fact, a single bite made them mortal."

"But it cleansed them first," Isabella replied. "We're already mortal, so we just need the cleansing part."

"Let's hope the tree hasn't gone the same way as that cherub thing." Drake pushed his slick hair back. "Which way?

Isabella pointed. "Always head toward the light on the hill."

Drake turned to see a soft starlight pinprick of light a little higher than the surrounding trees.

He half smiled. "Our guiding light."

Isabella turned. "Everyone keep your eyes open. We have no idea what to expect in here."

She waved her team forward. "Rocco, Marco, take point. We move two abreast. Let's move."

They headed in with Drake and Isabella just behind the two lead Knights. Drake marveled at how something could exist like this, and for any of the first people finding this, it would have seemed like a religious experience.

Overhead he thought he heard something and looked up. He wasn't the only one as Isabella's brows were drawn together and she stared upwards as well.

Several of their flashlight beams moved across the dark sky above them, and a few times they just caught a glimpse of something up there. Something big, dark, and bristled.

"We've got company," Drake said.

"It's moving too quick to see clearly," Isabella said. "Everyone, keep your…"

The buzzing grew furiously and then something like a small truck zoomed in at them. There was a thump amongst them, and then a grunt, a sharp scream, and whatever it was had vanished before they could see what it was that attacked them.

But Aria was gone.

"*No, no, no*." Isabella ran a few dozen paces after it, as the screams of the woman grew fainter.

She continued to walk into the forest, looking upwards.

"*Bastardo*!" Isabella screamed.

"Get back here!" Drake yelled.

The buzzing came back, and the remaining flashlights swung toward the sound. In the combined beam, they saw the massive fly with the face of Octavius Conti, coming right at them, or rather, this time right at Isabella.

Drake and several of the Knights began to sprint toward her. But Isabella spotted the threat and all she did was face it head on, widen her stance, and in seconds it was on her before Drake and the other Knights could even get close.

But Drake had never seen a human being move so quickly. In a blur, she had drawn her sword, and in an arcing loop brought it around and into the face of the speeding monster.

The mass and velocity of the thing didn't allow it to slow down, and its usual super-fast insect reflexes were no match for Isabella's.

In a crackling slice, the blade passed all the way through the giant blowfly from the bulbous eyes in the grossly human face, punching through the thorax and bloated abdomen, and out the pustulant end.

The Conti fly was cleaved into two halves that passed either side of the woman and skidded in the dirt.

Drake pulled up in awe of what he had seen. "Wow."

"Yech!" Isabella yelled as she was covered in the contents of the disgusting abomination. She rushed to one of the small ponds and threw herself in, rubbing herself and also cleaning her blade. In seconds more she climbed out.

"You okay?" he asked.

"I am now." She looked back at the butchered fly. "That was the thing that escaped from Hell."

"The feet," Marco said. "That's what made the tracks."

"Yes." She walked closer to the monster, and her mouth turned down as she saw the half face. "Octavius Conti." She spat. "So this was your reward." She leaned closer. "Was it worth it?"

She turned away in disgust. "Yes, it explains the pug marks. But not the boot marks. We have to assume there will be other threats trying to thwart us." She sheathed her sword and pointed to the hill. "Let's hurry."

They threaded through the dense forest, and from time to time, birds spirited from tree tops, and small furry animals bounded from their path. Each seemed to take their time as if they didn't know what a human being was and therefore perceived no threat.

Once again, Drake wondered whether the bible stories were true – did a man and woman really live here for thousands of years, and then only left when they disobeyed their God's rules?

The things he had seen were testing his reluctance to believe in some sort of omnipresent being or deity, but he couldn't deny there was something mystical about this place and everything he had seen over the last few months had few scientific explanations.

It took them another half hour to make it to the base of the hill. In the distance and up the slope was a huge tree, its limbs spreading for hundreds of feet and at its center something was glowing like a tiny star.

Isabella stared up at it, and then turned slowly. "This is too easy."

Drake turned, noting how the undergrowth was flattened in these areas.

"Maybe it is meant to be," Leonidas said. "The Garden of Eden was a place of warmth and joy. That revolting beast you slayed forced its way in."

From out in the shadows there came a sound of heavy sliding and breaking undergrowth.

"Maybe, just hold that thought," Drake said softly.

The group were spread along a pathway that was more an opening in the forest between trees and bushes.

The light was already muted so underneath the canopies there were pools of shade and an ominous darkness.

"At arms," Isabella said and drew her sword again.

The Knights pulled their guns or swords.

"Hold," Isabella said. "All quadrants."

The group knew what she wanted and some turned to face the left, others to the right, and the ones at the rear faced backwards, while Rocco out front held his huge broadsword pointed that way.

The snapping and sliding came again from out to the left this time. Then it vanished, but minutes later it came again from behind, and then the right side.

"Whatever it is, it's circling us," Drake observed.

It sped up, circling faster, and getting louder as it got closer.

"Anyone have eyes on it?" Isabella said.

"Movement!" Drake shouted as he caught a glimpse of something shiny that went by a break in the bushes fast. From further ahead a tree was pushed aside and then another that was only twenty feet out from them.

"It's right here." Marco raised his gun trying to track it.

"Hold your fire," Isabella said.

Drake knew the man didn't have a target, and once he fired the sound would make it impossible for them to track the thing.

Then the forest exploded from the left side. Gunfire did erupt then along with shouts.

But it all happened so quickly that one minute they were trying to see into the green depths, and the next something came out of the trees – huge, fast, and torpedo-shaped. The following impact, and then the muffled scream, told them it had taken one of their own.

The thing kept travelling through the group and bullets smacked into its enormously long and scaled body, but if they penetrated the armored plates it didn't seem to show it.

"*Snake!*" Drake yelled, hardly believing something so big could even exist.

"We lost Matteo!" Marco yelled.

The group pulled in closer together as the monster snake came at them from the other side, once again coming through their group like an unstoppable freight train. And once again the mouth opened and its passage was punctuated by the death scream of someone's life being cut short.

"Knights, we are leaving." Isabella had her sword in her hands and pointed to the light on the hill. "Move it."

The remaining men and women began to sprint up the hill. Drake noticed that this time the huge Rocco was missing.

He could still see trees being pushed aside just behind the wall of brush, and knew the thing was still there, dogging them. Drake had heard that in Earth's primordial past there were giant snakes, and he read that just a few years back in India they discovered the fossil remains of something called a *Vasuki indicus*, a fifty foot snake.

Could this thing be a remnant? he wondered. Or could it be the thing that was woven into the Garden of Eden story about the snake.

The crashing of the underbrush behind him snapped him from his thoughts and he spun in time to see the massive green and golden bullet-shaped head emerging along the path they were using.

Its black glass-like eyes were fixed on the slowest moving of them, Bianca, and Drake flipped his gun to full automatic, and waited.

As it bore down on her the massive mouth opened, and instead of two fangs, there was a row of teeth that looked like a serrated saw. And that was the moment he hoped for – Drake fired his gun, keeping his finger locked on the trigger and aiming for inside the mouth to the softer palate where there was no armor plating.

He didn't know how many bullets hit their target of those he fired but it must have been enough to dissuade the monster, as it veered away into the brush, and Bianca stood with sword raised to strike, frozen.

After another few seconds her shoulders slumped, and she lowered her sword. She turned to Drake to nod.

They continued up the hill, the remaining group now in tight and wary of every shadow. Not a single Knight holstered their gun or returned their sword to its scabbard. The glow from up ahead drew them on, and in a few more minutes they came to the top of the hill and saw where the glow was coming from.

"The tree," Francesco whispered.

"It's true, all true." Marco smiled and pointed.

Ahead of them was an enormous tree like a mighty fig, but it was a fruit tree that seemed as old as time. Its gnarled branches stretched for hundreds of feet, and in amongst its leafy ends, they saw apples growing there.

The trunk glowed a ghostly white, and had been the source of the emanation that had drawn them to it.

"It's magnificent." Isabella held her arms wide as she walked a little closer.

But then she froze as a figure walked out from underneath the spreading branches. Isabella backed up a few steps, and the other Knights spread out, lifting their weapons.

Drake frowned as he walked forward. He couldn't believe what he was seeing. "Ethan?"

It was his twin brother, exactly as he remembered him – tall, strong, and with that confident smile. He held onc hand out, and in it, there looked like something burning there.

"Ethan." Drake raised a hand, feeling a swelling in his chest at seeing him again.

"That's not Ethan," Isabella warned as she edged toward Drake.

Drake couldn't help himself but feel pulled forward. He wanted to embrace his brother, cure him, find out what had happened to him. He had so many questions for him.

"Stop, Drake." Isabella's voice rose. "Remember what he did to Addison."

"Brother," Ethan said, holding his arms out and continuing to advance. "Join with me."

"Spawn of the Devil, I see you," Isabella growled and turned to Marco and Bianca. "Take him down."

The two Knights advanced, Marco with his sword, and Bianca holding a gun. They didn't wait, and Bianca, with her gun in a two hand grip, began to fire. The bullets smacked into Ethan, and he pushed back a step, but the wounds didn't bleed and just left black holes in the flesh.

Marco charged, raising and swinging his sword in an arc, bringing it down toward the man. Ethan moved unnaturally, his body bending backwards in a way that wasn't possible for a human being. And no matter how Marco sliced, stabbed, or thrust, he couldn't hit Ethan.

Then Ethan came upright and caught Marco's blade in his bare hand. In the other, he still held the fiery something, and he thrust his arm out to press it over Marco's lower face and held it there.

Marco's eyes went wide, and he gave a muffled grunt of fear and pain.

His face lit up with red fiery veins, and Ethan, grinning, then let him go.

"*Marco!*" Isabella screamed.

The spidery veins travelled down the Knight's body, right to his fingertips, and then with a juddering scream, the man exploded and the bits of Marco showered the area with all of them still steaming like roasted meat.

Ethan then threw the flame like a bolt at Bianca, and it covered her like flaming glue. Her screams as she caught fire were unnerving in the twilight darkness. Drake rushed to her, and had nothing but dirt to try and kick over her, but he was too late and in seconds she was nothing but a smoldering pile of bones on the ground.

"You came for the tree?" Ethan laughed out loud. "The cure to everything."

He turned to glance at it behind him, then back at Isabella. "But there will be no cure for you. The Master is already rising. Soon the world will belong to us, and we will have great fun hunting down the last of you pathetic humans as sport." He grinned evilly. "And food."

"It will be you that is brought down, scum from Hell." Isabella advanced, holding the jeweled blade tightly in both hands.

"No tree, no cure." Ethan turned and threw the flame at the center of the tree. It hit the trunk, spread over it, and the massive tree burst into flame. Branches, leaves, and fruit, all began to wither to blackness. The flames quickly moved from the trunk to the branch tips.

"*No!*" Isabella screamed.

Leonidas ran forward, pulled his blade, and threw it – thc sword travelled with great speed and unerring accuracy to strike a branch tip, severing it just as the flames reached the outer branches. The last three apples that grew there fell to the ground.

Ethan growled and went to throw a fiery ball at both Leonidas and the apples, but Isabella let out a battle cry and charged with her sacred blade.

Ethan turned to her and instead threw the hellish blast at her.

It struck Isabella mid chest, and she was blown backwards off her feet as her sword spun away in the air. The agonizing flames spread over her torso.

"*Isabella.*" Drake sprinted to her, and ignoring the pain, reached for her fragmenting top and ripped it away, leaving her bare breasted. The suit top quickly turned to melted mush but he had made it in time as the fiery substance scalded her skin but didn't make through to the subcutaneous layers.

She moaned, semi-conscious, on the ground, but reached up to grab his forearm. "Only you. Only you can."

Drake turned to see Ethan was going for Leonidas, who was crawling away with the apples held tight to his body. The remaining Knights had formed a line between him and Ethan, but Drake knew they stood little chance against this creature that wore the skin of his brother.

Tears welled in his eyes as he knew what he must do.

He went and picked up Isabella's blade and began to walk, and then run at Ethan. The blade glowed a soft blue in his hands.

In the last seconds, Ethan turned, and by then Drake had the blade held high.

Ethan threw up a hand. "Drake, don't," he pleaded.

Drake brought the blade down in an arc, and managed to chop

deeply down beside the man's neck and into the shoulder.

Ethan barely reacted, even though the blessed steel sizzled in the flesh. But in the next second Ethan opened his mouth. Something began to emerge, like a horn of bone.

It was covered in a slimy black mucous, and it kept coming, getting bigger, and then with a bone crunching and tearing of tendons the jaws dislocated as what came out of his mouth began to take shape as some sort of deformed head, complete with jagged horns.

Drake could only stare, feeling both revolted, and more terrified than he had ever been in his life at what was happening to his brother.

Next, a long taloned hand reached from the torn mouth and began to peel Ethan's sagging body down like an old sack as the beast continued to emerge.

The head lifted to look at Drake, and he stared into multiple black eyes of a spider pressed into its bloody forehead, and the viper teeth of a deep sea fish. He recognized it as a thing from Hell and not of this world.

In seconds more, as Ethan's former body dropped around it like rags, the beast fully revealed itself.

The flame that was in its hand now covered its entire body and it straightened to about eight feet tall, but still with the blue glowing blade embedded in the meat of its shoulder. And Drake saw that the wound was getting bigger as the blade continued to melt into it.

The beast's form was crowded with horns over its head, back, and shoulders, and still running with black slime and viscera from its climb out of Ethan's body. The eyes burned like hot coals as the huge taloned hand reached up for the blade. But when it gripped it, its hands immediately began to sizzle and rot. It screamed a sound that hurt the ears of the surrounding Knights.

It tried again with its other hand, but it too burned.

"Now, Drake!" Isabella yelled.

Drake heard her and reached forward to yank the blade out. The wound immediately began to knit closed.

"This is for stealing my brother's face, you fucking demon."

He then spun to gather momentum, and this time cut right through the neck. Ethan's head spun through the air, and the flames over the demon went out.

Drake ran to Isabella and helped her sit up. There was a furious-looking burn on her chest, but she coughed and nodded.

"That hurt." She swallowed and grabbed his arm and used it to get to her feet.

Drake came up with her and he turned to watch the magnificent huge tree begin to crumble to cinder dust.

There were just four of them remaining, as other than Drake and Isabella, there was just Leonidas and Francesco. The two Knights came closer, with Leonidas carrying the small branch with the three apples attached. He held them out.

Isabella picked one and held it in her hand, and then closed her eyes. "I can feel it. Feel its power." She handed it to Francesco. "We need to test it."

She reached into her backpack, and drew forth the small glass jar that held the severed finger of the beast from the Kurdish village. The disgusting thing was a greenish-grey and curled up like a rotting grub. When she held it up, the thing started to move and inch around the bottom of the jar still seeking a way out.

Isabella had Francesco cut a tiny sliver of the apple. He held it ready and she opened the jar.

The revoting thing inside coiled itself, ready to spring out, but Francesco dropped the apple sliver in and she quickly sealed the jar. The apple piece fell onto the finger and the reaction was immediate. The finger began to swell and then exploded into a grey steaming liquid. In seconds more it dried to nothing.

"Now that's what I call a positive field test," Drake said.

"It has all been worth it." Isabella smiled. "We need to get these home and synthesize whatever compounds are inside."

She turned to the smoldering remains of the magnificent tree. Everything was gone other than a huge pile of ash. Most of it had burned so hotly that it devoured the tree rapidly and completely.

"Put the rest of that tree out. Till the soil, and when it is cooled, we will ensure the tree lives again."

She held up the apple she had taken a slice from. "From small things big things grow."

Francesco placed the other two apples in an airtight cannister, and twisted the lid, and it immediately frosted. He then slotted it into his backpack.

The group did as Isabella asked, spreading the ashes which would provide rich minerals to sweeten the soil. The apple was buried, and covered over, and then they emptied their water cannisters there.

Isabella stood back and smiled down at it. "Thank you."

She backed away and then turned. "We need to get this back and hopefully there's still a world out there when we get home."

The group headed out through the garden forest, and with only four of them remaining, they were on guard against the huge snake. But they left unharmed, and came to the dark pond once again. At the water's edge the group kitted back up for the swim.

Isabella nudged Drake. "After all you have seen, the Garden of Eden, Hell, and even the Devil, are you a believer yet?"

He chuckled softly. "Let's just say I have a more open mind now."

She laughed softly. "Then that will do." She slowly pulled the wetsuit over her painful burn. "For now."

They entered the water.

CHAPTER 39

When they emerged from the water, Enzo was waiting for them with sword drawn. His whole body sagged when he saw how few of them there were, and Francesco shook his head.

The Knight went to Enzo and embraced him. But then pulled back and pulled the glass canister out with the two apples.

"We have succeeded, brother." Francesco gave him a sad smile. "But the price was high."

"Then the sacrifice was not in vain," Enzo replied and sheathed his sword.

It was a somber trip back home made worse when they passed through the village of the Elbaşi Kurds.

"Ethan," was all Drake said.

Isabella nodded as they looked over the grotesque massacre of every man, woman, and child in the village. It had been an orgy of physical desecration. And the ferocity and brutality showed them it was done by something with a visceral hatred of the human physical form.

The boat was still waiting for them, and it seemed oversized now that more than half their ranks were gone.

Even travelling via the high speed links they had set up it took two days to return to Rome. Most of the stops along the way had been surreal as many towns had been either abandoned or ravaged, and they needed to fire upon roving bands of the skinless-looking creatures that in some cases still wore the clothing of their previous human lives.

It was both saddening and revolting when they saw one small creature wearing the clothing of a little girl – it seemed no one and nothing was spared.

A Vatican convoy was waiting for them at the airport that was guarded now around the clock by the Italian military, as, Drake assumed, was most of the critical infrastructure all around the world.

From the intel he had gathered along the way, some countries had gone totally dark. It would take a generation to recover, and that was only if what they brought back could somehow be mass produced and weaponized.

Even though exhausted, Drake and Isabella were ushered directly to the Vatican laboratories beneath the walled city.

Cardinal Tommasini was waiting for them. "Show me," he said.

Isabella handed over the canister. Drake wasn't surprised to see that the apples hadn't degraded at all, and perhaps they never would.

The Cardinal crossed himself and then took the canister and closed his eyes as he held it.

"It was all there," Isabella said. "The garden, the gates, the tree, and the snake."

Tommasini nodded. "Faith is a burden and a battle every day. Until you see something like this and you know you were right all along." He turned away. "We must hurry. We need to find out what it is that makes these special."

The trio headed down to the older lower level, and went from a stone hallway, through a heavily fortified door, and then into a pristine white corridor. It never failed to amaze Drake that the ancient walled city of the Vatican hid a hi-tech world that rivaled the best of anything on the planet.

They entered the laboratory and there was a small team of white coated scientists and doctors waiting. They bowed, took the canister, and then opening it, used forceps to remove one of the apples.

They then sliced away several slivers and each was headed for a different device – an electron microscope, mass spectrometer, chromatography systems, and thermal cyclers. Each of these devices would employ different techniques to analyze the physical and chemical properties of a sample.

It was the X-ray Fluorescence Spectrometers that was used to determine elemental composition of materials that found the first anomaly.

"Something here that shouldn't be." The scientist put the findings up on the wall as a projection. The graph showed the spikes of the chemical composition. "There are all the basic chemical components – sugars like fructose, glucose, and sucrose, minerals like potassium and calcium, also polyphenols-containing compounds like quercetin, catechin, phlorizin, and chlorogenic acid. All normal." He went on to list dozens of other things he was expecting.

He stopped, turned, and pointed at one particular spike. "But then there's this compound." He half smiled. "I have no idea what it is. The computer's global flora encyclopedic database has no idea what it is." He half smiled. "As far as it's concerned it's…" He beamed, "…non-Earthly."

"Isolate," Tommasini said. "Then we test it."

They did, and they tested it on a captured subject. An almost microscopic amount of the substance caused the creature to shudder violently, fall to the ground, and then simply turn to dust.

"Three seconds." Tommasini nodded. "Good result."

Isabella stepped forward, and dragged her sleeve up. "Test it on me, the uninfected. We must ensure that it is safe for the population."

"No," Drake said, and reached out for her.

She turned. "We don't have much time and we need to know if it's safe. Right now."

The scientist's eyes went to Cardinal Tommasini. He gave an almost imperceptible nod.

He administered the same amount to Isabella. She waited, and the whole room stood in silence, watching.

Drake felt his stomach flip from nerves. He should have offered himself, he thought. He should have…

"Three seconds," Tommasini exhaled.

She smiled. "Nothing."

"How do you feel?" Drake asked.

"Good, fine." She drew in a breath and let it out. "Better than fine."

Drake smiled, and pointed to her chest. "Show me. Show me the burn."

She felt it, and then frowned. She quickly opened her shirt and peeled it open above her breasts.

The burn was gone.

"Better than fine,' Drake repeated.

Cardinal Tommasini crossed himself, but then his face grew serious and he turned to the scientists. "This wondered element or compound. Can it be reproduced?"

"Doctor," one of the other scientists pointed, "the sample."

The lead scientist walked back to where they had the sliver of apple in a beaker of distilled water. The level was higher and it was all milky. He took a sample and placed it under the microscope.

"What is it? Is there a problem?" Tommasini asked.

The scientist began to smile as he changed the magnification. "No, no problem. But we don't have to worry about synthesizing the substance." He looked up. "Because it is self-replicating. It is growing. The unknown component is alive."

"It is the antithesis of the Hell plague micro-parasite." Cardinal Tommasini closed his eyes. "Thank god." He opened his eyes, his gaze intense. "How long until we have enough to begin mass delivering it? Like via some sort of crop dusting process. We also need to get it out to every country in the world. So they can produce their own."

The scientists looked back at the sample. "Only as long as it takes to set up growth tanks. The rate of replication is astounding."

"How long?" Tommasini repeated more forcefully.

The man smiled. "Days. Maybe hours for the first batch."

CHAPTER 40

The first thing the Vatican did was spread the news to every government around the world – from China to the USA, to Australia and beyond. A sample was then sent via high speed delivery with instructions for growing and dispensing.

Across Europe the spraying had already begun and every plane that could be modified was utilized to deploy the substance.

Another thing they found was that although the substance could be destroyed by heat, high impact had no effect so dispersal bombing could also be utilized by creating inoculation bombs for highly over-run areas.

Over the next few weeks, it became a time of joy from every country with feedback of the hordes being decimated so substantially and so quickly. Updates on eradication changed from years, to months, to weeks, almost daily.

Though there would be pockets of the creatures hiding in basements, barns, and old mine shafts, they too would eventually be hunted down.

There was one last area of infection to deal with – the ground zero, and that would be next.

CHAPTER 41

The high altitude bomber was nearing the drop zone in the South Pacific. The pilot had his undercarriage cameras rolling and he relayed what he was seeing to home base. In addition, the feed was provided to most countries.

"Coming up on target."

Thc commander in chief and his war room all watched in silence. Coming up on screen they all saw it and the room filled with gasps of disbelief and horror.

"Oh my god," the President whispered.

What was once the Devil's Peak was now a mountain of colossal, mottled tentacles hundreds of feet across and thicker than redwood trees. The water that was once a magnificent steel blue was the color of blood and they could see dead sharks, whales, and other sea life floating lifeless on the poisoned surface.

But there were other things living in it – all the abominations that had been released from the pit of Hell, the leviathans, the Kraken, and other gargantuan monstrosities, were in attendance to their Master.

There were other huge malformations clinging to the bottom of the peak, that were neither fish nor animals, but a revolting mix of things that looked as if borne from a madman's nightmare.

"Coming up on target in, five, four, three…"

The world watched and waited.

"…two, one… *away*."

The thirty thousand pound, pilot-guided device was released from the undercarriage, and immediately small wings were deployed. The copilot took control and via a nose camera steered it all the way to the center of the hellish bloom.

It entered the heart of the great beast and detonated. There was no fiery blast, but the impact and the following bloom of greenish mist spread to cover the entire Hellborne horror and the sea surrounding it for hundreds of yards.

What followed was an absolute explosion of activity as the Garden of Eden compound met with the monstrous Father of Flies.

The bomber had already banked away and was several miles clear when the secondary detonation occurred.

This one was a volcanic eruption, and a geyser of magma shot skyward. Surrounding the remnants of the Devil's Peak, the leviathans had all vanished and the sea churned as if in a violent storm.

Tidal waves roared away from the peak, and in another half hour, the magma stopped flowing, the sea calmed, and the clouds cleared.

The bomber pilot returned and scouted the area.

Other than a ghastly slick on the ocean's surface, nothing remained of the peak at all.

"Target destroyed," the pilot intoned. "Coming home."

He banked away, just as the sun was coming out again.

***

All around the world fist-sized blowflies fell from the sky and immediately began to rot. Areas where swirling purple clouds had formed to drop miserable rain suddenly vanished.

Some people came from their cellars, from train tunnels, and from wherever they had been hiding. And other beasts, the skinless ones, the abominations did the opposite, skulking back into the sewers, mine shafts, and deep holes in the ground.

Thousands of miles away, in a corner of Turkey, in a valley that it is forbidden to enter, and through a pond, below ground, and then into a hidden garden, a tree sprouted on the only hill.

It would be years before it could bear fruit.

But it would fruit.

CHAPTER 42

USA, Texas, the Stoker Ranch – six months later

Drake and Isabella rode out to a hillside and looked back out over a valley that was green, and dotted with grazing cattle. They sat there as the sun neared the horizon.

He turned to her. "You know you can stay here. With me," he said, not looking at her.

She laughed softly. "And what would I do? Not much call for a Vatican warrior in Texas. I couldn't even ride a horse until a few months ago."

"There'll be a lot of work now. Going to take years to rebuild everything that was destroyed. There'll be big calls for construction work. We'll be travelling around. Going to be busy."

She continued to look out over the landscape before finally turning. Her brows were raised. "So, a business partner?"

"Well, no, you know I lo…" he sighed.

"Go on." She smiled. "Sa-*aaay* it."

He grinned and shook his head. "This is harder than I thought."

"Big tough Drake Stoker afraid of a little sentence." She waited, smiling.

His face grew hot and he turned away. "I love you."

"What? I didn't hear that." Her grin widened.

"*Aggh*." He tilted his head back on his neck and then turned to her, his cheeks fully red now. "I love you, Isabella."

"A-*aaand*?" She leaned forward in the saddle.

"And I want you to stay with me," he said in a rush.

"Anything else?" she huffed. "I'll think about."

He shook his head, exhaling.

She half turned, looking at him from the corner of her eye.

"Okay, okay, will you marry me?" he said at last.

She lifted her chin, beaming. "That's more like it." She nudged her horse closer to his. "Yes, Drake, I would love to marry you."

He reached out one big arm, grabbed her, pulled her onto the saddle in front of him, and hugged her, leaning over her shoulder as she faced him so he could kiss her.

They broke apart and she reached up to pinch his chin. "I have to anyway. Who else is going to save you from Hell next time you get into trouble?"

She still held the reins of her horse, and he began to walk his steed back down the hill to the ranch.

"I haven't got a ring for you yet," he said.

She turned to look at him. "I haven't picked one out yet. But I got you something." She reached into her pocket and pulled out a small box. She handed it to him.

"What is it?" he asked.

"Well, open it and find out." She smiled.

He did, and inside was a small silver antique cross on a chain. He laughed softly. "Okay, it's beautiful."

She turned in the saddle to face him, took the cross and put it around his neck.

"There, perfect," she said.

"You think I need it?" He raised his eyebrows.

She shrugged. "It can't hurt. But I think it is already in here now." She pressed his chest with her hand.

She turned around to the front again and leaned back against him. After a moment of thinking about what she said, he had to ask, even though he wanted to try and bury the memories forever.

"Do you think we beat him, the Devil?" Drake asked.

She thought about it for a while and then shook her head. "No, he is eternal and eternally patient."

Drake frowned. "Does it matter? We closed the opening to Hell."

She scoffed. "No, we closed *an* opening to Hell. In a hundred or a thousand years he'll try again. We need to be vigilant, and we need to remember."

"That's where the Vatican comes in," he said

"Yes," she said softly.

The horse slipped a little and then bounced as it cantered for a second or two, jolting the pair.

"Ouch, that's hard," she said.

"Sorry, horse slipped," he said.

"No, not the horse." She turned and smiled.

He laughed. "That's your fault. Stop rubbing up against me."

"You better get me home, cowboy," she whispered.

"Yes ma'am." He nudged the horse to travel a little quicker down the slope.

EPILOGUE

Canada, Yellowknife – the Giant Mine

The former gold mine had been abandoned for years. It was deep, and toxic as it was found to contain significant amounts of arsenic trioxide, posing both a biological and environmental danger.

Miles below the surface, the remnants of the skinless dog-like creatures had gathered there, hundreds of them, trapped above the Earth when the Father of Flies had retreated back to the underworld.

But they dug, and burrowed, and never rested. Many of them wore their claws down to nubs of bone. But already the shaft was five hundred feet deeper than it had been.

They would never stop, never cease their work, like a group of mindless army ants, working on instinct alone, they would continue until they broke through to the underworld.

And then, they would start their conquest again.

The End

SEVEREDPRESS

@severedpress
/severedpress

Checkout other great books by bestselling author

Greig Beck

TO THE CENTER OF THE EARTH

An old woman locked away in a Russian asylum has a secret—knowledge of a 500-year-old manuscript written by a long-dead alchemist that will show a passage to the mythical center of the Earth.She knows it's real because 50 years ago, she and a team traveled there. And only she made it back. Today, caving specialist Mike Monroe leads a crew into the world's deepest cave in the former Soviet Union. He's following the path of a mad woman, and the words of an ancient Russian alchemist, that were the basis of the fantastical tale by Jules Verne.But what horrifying things he finds will tear at his sanity and change everything we know about evolution and the world, forever.In the tradition of Primordia, Greig Beck delivers another epic retelling of a classic story in an electrifying and terrifying adventure that transcends the imagination."Down there, beyond the deepest caves, below the crust and the mantle, there is another world."

THE SIBERIAN INCIDENT

100,000 years ago the object hit the lake at the deepest point, quickly sinking into its mile-deep stygian darkness. With it came something horrifying that would threaten every living thing on the face of the planetOver the centuries, legends grew of people vanishing, of strange, deformed animals, and of an unexplained luminescence down in the lake depths.When Marcus Stenson won the lucrative contract to create a sturgeon fish farm on the site of disused paper mill on the shore of Lake Baikal, he thought he had hit the jackpot. He refused to listen to the chilling folktales, or even be concerned by the occasional harassment from the local mafia. But then animals were found mutilated in the frozen forest, and people started to go missing. And worse, some came back, changed, horribly.In the depths of the lake, something unearthly that had been waiting 100,000 years was stirring. And mankind will become nothing more than a host.THE SIBERIAN INCIDENT - a tale of invasive Alien Horror from international best selling author, Greig Beck.

Made in United States
North Haven, CT
17 November 2025

82506691R00128